DANGEROUS C...

JACK

Dennis O'Donnell

> *Dangerous conceits are in their natures poisons*
> *Which at the first are scarce found to distaste*
> *But, with a little act upon the blood,*
> *Burn like the mines of sulphur.*
> **Othello**

Copyright © 2010 Dennis O'Donnell

All rights reserved

1

It was the same all through August. Every morning dawned bright, fresh and sunny, still damp around the edges, the sort of morning that would have smudged if you'd held it anywhere but by the corners. Afternoons, the sun got as hot as a nun at a wrestling match. My little office above the Chinese takeaway in King Street flared like a wok, even when I had the windows wide, the door wedged open and my electric fan whirling on the desk. I sweltered every afternoon from two till six, then closed up and went to Mulholland's for a jar to rinse away the stour of another wasted day. When I got up next morning the sun was shining again. And it stayed shining all day, right until it slid down the sky in a crimson smear around about evening time.

The sun cracking the flags one day a year is a rare enough event for our part of the world. The good people of Bathgate loved the heatwave. They worshipped the sun like Aztecs. Shimmied around the streets in light summer clothes. Workmen stripped to the waist. In the Public Park and on every other available strip of grass, folk basked like lizards and topped up their skin cancers. Quite right. It couldn't last for long; they might as well enjoy it while it did. Make hay.

Me, I was going through one of my many fallow spells. Work was as slack as a moron's jaw. And killing time is never easy. Time dies very slowly and fights like hell. Day in, day out, I did the same thing. Mornings, I opened up, read *The Scotsman* and *The Herald* from cover to cover, then did the crosswords and read some more Shakespeare before I went out and bought my sandwich for lunch. Then I took the air, the hot air, around the Steelyard.

After lunch, I took my jacket off and let the damp circles under my oxters air a little, while I waited for a client. I turned my waste-paper basket on its side and putted those five old golf balls into it from every angle in the room. When that got flat, I putted with my left hand for a while, to add some spice to it, then putted backwards between my legs. I got so that I could get those dimpled little spheres into the basket with my eyes shut. Then I laid the basket on its side on the chair and flipped beermats into it. Awarded myself ten points for every one that went in clean, twenty points if they landed standing up, and five points for a rim shot. Just to juice it up a little, I deducted five points for every one that missed. Once, I got to 445 points in the black before I felt my brain crash and go Cyrillic. I shut my eyes and cried softly for five minutes, then I rebooted and read another whack of Shakespeare. I tell you, Old Shakey kept me sane that August.

It was a day like all the others, only more so, when Grace McGuire came into the office. About twelve noon. The sun hadn't quite got to burning holes in people yet. I'd read the paper, done the crossword, and followed Lear about the heath for a while. I had intended to have lunch but my BLT sandwich wasn't promising. Bored out of my gourd, I was rolling my pencil on the desk when Grace McGuire came in. I goggled. It was one of those hormonally-induced non-blinking episodes.

I pegged her as in her early forties. She had collar-length brown hair and big puppy-dog eyes. Her nose was long, but then so was Nefertiti's, they say. Or maybe that was Cleopatra. I can't comment. Personally, I've never gone in for those ancient Egyptian babes. I know that my description makes her sound like a borzoi but, just take my word for it, the features all worked. Later, when she used it, she had one of those rare smiles that's been described by lesser writers as 'radiant'. It had all the strangeness and charm of a sub-atomic particle. An Ideal Tooth Exhibition. She also had a fine set of curves that were pleasantly wrapped in a tan V-neck top and a pair of fawn slacks. But it was her legs that were the piece de resistance, as Marcel Marceau would say – fine, shapely, state of the art legs. With pins like that, you'd keep a spare pair in the cupboard under the stairs in case of accidents. She deserved one of those throaty gurgles that Roy Orbison does in *Pretty Woman*. She looked like she'd been around the block often enough to know where everything was, but still might be enthusiastic if you offered her a sentimental journey round it one last time.

She came up the stairs from the waiting room hesitantly. First time clients were unsure of the lay-out because the windows on the street had my name in black letters, but the stairs and door were round the back. Go in the front door, no matter what your problem was, all you'd come out with was number 32 with bean shoots.

I guess she would have knocked on the door, if I hadn't had it jammed open. The frosted glass bore the same legend in black lettering as the windows on to the street:

J. BLACK. PRIVATE INVESTIGATOR.

"Mr. Black?" she asked.

"Jack Black at your service, miss…" I replied gallantly and indicated the easy chair opposite the desk.

"Mrs.," she corrected me. "McGuire. Grace McGuire."

"Pull up a chaise longue, Mrs. McGuire. What can I do for you?"

"Well, that all depends," she said, and sat down.

"Depends on what, may I ask?" I asked.

"Well… are you really a private detective?"

"Sure am. Even got the BAPI certificate on the wall to prove it." And I jerked my thumb at the document in question.

She laughed self-consciously. "Funny. I half expected you to be wearing a fedora and a trench coat."

"That's all I need. Folk think I'm enough of a fanny just being a private detective, without hanging around the Steelyard in a get-up like that."

"You know what I mean – Humphrey Bogart kind of thing."

"Sure. I know what you mean.. 'Down these mean streets a man must go who is not himself mean', and all that."

"What?"

"Forget it. Not important. What can I do for you?"

"I suppose nowadays all your business is adultery. You know, seedy hotels and that kind of thing."

"Not so much as you might think. Times have moved on. Divorce is as a lot simpler these days than it used to be. Sure, I do some matrimonial work. But there's a whole spectrum of work for a private eye these days."

"Yes?"

"Sure. There's the marital stuff. Cohabitation reports. But there's vehicle and asset satellite tracking; telephone monitoring and tracking; text message and e-mail retrieval; insurance work; blackmail and fraud enquiries; computer forensics; surveillance; family members located; tracing beneficiaries – all sorts."

"Wow."

"Yep. What can I do for you, Mrs. McGuire?"

"Call me Grace."

"Grace."

"It's my daughter."

"You want me to trace her?"

Her eyes brimmed with tears suddenly. I stood opposite her and said nothing. She would tell me in her own good time.

"Do you mind if I smoke?"

"Nope. Go right ahead. In fact, I think I'll join you."

I flicked my Zippo open, reached across the desk and tendered the flickering flame towards her. Her lips pouted softly round the filter tip of her coffin-nail as she inhaled. I waited for her to start.

"No, I don't really want you to trace her," she said, sitting back and exhaling. "Not as such. I know where she is. Are you a religious man, Mr. Black?" she asked.

"Not me," I shook my head. "Not since childhood. I got disillusioned at Sunday School. Jesus didn't want me for a sunbeam."

"Mmm?"

"I didn't make the cut," I said, sitting down.

"I take it you don't believe in faith, redemption, heaven – all that stuff?"

I pointed up towards the ceiling.

"'Above us only sky'. As a wise man once said."

"You see, that's my position on religion, too. It was my husband's. I thought it was Laura's. But it seems I was wrong. Couldn't be much wronger, in fact."

"She's found religion?"

"In a big way."

"Maybe you should give me some details."

"My daughter's name is Laura McGuire. She's eighteen and very bright. She should be going to Edinburgh University this October to start her studies. But now she says she won't be. She's found the meaning of life. *She* says."

"So what's she studying? Or supposed to be studying?"

"Art. She's really into modern art."

"And what's happened now to change her mind? Where is she?"

"She is living with a cult somewhere up in Angus. Just took off the weekend before last. Said she was going into Edinburgh to check out the galleries again. Well, I'd no reason to doubt her. She went there often enough. And then, the next thing – out of the blue, I get a phone call saying that she's joined the New Dawn somewhere in Angus and that she's dedicating her life to the service of God. It's incredible."

"Right. And she'd never shown any sign of this before? Not a church-goer?"

"Not at all. She was christened, as a child, because our parents insisted it was the right thing to do. Neither her father nor myself believe in any of that. And now it looks like the born-again brigade have got their claws into her."

"Yeah. Waste of time, them being born the first time round, I always think. What did she say when she phoned you?"

"Just that – that she was entering the religious life with this cult; that this was how she wanted to spend her life, making something worthwhile of her life and being 'in the bosom of her true family' as she called it."

"So how did she come to fall in with that crowd particularly?"

"I'm not sure, Mr. Black, but there was a big spread on them in *The Scotsman* a couple of months ago. Nairn MacVicar did a kind of feature on them. Maybe she saw that."

She ground out the stub of her cigarette in the ashtray. I even liked the way she did that.

"Have you spoken to the police?"

"Yes, of course. They sympathised but said …" she shrugged.

"That she had reached her majority, that you knew where she was and that she was fine and in no obvious danger, and there wasn't much they could do about it."

"Exactly."

I looked at her and stubbed out my own fag.

"So why are you here? Is it just that you resent these people 'getting their claws' into her, or…"

"Not just that, no. Though that's part of it. I want to know that she's okay. That she's not been brainwashed. That she's not taking part in savage or sexual rituals."

"I can find that out for you."

"You can?"

"Sure. You think she might be involved in some bizarre stuff?"

"If I remember correctly, that's why Nairn MacVicar did the article in the first place. There was some suggestion of sexual shenanigans to do with the cult leader."

"Wouldn't surprise me. Sexual shenanigans are common enough. And so is brainwashing, unfortunately."

"MacVicar said that the rumours were unfounded, that the New Dawn were good souls, working the land and selling the produce. And waiting for the End of Days."

"But you still have concerns."

"Of course. I want you to find her and make sure she's okay."

"And if I do and she wants to come back...?"

"I want her back. At the very least, I want you to be able to reassure me that she's okay. That's the bottom line, Mr. Black."

"Okay," I said, getting more business-like, "basics. Do you work for a living, Mrs. McGuire?"

"I'm an English teacher."

"So Laura's been brought up in a house where education would be the expected career move at her age. Have you a recent photograph of her?"

She unclasped her handbag and passed me over a 3x2 photograph. Laura had her mother's eyes and nose. What else she had inherited, I couldn't tell from the picture. It was head and shoulders only. Hair glossy, brown and shoulder-length. She was wearing a black and gold hooped top. She was sporting a castor-oil smile, as if the photograph was the last thing she had wanted – typical teenager, smart-arsed and moody.

"That was taken on her 18th birthday, a month ago."

"Good. Okay. Father. What does he do for a living?"

"My husband teaches too. He ran away with a psychiatric

nurse when Laura was ten, Mr. Black. They live in Blackburn."

He must have been a psychiatric patient to run away from hotcha Grace, I thought. But then again, what did I know? Maybe she picked her feet and spat cherry stones into the fireplace.

"Lucky them. Has he seen her at all recently?"

"On her birthday. He always sees her on her birthday."

"Good relationship with her?"

"Good enough. She sees him regularly and he spoils her. Buys her clothes and music and all sorts of things."

"Is Mr. McGuire religious? Could he have influenced her?"

"No. Joe's positively anti. And I don't think he could influence Laura on a flavour of ice-cream. They're close enough but he's not the strong character that she is. She's got a mind very much of her own."

"Does he know she's gone AWOL?"

"Nope."

Something in her tone ...

"And you don't want him to know."

"Not unless he has to."

"Okay. Was there any kind of argument with yourself before she left? You know, any bad feeling between you?"

"No, none at all. We've always got on pretty well, I think. We're not joined at the hip or anything, you know? Not that kind of relationship. 'More like sisters than mother and daughter' – that kind of crap. But we've always got on well."

"Okay. Lastly. Is she in any kind of trouble? That you know of? Is she pregnant?"

"*Pregnant!* Laura!"

"It happens, Mrs. McGuire."

"I don't need you to tell me that, Mr. Black. No, Laura is not pregnant."

"You seem very sure."

"Oh, I am, Mr. Black."

"Is there a boyfriend?"

"Boyfriend? Well, there have been one or two."

"Most recently?"

"There was a boy from Broxburn, but they finished up weeks ago."

"Do you know his name?"

"Yes. Billy. Billy something ..."

She searched her mind. I let her search. Billy something from Broxburn wasn't a lot to go on.

"He was in the flute band, I think."

"I would imagine, so are ninety per cent of Broxburn boys called Billy."

"I can't remember his second name. McFarlane, I think. Or was it McCallum? I'm sorry..."

"No matter. If I need him, I'll find him. Right. I think that's all I'll need for the moment. You could maybe jot down your address and phone number on the pad for me."

As she wrote, she asked, "What do you charge?"

"It varies. Standard is forty-five pounds an hour; maximum hundred and fifty a day; mileage 65p a mile; expenses as and when, but never extortionate. I can sleep on a clothes-line when I have to. How did Laura get up to Angus?"

"She drove. She has a maroon Megane." She opened her handbag again and raked through it as she told me the registration, then passed over an envelope. "I hope that's an acceptable down payment."

"I haven't asked for one."

"Nonetheless."

I riffled through the notes in the envelope. Five hundred brick. Fifty lovely crisp pictures of Charles Darwin.

"Very acceptable, Mrs. McGuire."

"Grace."

"Grace. Very acceptable. Let me write you out a receipt."

She looked over the desktop while I was writing. She picked up my paperback copy of the *Complete Plays*.

"Funny."

"What is?"

"You don't strike me as a Shakespeare man."

"Appearance and reality – one of his major themes. Why don't I strike you as a Shakespeare man?"

"Just from the way you talk, I suppose."

"Mrs. McGuire," I said without intonation. "The sign on that door reads 'Private Investigator'. People don't come in here for elocution lessons. I'm a private investigator and I'm good at it. I live in Bathgate and I'm a fairly basic kind of a guy. If I talk coarse at times, that's just the way I've got over the years. It doesn't mean I haven't had an education."

She coloured slightly and adopted a brisker tone. "You're quite right, Mr. Black. I apologise. My remark was unthinking."

"That's okay," I smiled at her. "I like it when people make assumptions about me. They're usually wrong. It helps in my work." I passed her the receipt and said, "Don't give it a second thought."

She smiled and stood up. I stood up too.

"Well, I hope to hear from you soon, Mr. Black. Don't hesitate to get in touch if you should need anything."

"I won't."

We shook hands. And she was gone. It wasn't the hardest thing to do, to watch her sashay out of the place. I checked over her address. A house in the big new estate in Armadale. Well, the 'Dale was certainly attracting a better class of resident these days. I looked again at the snap of her daughter in the bum-bee tartan top. Good-looking girl. Now why would a smart youngster like Laura McGuire fall for that ole-time religion? I wondered.

I went out and up the street. The Steelyard glittered in the glare of sunlight. That's a thing it hasn't done in years: glitter. The Steelyard is Bathgate's town centre. When I was a grub, it was the centre of a bustling town, the busiest and biggest town in the county. There were big department stores like Greig's, gentlemen's outfitters, drapers and haberdashers. The Steelyard was full of benches and shaded by leafy elm trees. Now, Bathgate is a ghost town compared to what it was. All it's missing is the tumbleweed.

History has left us by the wayside in West Lothian. The land that time forgot. I stay here because it's one of the last outposts of Community. They've taken most other things from the people here; that, they haven't been able to. I still know plenty folk I pass on the street. Them or their parents. I sometimes think *that* sense of community is all that we have left.

2

I drove home to Boghall. I parked the banger where the neighbourhood kids couldn't bounce a football off it. Then I went inside to chill for a spell. I live in a three-apartment semi-detached near a block of flats.

There's only me here. Me and Black Jack. No wife, no partner, no regular girl. Once in the bluest of blue moons – O, the darkest blue moon, like maybe a Prussian blue - I get lucky and bring a bedmate back for a night's entertainment. But she never stays longer. And these occasions get less and less frequent as time goes on. Such is life. You get used to it. Custom calls me to it, as Shakey says - that monster custom.

I keep myself simple here. In the living-room there's a TV set that's never on and a hi-fi, apart from the sofa and a couple of chairs. I like to chill out and listen to music. Helps me think. I have a catholic taste in music. Small 'c'. I don't mean I like to listen to Gregorian chant or choirs singing *O Salutaris Hostia*. I don't indulge myself in much but I do in music. CD's and old vinyl are everywhere in the room – on shelves, in racks, stacks and alphabetised boxes. I inherited my father's collection of 60's LP's and have added to it on disc. I like the Beatles, especially once they got into drugs around the time of Rubber Soul and Revolver. The early Stones – before 1970, when they were still capable of being a reasonable wee blues band. I like Dylan. But most of all I like the blues.

I slid an old Sonny Boy Williamson LP out of its inner sleeve and put it on the turntable. The finest exponent of the blues harmonica ever. The old black semi-literate bluesman who found fame and acclaim late in life. In Europe. After busting his old ass around the States, he was lionised at the end in the early 60's by a bunch of white kids in Europe who'd discovered the blues. He came over here on a tour and lapped up the attention. Bought himself a brolly and a bowler, looked like a London business man. A two-toned suit like some old sharecropping Pied Piper. Wheezed his sly innuendos into the mike and blew his harp like a old bad angel. The finest on the Chess label, in my arrogant opinion.

The strains of Don't Start Me to Talkin' blasted from the speaker.

I opened the back door and Black Jack came stalking in from what passes as a garden. Black Jack never mews; he's got dignity. He's been left to shift for himself so often and so long that he's developed a kind of fuck-you independence that I like. I hadn't seen him from the time I put him out the night before, so I knew he'd be hungry. I tipped some cat biscuits into a dish and he set to. Then I eased my length along the settee and listened to Sonny Boy, thinking.

A case at last, after weeks of zilcho. And a very welcome capital D in an envelope to spice things up a bit more.

Black Jack jumped up and lay on the arm of the chair. Black as the Earl of Hell's waistcoat and not to be wooed or coochy-cooed. I didn't ask him where he went to at night or who he saw, and he paid me the same courtesy. Sonny Boy sang knowingly in the background. Lots of people talkin' but mighty few people know.

Right. First thing: get the laptop out and check the MacVicar article on the New Dawn. I would need to snag MacVicar too, in all probability; get some insider trading on the set-up from him. See how easy or otherwise it was to get in. Very otherwise, probably. Cults are notoriously suspicious. There had to be a way – MacVicar had managed it. I might try and unearth the Billy Boy boyfriend, too. Might be some mileage in that. The absentee father would be easy enough to trace. Grace McGuire didn't want him in the loop, at least not yet. But it would do no harm, in any case, to find out where he kept his pyjamas under the pillow. Who knows? I might need input from him at some point.

I Googled the Scotsman site and pulled up Nairn MacVicar's article. There wasn't that much to it. He had, though, spent a couple of days among them, which interested me. It's rarer than hobby-horse shit for cults to allow outsiders access. I would have to find out how he did that. Other than that, the article described how they worshipped together at prayer groups called 'Meets', how they spent the rest of their time in various country activities and how they sold the produce – honey, cheese, milk and so on. A commune, my father would have called them. A kibbutz.

Undoubtedly a bunch of weirdoes. Religious fanatics; born-againers most likely. But they had started to draw a little heat on themselves. The local yokels had been lukewarm on them at first. Just pegged them as a bunch of hippies, growing sunflowers and smoking dope. But things were not quite as simple as that. Hence the reason for MacVicar's spread in the first place. The high heid-yin had a harem of wives. MacVicar's Square One had been that the pointy-heads were accusing these weirdoes of stealing their lassies and brainwashing them into becoming this guy's sex slaves. All at once, Laura McGuire's situation took on a new dimension.

The New Dawners had started off being A1 at Lloyd's with the hillbillies but now were past their sell-by date. I assumed that these people were just another bunch of Apocalypse nutters. Fruitcake religious groups had proliferated around the Millennium.

MacVicar's piece was quite soft on them, pretty much pooh-poohing the shagging and saying that, if the adults wanted a Born Again Bonkerama, then that was up to them. The basic hard facts I gleaned were that the group called the New Dawn had bought Scriddan House, an old mansion and grounds near Edzell up in Angus, and changed the name of the place to Eden.

I would try my luck with MacVicar the next day. I had a hankering to meet the man. I had read his columns and articles for several years and liked his style. Pity about the name. He could hardly have had a bigger caricature of a name if he'd been called Alba McScotia. But that wasn't his fault, I don't suppose. Everybody's got to be called something.

3

I'd just got into the office the next morning when the phone rang. Bert Saunders. DI Saunders of Lothian and Borders Police, F Division. Bert and I go back a long way. I give Bert and his boys handers now and again. Especially with computer work. There's a lot of that these days. The Bow Street Runners call me in sometimes, to check on some scoutmaster's PC. See if he's been downloading what he shouldn't and tweaking his woggle at the same time. I'm something of a nerd when it comes to all that stuff. Bert, on the other hand, thinks a toaster is a pretty slick piece of technology and that Einstein invented the remote control. He greeted me in his usual way.

"Aw right, Seamus?" He'd obviously read an American detective novel once and picked up on the word 'shamus', although not the pronunciation. I told him how it was pronounced, but he kept doing it, anyway.

"Bertie boy, how you doin' these days?"

"Fine and dandy. You busy this mornin'?"

"Not too. I've set up a meeting at lunchtime in Edinburgh. But before that, nowt."

"You hear about the body at Old Bangour?"

"No. I didn't have the car wireless on, this morning."

"Oh, you'll like this one. You might even be able to help us out. There's a wee detail that's got us thinkin'. And I said to myself, 'This is a job for Seamus'. Got time to come out here?"

"Sure. Gimme half an hour."

"Okay. And Seamus…?"

"Yeah?"

"Nobody's called a radio a 'wireless' since 1955."

A pleasant drive out to Livingston. Sunny. Green. Not too busy. The police headquarters are in Almondvale, the main shopping centre. From a distance, the complex is almost eye-catching, with its domes and towers. Xanadu by the Almond. When you're there, it's glass and concrete like everywhere else.

Bert ushered me into a small room and sat down behind the desk, indicating I should take the chair opposite. "You want a coffee or something?"

"No ta."

"Right."

He opened the top drawer of the desk, took out a photograph and slid it over to me. It was of a dead man. He was lying on his front, his head turned to the left and his left arm up by his face. He looked like he was sleeping. Except he had a black and bloody mess where the back of his head should have been. Someone had obviously been keen to admit fresh air and daylight to that head, for whatever reason. The guy looked like he was in his 40's maybe, a good-looking man before his assailant got to work on him. His hair was thick and slightly wavy, his features patrician and finely chiselled – a piece of craftsmanship to contrast with the rough work done at the back. It wasn't the way his mammy would have wanted him to be. The ground he lay on was path and woodland.

I examined the photograph carefully before dropping it on to the desk surface. Bert lifted it and looked closely at it.

"Somebody did a good job," I said.

"Aye. A bloody good job."

"Do you know who he is?"

"Brian Cairns. East Calder. Forty-three. Married man. Father of two. Self-employed builder. Two or three guys workin' for him. Fairly well off. Teetotaller. Football fan. Season-ticket holder at Easter Road."

"Yeah?"

"Found on the mortuary road at Old Bangour. Some old codger from Dechmont, retired guy probably, out walkin' his dog. Found him last night. Noo that's what I call an irony."

"What is?"

"You know why Cairns would be at Old Bangour?"

I puffed out my lips and thought. Bangour Village Hospital, to give it its correct title. Old Bangour is just its Confirmation name. The county's asylum, built long ago to house lunatic paupers of the city of Edinburgh. The Edinburgh District Lunacy Board bought the site, fourteen miles away from the capital. The name "Bangour" means "Hill of the Wild Goats" in the ancient Celtic tongue; and the estimable burghers of Edinburgh preferred *their* wild goats to be tended as far away from the hills of their own city as possible. It was the Seventies before they accepted West Lothian as sole catchment area. My father had been an in-patient in Old Bangour.

But it was shut completely in 2004. Been a derelict site of ghostly villas ever since. There was talk of building an estate of premium quality housing there but so far nothing has materialised.

"I don't know…" I drawled. "A bird-watcher? Or a former patient on a sentimental journey?"

Bert smirked. "Old Bangour is where the doggers go."

"Is it? Get along, little doggie."

"Aye. Sex in cars. Open air rumpo. So called because their alibi is supposed to be that they're walkin' the dug. The irony is that Cairns's body was found by probably the only genuine guy walkin' his dug in the grounds this year."

"Really? Is that where they go? I often wondered."

"Did you?"

"Well, not *that* often, to be honest. It crossed my mind."

'Well, now you know."

"I'm not convinced about your etymology of the term, either," I said. "I think it's from 'dogging' meaning following people."

"Who gives a tin shit?" said Bert.

I thought for a second.

"Is it just me or is that a sad thing to be doing?" I wondered.

"What? Watchin' strangers shaggin' in cars? Aye, I think it is."

"I mean, when did shagging get boring? I missed that. Was it in the papers?"

"I'm just glad to know that it still goes on, mate," laughed Bert.

"You too?" We laughed together. But briefly. It wasn't that funny.

"I suppose it's meant to be sophisticated," said Bert.

"Yeah, I suppose so. Like live theatre instead of the pictures." Then I said, "So Mr. Cairns liked a bit company when he was getting his rocks off. Maybe he strickly have got next to someone."

Bert repeated in a singsong pisstake falsetto, "Strictly have got *next* to someone? Is that fae that plantation music you listen tae? What the fuck does it mean?"

"That he got too involved, possibly. Think things went a bit too far with somebody, maybe?

"Could be."

"Might have tried it on with somebody's wee jelly roll, you know? In the heat of the moment. Guy didn't like the notion of somebody else cutting his grass...."

"That's what they're there for, Jack. It's lawnmowers at dusk."

"Or somebody's missus preferred the way Brian did it as compared to her husband. Wallop! Tap on the crust with a toffee-hammer. Find the weapon?"

"No yet. We haven't found much, to be honest. I've got the guys doin' a fingertip search now."

"Think it might be related to the dogging?"

"I think it might be, Seamus, it might be. What I wanted to ask your advice aboot was this. Found it on his person." He took a sheet of typing paper out of the drawer and passed it to me. "Of course, this isnae the original. Forensics guys have got that. I just typed up what it said. And the original was typed, tae. No handwriting analysis possible, I'm afraid. Nae prints either, it seems."

On the sheet were two lines.

O unseen shame! invisible disgrace!
Thy grace being gain'd cures all disgrace in me.

Bert said, "What is that – poetry? The Bible? A proverb?"

"It rings a bell," I said. "I think it's Shakespeare but I can't be a hundred per cent sure. Quotes from two different sources, I think."

"You mean you dinnae ken?" Bert said. "I'm disappointed in you, auld son. Was a' that good classical education wasted?"

"Fuck, I don't recall every single line the Swan ever wrote.

I'm not *that* good. I've a feeling it may be one of the less known things. Why'nt you just Google it?"

Bert looked disappointed.

"When I've got a tame smart-arse like you around? I need to know what it means, not just where it's from."

"I'll look it up for you. Must be a clue. Where was it?"

"Folded in his wallet. I don't think Brian Cairns was the kind of guy to carry quotes about with him. So somebody left it there. The one who killed him, most likely."

"Strange thing to do, though, Bert. Why leave any clue at all? Unless ... there's a point being made here. The killer wants the police to know *why* he was killed."

"Aye. And the word 'disgrace' is important. Somebody disapproved o' what he was up to. It's a religious thing, isn't it?"

"A moral one at least. His wife, maybe."

"Maybe."

"Children?"

"Unlikely. His son's at university in England, away workin' in India for the holiday. His lassie's as mad as a mongoose. Up in the locked ward at St. John's. Severe depression. Self-harmer. Several suicide attempts. Oh Jesus, I'm sorry, Jack."

"No, no. 'S all right. Shit happens to lots of people besides me."

"Still... nae prizes for diplomacy."

"Forget it. I still think it's not a natural thing to do. It's artificial. It's stagey, don't you think? Especially for a crime of passion. You don't bludgeon somebody to death when the red mist comes down and then look up a nice wee quote to stick in his pocket once the red mist thins out again. I don't like it. It's all been pre-meditated and arranged."

"You got time to visit the scene?"

"Sure." I looked at my watch. "If we go quickly."

4

The mortuary path runs from the back streets of the village of Dechmont into the grounds of what was once Bangour Village Hospital. It was a suitably wooded and spooky place for a stiff repository. I could imagine some poor nurse walking home to Dechmont past the sombre building on a windy night. She'd be braver than me, I can tell you.

We crossed the blue-tape line and strolled some way up the path. Bacon was much in evidence, uniformed and plain clothes.

"Found the guy there," said Bert. An area was cordoned off at the edge of the path and the woods.

"Fairly far down the path then, from the hospital itself," I mused.

"Aye," agreed Bert. "The actual hanky-panky itsel' takes place up at the back of the old admin buildings. So I'm told," he added, seeing me smile.

"Right. I didn't think there would be any sylvan shenanigans," I said. "Coupling in the trees like nymph and satyr. Well, for one, the guy's fully clothed."

"Aye," said Bert slowly. "Pursued down here by his assailant. First blow prob'ly killed him. So the path guys think. The rest was just savagery."

"Got the path report already?"

"Naw, fuck. Nothin' official. Just verbal reports. Impressions. Hodge thinks Cairns was killed wi' an axe or somethin' like one. Some of the wounds suggest that. Mind you, there's not that much of his skull that isn't pulp. But it looks that way at the moment."

"If Paul Hodge says it, it'll be true. He knows his stuff, all right."

"Nae point in having a pathologist if you don't back his judgement."

We turned and started to wander back down the path.

"Gonnae be hard to get folk to talk now," Bert mumped.

"Yeah. I don't suppose doggers would be too keen on admitting to the polis what they get up to at the best of times. They're going to vanish like snow off a dyke now that this has happened."

"Naw, we won't get one bonker up here for months now. If ever again."

"Sure. They'll most likely move on. Find somewhere else for their gardening."

"Well, let us know if you find anything on that poetry or whatever it is, won't you?"

"Will do, Bert. I'll get on to it a.s.a.p. Off to Edinburgh now. But I'll give you a bell later on."

"Cheers, Seamus. Take care."

I headed back to my car. Bert stopped to speak to a uniform sergeant.

5

Just why Bert or his boys didn't do what I did straightaway, I have no idea. He isn't a neanderthal, by any manner of means. Maybe he just isn't all that literary. Still, you would have thought somebody might have suggested it. I suspect that he was bringing me on board. He thinks I'm a pain, but he knows I'm a pain with one or two good ideas.

I drove straight to the library on Hopetoun Street and looked up a Dictionary of Quotations. Of course, it wouldn't include everything but that was the obvious first place to look.

The lines were there and I was right. Shakey. Two sources. 'O unseen shame! invisible disgrace!' From *The Rape of Lucrece*. 'Thy grace being gain'd cures all disgrace in me'. From *Love's Labour's Lost*.

That would explain why they didn't spring immediately to mind. I'd only ever read *LLL* once and that was at university. I didn't like it much. Not many people did. I suspect even Shakey himself was a bit iffy about that one, didn't include it on his CV too often. It was rarely staged and even more rarely read. *Lucrece* is a poem. I'm not as big on Shakey's poems as I am on the drama. So. Two quotes from obscure sources. Common theme – disgrace. Why disgrace? Dogging, obviously. To be exposed as a dogger would be a disgrace. But 'thy grace being gained *cures* all disgrace...' What was gracious about him? Who wanted their disgrace cured? Rape! The Rape of Lucrece. Did he rape somebody? Was this revenge? Did his murder cure his victim's disgrace? Love's labour was lost?

Could that be the reason for Cairns's brutal murder? Disgrace could result from *any* offence, sexual or otherwise; I knew that. But it had to be sexual; had to be. The choice of setting for the murder and the lines from Shakespeare indicated that. I decided to hang on to this information an hour or so longer before I shared it with Bert and the boys at Almondvale. An idea had just occurred to me.

I got back to the office. I had half an hour to kill before I left for Edinburgh. I flicked through my personal phone book and dialled a number. A man answered it after six rings.

22

"Hello?"

"Keith! Hi, it's Jack Black."

"Jack! What can I do for you?"

"Some information, Keith. It'll be privileged, but anything you can get would be appreciated."

"Go on."

"Patient in the locked ward. Female. Name of Cairns. Um, suicidal, depressive, several serious attempts to do away with herself."

"Aye…?"

"I need to know if there's any suggestion of sexual abuse from the father."

"Fucksake, Jack! You know that stuff is confidential. I'd get my ballocks ripped off if they found me passing that kind of information to a third party."

"I know, Keith, son. I know. Just … any information, however insignificant it might seem to you, would be invaluable."

"This for a case?"

"Yeah, I wouldn't ask otherwise. Nothing trivial, pal. You know that. All received in utmost confidence of course."

He sighed. "How soon do you want this stuff?"

"Yesterday."

"I'll see what I can do."

"Ah, you're solid gold, Keith son, solid gold. I won't forget this."

"Yeah, right, Jack."

And he hung up. Keith Young was a good man. He'd nursed my father in his last years.

6

MacVicar had agreed to meet me at lunchtime to give me the SP on the New Dawn. I travelled through to Edinburgh by train. I reasoned that a journalist's lunch was most likely to consist of three liquid courses and a pie, so why risk taking the wheels? Most journos are on the bottle more than a baby. The station is directly opposite my office and the journey is pleasant enough. It takes slightly less than half an hour and rattles you along nicely through the West Lothian countryside. Then Edinburgh's outskirts start springing up around the line in towers of flats, furniture repositories, goods yards, housing schemes and playing fields. The whole experience would be fairly enjoyable if it weren't for the invention of the mobile phone.

Now, I realise I'm being as old-fashioned as spats here and that I'm pissing against the wind. But I loathe the way that, because people *have* these things, they feel obliged to use them all the time. Today, at three locations along the carriage, terminally irritating people were babbling on them. I looked out the window hard and hated in silence. I tried Transcendental Meditation. It didn't work. But, eventually, the train pulled up at Waverley and I got a taxi down to the *Scotsman* building at Holyrood. Come what come may, time and the hour runs through the roughest day.

MacVicar turned out to be quite different from my expectation. For one, he took me to a bijou restaurant not far from the paper's office where we ate crab salad, and he drank mineral water throughout the meal – which I paid for, naturally. He was, however, fat and heavy, short of breath, with greasy curls that badly needed cutting and a faceful of raddled leading-man good looks. His byline photograph must have been taken some years before, judging by the avoirdupois he had piled on. He was carrying more weight than Atlas. What's more, he constantly leaked beads and streaks of sweat during our conversation. I guessed something was amiss with his ticker. Knocking on heaven's door.

Chomping his way through crab and lettuce, he said, "So why are you interested in the New Dawn?"

"A client of mine says her daughter has joined them. The girl is 18, was due to go to Uni in October. Never shown any interest in religion before. Now she's playing Isabella."

"Isabella?"

"The heroine in *Measure for Measure*. Cloistering herself from the world. Her mother wants me to find a few things out. Maybe bring her back, if I can."

"So, are you really a private eye?"

"Really." I showed him my card.

"I don't think I've ever met one before. What do you do?"

"All sorts. Right now, I'm trying to find Laura McGuire."

"What do you need to be a private eye? I don't mean qualifications, though I suppose you have them…"

"I do."

"… but what I really mean is what qualities do you need? I suppose being a hard man with a nose like a bloodhound helps."

"I wouldn't class myself as a hard man. I can look after myself okay. That's about it."

"Do you have a gun? Have you ever shot anybody?"

"No and no. But I do know how to use one. I got myself trained. No, what you need, more than anything, in this job is patience. And lots of it. You need to have the patience of a piano-tuner. Most of my job is waiting and watching. Watching and listening."

"Makes sense. Tuned any good pianos lately?"

"Well, right now, I'm trying to find a baby grand called Laura McGuire. And I'm trying to find out about this New Dawn shower."

"Forgive me, Mr. Black. I'm just interested. The Dawn? Well, they're pretty much as I described them. Bunch of fundamentalists who believe we're in the Last Days and are trying to prepare themselves for the Big Finish. They believe *they* will be on the right hand side of the Lord when it all kicks off, of course. But don't they all? Meanwhile, they till the land, and they milk cows and they flog their dairy stuff to keep themselves alive."

"How did they get a hold of this old manor place – this Scriddan House?"

He took a sip of mineral water, but I could tell he would rather be drinking something with a bit more zing to it. He didn't get that shape by drinking Highland Spring.

"They were given it by an Angel. They call themselves 'Angels', by the way. The place is now called 'Eden', you see? Makes sense. Brother Matthew, I think was the name. One of their oldest converts. His wife had passed on and he had no family. So the New Dawn got it."

"These fuckers always fall on their feet, don't they? Tell me about the leader, the one that's suspected of plenty of sex."

"That would be Brother Gabriel."

"Right."

"There were rumours of sex with minors when I was up there. Which is the main reason I went. I found no evidence of that. While there is plenty of hochmagandy – group sex is encouraged, for one thing – there was no evidence whatsoever of underage stuff."

"But they like their jollies."

"They certainly do. And Brother Gabriel, being the Patriarch, gets his fair share, let me tell you."

"Tell me about him."

"Well, he is an extremely charismatic guy. Which explains why these people hang on his every word. They believe that he is the latest prophet. The latest, and the last. Like I say, they believe the end is nigh. And they believe that Brother Gabriel will take them with him to Heaven. It also explains why so many of these babes are willing to warm his lonely bed at night. Makes sense."

"Young?"

"No. Middle aged. Tall, slim, white haired and moustachioed like a patriarch should be. Good looking. Has a winning way with everybody."

"I wonder who he is," I mused.

"Oh, I know who he is," said MacVicar. "I did a little digging after I'd been there. It's not only private eyes who can find things out."

"Well of course not. Otherwise, my job would be impossible."

"His name is Dominic Tweedie…"

"What! Not from Linlithgow?" I nearly coughed up a pellet of crabmeat.

"Yes! He was born in Linlithgow. Do you know him?"

"Well, I know who he *is*. He was at university with my father. Both from West Lothian schools. My father was at St. Mary's. Tweedie at Linlithgow Academy. They ended up on the same English and History course. My father said he went to one or two parties at the end of the 60's when he was there and started to hang with him after that. He was charismatic then, too. Always had a dame on the go. Picked them up and discarded them all over the place. The gutters around the university were full of discarded females when Tweedie was around. Yeah, he was good looking as a young man. He was the first one my father ever saw roll a joint, too. Fucksake! Dominic Tweedie! It's a small world, right enough. It's probably a small next world too. So that's what the bastard is up to nowadays. Listen, Nairn. How did you manage to wangle your way in there? I mean, most of these communes are as tight as a clam's chuff. The last thing they would want would be guys like you snooping around, I would have thought."

MacVicar pushed his plate away and jabbed a toothpick into his mouth. Not an improvement.

"Yeah, I would have thought so, too. I'll tell you, I didn't expect to get very far with them. But one of the guys in the office got the landline number and I just dialled it. Got hold of a guy called Brother Ira. Ira is … well, I suppose he's their version of a PR man. Big, black guy, a Jew from Chicago. He couldn't do enough for me. I imagine he saw the need for positive publicity, once I'd explained that I was scratching around the sex angle. The only stipulation he made was no photographers. *He* gave me the mug shot we used for the spread. Probably had one of the Angels take it."

"You got that phone number?"

"Sure."

He rooted in his inside pocket, produced an address book and read me off the number. I jotted it into mine.

"I don't think Ira will be quite as accommodating if you tell him you're a private detective. Hardly the same thing."

"Which is why I'll take a different approach."
"Makes sense. What?"
"I don't know yet. I'll think of something."
"Well, good luck. Happy hunting."
"Cheers. I owe you one."

7

The train ride back to Bathgate was a bigger drag than a dead walrus. I was full of shellfish and greens and starting to quease up by the time I emerged into the afternoon sun on King Street. I checked the phone in the office. Niente. Then I strolled up to Mulholland's. I knew I'd find Charlie Peel – Orange Peel – in there at this time, in the corner in his dungarees and cloth bunnet, having a couple of snorters after his shift to give him the courage to go home and face another evening with Betty. Sure enough, there he was with his big red face, his pint half empty by his elbow.

"Jack?" said Rab the barman.

"Pint, Rab, please. Aw right, Charlie? Just finished?"

"Aye. Gled tae see the back ae it."

"For a pint?"

"Gaun then." He immersed his face into the pint glass. It emptied with a sizzling sound.

"And a pint for Charlie," I said. Then I stood next to Charlie. "Know anything about the flute band in Broxburn?" I said.

"Wan or two things," he said. Charlie was high up in the Orange Lodge in Bathgate, hence his nickname.

"Ever heard of a boy called Billy McFarlane, or Billy McCallum maybe, that plays with them?"

"Naw, Jack. I widnae ken aw the band members anyway. I ken the band leader's a block called Gavin Sherp. An' I ken they practise on Wednesday nights in the Academy. If you go through tae the Bronx the night, that's where you'll find them. Seven o'clock onwards. If you need tae talk tae this boy, that's whit I suggest. If it's ony use tae ye."

"Loads a use, Charlie, thanks," I said.

"Tell Gavin I sent ye, if it'll help."

"Even better."

Next I drove over to the Local History library in Blackburn. Beryl, the librarian there, is an extremely useful contact for somebody like me. She knows everything about her subject and is clued up on local current affairs too. She's ten years or so older than me but by no means a blue stocking. Slim, elegant, with a very pleasant smile. I've thought about pitching a woo once or twice but never got round to it. I suspect if I tried it, she'd hit it out of the park.

Today I just wanted to check up on some back numbers of the local rag, 'The Courier'. There are always a handful of folk in the main room, trying to shake apples from their family trees. I told Beryl that I wanted to look up the name Dominic Tweedie.

"Oh yes, the man who ran *Flash* computers?"

"The very he," I agreed. Told you – what Beryl doesn't know isn't worth knowing.

She looked up the name on a computer, fetched a box from a drawer, pulled a spool of film from the box and threaded it through the capstans of a viewer and, reminding me how to feed the spool on and how to zoom in on the information I wanted, let me get on with it.

I found what I wanted quickly enough. I'd remembered Tweedie had been something of a big shot in the 80's and that things hadn't quite worked out for him. In here was the whole dope on the sting.

Dominic Tweedie had set up *Flash* Computers Ltd in Livingston with a coffle of about a hundred workers. The operation was financed by share issues, fixed term bank loans, grants from the Local Enterprise Board and the European Commission. *Flash* tendered to supply computers for local schools, won a contract to equip the Computer and Business Studies Departments of three Secondaries and the FE College in Bathgate. The contract was completed satisfactorily – although the firm's working capital in relation to its cash flow cycle not ideal. (No, I don't know what that means, either. I did Latin.)

The next year, *Flash* tendered won another, more ambitious, contract. Things were looking good but, after six months, it became obvious that the workforce couldn't meet delivery dates. Overtime working was introduced and some component production contracted out.

Despite difficulties, contract completed in time but the extra costs had peeled away already narrow profit margins. HP instalments on machinery fell into arrears, as did repayments of bank loans. Suppliers were not paid for two months. There was no profit for Dominic Tweedie, no dividend for the company's shareholders, and no candy all round.

Following year, *Flash* lost the Local Education Authority contract. Unable to find any other customer, they found themselves negotiating a well-known stretch of polluted water without any means of steerage.

And the shit got deeper and miles more fragrant. Eventually, creditors passed a resolution at a meeting in a Livingston hotel to appoint a Liquidator, in terms of the Insolvency Act of 1986. *Flash* Computers Ltd. were wound up. Tweedie was liable for all of *Flash*'s debts up to the limit of all personal capital invested. Directors and shareholders lost their shareholdings in the firm. Tweedie disappeared completely off the face of the earth. Just disappeared up his own PC with a flash.

This was the Tweedie that the West Lothian public had read about in the blatts. There was reference to one or two other big money ideas that had bombed. That place outside East Calder, The Foxhole, a concrete pillbox like a nuclear fallout shelter. He'd turned it into a rave venue and the kids had come from far and near, paying big bucks for their jigging to electronic Jew's harp music. The place got busted and he fucked off into the sunset again. Every time, Tweedie had either popped the pod before the faeces struck the ventilator or had gone to earth as soon as it had. Nice man. Now, if MacVicar was right, he had turned from Mammon to the service of the Lord. How likely was that?

Well, maybe less *un*likely than might be imagined. Few other people knew what I knew about Tweedie: that he was as mad as Merlin. He had had several sojourns as an unwilling guest of the psychiatric services in West Lothian. Hallucinogenic drugs had fucked him up. Drug-induced psychosis. He had spent months as an in-patient in the locked ward at Old Bangour, in several admissions. My father had been a patient there, too, a couple of times but his problem was different. His problem was profound depression.

I visited the pater up in Old Bangladesh once. He was in an

armchair by the window. This time, he was talking. Most times you went in there, he stayed silent and looked through you to the edge of the universe. But this time he talked. He was interested in a fellow patient, a man who had been admitted the previous day. This man was standing by the window, looking out over the rather special view across the wooded valley. He stood with his hands behind his back, for all the world like a man standing looking out of his window at home. He was tall and slim, with collar-length fair hair.

"That's Dominic Tweedie," my father had said. "I was at university with him. Very clever man. A bugger for the ladies, though. That and the old acid. Very 'I Am the Walrus', that one!" And he had wheezed that smoker's laugh that was so characteristic of him and that he so seldom used those days. "Probably in here because he's tripping like a bus to Burntisland!"

The man had turned from the window and walked away towards the snooker table without acknowledging us. He was very good-looking, with eyes honed blue and sharp as a Gillette blade. Dominic Tweedie. Tycoon and lunatic. Now a fisher of men.

8

I tooled the Nissan east along the A89, headed towards Broxburn by the bings. Bings are slagheaps. Most mining areas used to have them, even if they no longer do: black, conical hills of coal waste that scarred the landscape. In West Lothian, we had them but we also had pink bings. West Lothian was the site of the world's first oil industry, back in the dinosaur days when men used to dig oil-shales out of the ground and blast them in furnaces long enough to trickle the black gold out of them. When that was done, all that was left were useless pink husks, so they made mountains out of them. There were dozens of these table-mountains scattered around the county and folk used to complain about how they were huge eyesores that ought to be levelled.

Me, I liked them. Beautiful, colossal pink bings that looked like buttes and mesas way out west, when the sun was going down in the evenings. Nowhere else in the world had these features, nowhere. In a couple of generations, nobody would know, unless they looked it up in Wikipedia, that they were bings – they would just be the pink mountains of West Lothian. But there's always some bozo with an eye to the main chance. Some guy bought the Deans bing for a handful of reading-sweeties and then made a fortune selling it to the construction companies that were building the motorways through the county. They used it for bottoming the roads. So even the bings came to have a value, and they started removing them. I regret it. They're removing a unique feature. But there are still some around and most of these are in the Broxburn area.

I had no great eagerness to be anywhere near a flute band, practising or perfect. They are just one aspect of the religious shit that has bedevilled Scotland for years. I hadn't been joking when I told Grace McGuire that I was not a religious man. I am spectacularly not a religious man.

The Academy in Broxburn hides away up a warren of streets with couthy Scots names like Galmeilen, Liggat Syke and Timmeryetts. 'Timmeryetts' means 'wooden gates'. 'Galmeilen' might mean 'home of the drug dealer with the savage big dog' for all I know. This was not the most des.res. district of West Lothian. I'd been here before, and I knew.

There were several cars in the school yard. I parked beside a Suzuki 4x4, painted in the kind of purply pink that really ought to be a shade of lipstick, and went in. The janitor jumped out of his little howff by the front door like a troll and stopped me. He had greasy black hair, shiny stubble and a nose that could have picked peas out of a milk bottle. His breath smelt like he licked out ashtrays for a hobby.

"Where ye gaun, pal?"

"I want to talk to somebody in the flute band."

"Musical education, you mean?"

"Eh?"

"The let is allocated in the name of 'musical education'. No the flute band."

"Right. So some weeks it's the flute band, and some weeks it's the Royal Philharmonic with Sir John Barbirolli."

He looked at me. He didn't like me, I could tell. I wasn't exactly smitten, either.

"Smart cunt, eh?" he said.

"I'm Jack Black," I replied, flashing him my ID. "I'm a private investigator on a case, which makes me the smartest and the cuntest. I'd like to talk to a member of the band, if that's no gonny rain on your parade."

That tickled him. He pursed his lips. Then he gave me a smile. I wished he hadn't. He had a mouth like a plateful of Sugar Puffs.

"Righto," he said. "Aw right, then. It's jist, Ah've goat tae be aware ae a' whae's here. Security 'n' that, ye know?"

"Right."

"They're through there." And he nodded in the direction of the hall, from which sounds were emanating that could only have been made by a flute band.

I don't know if you've ever heard a flute band, but it's one of the most unusual sounds you'll ever come across. The skittering of the side drums, and the pulse of the bass drum are the underpinning for the shrill sound of the flutes. Only, it's not an actual flute that they play. It's a fife, a much simpler instrument, originally military, that produces a harsh and piercing sound. What the Swan calls 'the vile squealing of the wry-neck'd fife'. If you hear a whole band of these ear-piercing pipes blowing in unison, it's unsettling, to say the least. Probably the intention.

When I walked into the hall, it was like walking into the gym hall of any school. It all came back to me in a guff of sweaty feet. The band were not actually practising yet, just goofing around, blowing fragments of tune or practising their wallops on the drum. A dog-faced boy near the door had a flute in his hand and was looking at it as if he hadn't quite worked out what to do with it yet. I spoke to him.

"I'm looking for a man called Gavin Sharp."

"Ats him ower 'err," he growled without in any way indicating where he meant me to look.

"Where?"

"Him wi' the baldie heid."

I identified Mr. Sharp, leafing through some music sheets, with his back to the band. I strolled over to him, my footsteps sounding on the boards of the floor.

"Mr. Sharp?"

"Aye," he said, turning round. "What can I do ye for?"

"My name's Jack Black," I said, showing him my card. "I'm a private investigator. I'd like a word with one of your bandsmen."

"What aboot?"

"Ah, well. That's private. I was told to mention Charlie Peel's name to you. Charlie said you would see me all right."

"Charlie, aye? How's he daein'?"

"He was fine when I saw him in the boozer."

"Aye, he likes his ale, dis Charlie. Right, Mr. Black. Whit one is it you want to speak tae? I hope whoever it is hasnae got himsel' in bother."

"No, no. I don't think so, Mr. Sharp. The fella's name is Billy."

Sherp smiled.

"Billy McCallum. Or McFarlane? A name like that."

"McPartland?"

"Aye, that'll be him."

"Billy! Man here wantin' tae talk tae ye," he yelled at a

group of young men. Then he said to me, "There's a room ben the corridor there. Give ye a bit a privacy, if ye want."

"Thanks."

Billy McPartland slouched over. Exactly what I expected: tall, athletically built, reasonably handsome with a plook or two blemishing his cherubic complexion, and all his brains in his ballop. He was wearing a denim shirt, open enough at the neck to reveal that his chain bore an RFC badge. Rangers Football Club. He reeked of aftershave. He looked at me resentfully and jerked his head upwards in interrogation.

"Who a' you?"

"Can I talk to you for a minute or two, Billy?" I said. "It's quite important. Mr. Saerp suggested we use the room down the corridor."

"You the polis?" he asked suspiciously.

"Not quite," I replied and preceded him down the corridor.

The room was small and stacked with desks. A strip light hummed on the ceiling. A greenish blackboard fixed to the wall had a stupendously breasted nude scrawled on it in chalk and the legend FTP done in various hands.

"I won't keep you long, Billy," I said reassuringly, and flashed my ID again. "I'm Jack Black and I'm a private investigator."

"So what are you wantin' wi' me?"

"Do you recognise this girl?" I asked as I passed him the photograph. He replied immediately.

"Aye, it's Laura. Laura McGuire. How? Has anythin' happened to her?" He handed me back the snap and I carefully replaced it in my wallet, before carefully not answering his question.

"When was the last time you saw her, Billy?"

"Aboot a month ago. Maybe a wee bit mair, maybe a wee bit less."

"Mm-hmm. Were you fond of her?"

"I went oot wi' her for a wee while, aye. What's a' this aboot?"

"All in good time. How did you split up?"

"We'd a fa' oot. She said I was seein' somebody else, got a

36

wee bit jealous, like, ay? I said I wasnae mairrit tae her. We were jist gaun oot, it wisnae anythin' serious. An' well … wan thing borrow't another, an' she just walked oot on me, ay?"

"Where was this?"

"Club Earth."

A nightclub in Livingston, m'lud.

"And *were* you seeing anybody else?"

"What's it tae you?"

"It might be relevant."

"Ah go oot wi' a lot a lassies. Ahm young. Nae commitments, eh? Ah tell them, like, try tae be fair tae thum. Ah say tae thum that Ahm no the serious type. Jist a guid time an' a few laughs, know what Ah mean?"

"I know exactly what you mean. How did you get on with her mother?"

"Aw, her mother wisnae keen on me gaun oot wi' her at a', I don't think."

"Why would that be?"

"Well, Ah mean … come on, think about it."

I thought about it.

"Nothing's jumping out at me."

"Well, 's obvious, ay?" He flicked the RFC badge on his chain and smirked. Nodded towards the sound of the band just starting to play. "Ah am what Ah am, and they are what they are."

"And that is?"

"Well… wi' a name like McGuire… eh? Cath'lics."

"Right. So you think Mrs. McGuire disapproved of the relationship because of the religious thing."

"Aye. 'S obvious, intit?"

I looked at him. He was a cocky young fucker, and no mistake.

"Did Laura and you ever discuss the religious thing?"

"Naw. She never mention't it. An' Ah certainly didnae. Ah don't think she was a' that bother't wi religion, anyways, you know?"

"Was it a sexual relationship?"

"Mind yer ain fuckin' business!" he snapped. "What's that tae you?"

I shrugged. "Might be important. Did you hit her, Billy?"

He coloured furiously. "Naw ah never. How? What's happened tae her? Hus she hud an accident?"

"No. She's left the area. I just wonder why a girl like Laura would take off the way she has. There must have been a reason."

"Aw, so you're tryin' tae find her?"

"Something like that."

"Well, Ah didnae hit her an' Ah didnae hurt her. An' you're a cheeky cunt."

"Don't be offended, Billy. I just need to ask questions. Sometimes they're awkward. And you haven't seen her since that time at Club Earth?"

"Naw. Ah've moved on, man. Different day, different girl. Know what Ah mean?"

"I believe I do, Billy. One last thing before I let you get back to your musical soirée. Could you just tell me your address and phone number? I probably won't need to get in touch with you again, but you never know."

He gave me an address in Wyndford Avenue and a phone number. I jotted these details in my notebook and then slipped it into my jacket pocket.

"Well, thanks a lot, Billy. You've been most helpful."

"Right. Ah hope Laura's okay. She was aw right, you know? Ah hope she's okay."

"I hope so too, Billy. I hope so too."

We returned to the hall. The band were giving some tune I didn't recognise big licks. Billy went to the corner and found his flute. I nodded and waved to Gavin Sharp as I left.

Cinders the janny materialised out of his cubbyhole again like a djinn. He favoured me with another flash of his mossy green smile. It was obvious that he hadn't brushed his teeth in years. Maybe he combed them.

"Aye-aye..." He favoured me with another waft of old stogey breath.

"Hello again."

"Ah see that wis Billy the Buhll ye were speakin' tae."

"Billy, yeah."

"Ah'm no surprised. That yin's worth the watchin', believe

you me."

"Is he? In what way?"

"Fanny daft. He'd shag a ragman's trumpet. Ride a puddock if it stoapt jumpin' long enough."

"Aye? Well, there's a lot of young laddies like that. 'And, truly, in my youth, I suffered much extremity for love, very near this'."

"Eh?"

"It's a tendency of the young, to be overfond of the old hochmagandie."

"Aye, mibby. But that yin? If it's goat a fanny, he'll hae a go at it. Seen the purple jeep oot in the car park?"

"Yes."

"His. It's a shaggin' wagon."

"Well, I'd love to stay here just shooting the breeze with you," I said. "But I've my hair to wash."

He laughed again. He was getting to be fond of me, I could tell.

"Oh, one thing," I said, as if it had just occurred to me.

"Whit?" he said eagerly.

"Would you say Billy was a violent laddie?"

"Naw. No jist whit ye'd cry 'vi'lent'. He widnae go lookin' fur trouble. Bit he kin handle hissel'. He kicked a boy's fuck in, wan night in the Strathbrock, fur spillin' his pint."

"Oh well," I said, "so long as he isn't violent. I'll be off."

"Aye, well, nae rest for the wicked," he quipped.

The sun was slanting over the school yard. I strolled across and shook my head as I passed the Suzuki. You wonder if some folk have ever heard the word 'cliché'. I got in the jalopy and switched on Sonny Boy as I shot the crow. He was singing one of my favourites.

"Do me a favour, darlin', keep our business to yourself."

9

Three times that evening, I rang the number MacVicar had given me. The first time, I let it ring out for three minutes, but there was no answer. The second time, I rang it for another two minutes – same lack of response. I put Howlin' Wolf on the player and sat back in my armchair.

Black Jack flicked up onto the arm and sat upright, staring at me. I had no light on in the room and he was just a silhouette with two glowing green eyes. He fixed them on me steadily as I ran one or two ideas past him. I did that sometimes.

"That boyfriend one, that Billy the Buhll. I don't like him much. And I don't trust him, either. There's something about him that doesn't ring true. And, now that I think of it ... something he said doesn't quite square with what Grace McGuire said yesterday. She says she and the girl have no religion. They're not believers. But the Buhll said that Grace didn't like him going with Laura because he's a Protestant – well, an Orangeman – and they're Catholics. They can't both be right."

Black Jack didn't answer.

"Or can they? Maybe Grace just doesn't approve of the Orange stuff full stop. She could have disapproved of the lassie going with an Orangeman, plain and simple. But maybe it's something else all together. Billy didn't strike me as an intellectual gymnast. She would want somebody with a bit more class for her daughter, surely."

I sat and mulled this over for a while Black Jack waited patiently.

"And why should a young woman, with no previous interest in anything religious, end up shutting herself off from the world in a religious community? If she isn't religious. It just doesn't make sense, does it Jack?"

Black Jack yawned so extravagantly that I thought his head was going to split in two. There was silence for a moment.

"It does if something's happened to *make* her want to join a religious community, get out of the world for a while."

I looked at the cat as the thought struck me. "Well, of

course," I said. "She's baking one; I'm sure of it. The little lady is with child. And you want out, don't you? Right. First, we let *you* out on the ran-dan, and then we try this number again. The sooner we get a look at this Eden place the better."

I let Black Jack out and I shut the door again. I rang the New Dawn for a third time. This time, after about ten rings, the phone was picked up and a voice said, "Eden. The New Dawn."

This voice was basso and very profundo and the speech had a lazy American twang to it: the sort of voice that, before its owner found the Lord and moved on to higher concerns, would have had female hearts fluttering, the minute he opened his mouth. Even if it was just to ask for a pack of cigarettes in a drugstore.

"Am I speaking to Brother Ira?" I asked.

"You are sir," he replied. "And to whom am I speaking?"

"My name is Jack Black, Brother Ira, and I have a great favour to ask of you. Well, of your entire community and your Patriarch."

"Of what nature is the favour, Mr. Black?"

"I am a writer, Brother, and I have a commission from Frank Sexton of Cowgate publishing to write a study on closed religious communities in contemporary Scottish society. I read Mr. MacVicar's piece on the New Dawn in *The Scotsman* and was fascinated by it. It seems to me that the New Dawn would be the very type of community I should like to consider. I will, of course, be discussing traditional Christian closed orders but many people are interested in the newer sects such as your own that have come into being in recent times. I wondered how I might go about seeking permission to spend some time in your company so that I can write about your faith. I would, of course, make all of my notes and drafts available to your people at any time during the research period."

"Well, Mr. Black, such a matter would be for our Patriarch, Brother Gabriel, to decide. He has sole responsibility for such things."

"Might I speak to Brother Gabriel, Brother?"

The laugh was even more bass than the speaking voice.

"No, sir. Not quite. What I will do, Mr. Black, is I will convey your request to the Patriarch and, once he has made his decision, will communicate that to you in the fullness of time. If you would be so good as to provide me with your telephone number?"

I was so good. Both landline numbers and my cell. That good. Oh yes, even I owned one; that device of Beelzebub himself. I hated having to go over to the Dark Side but, being in the present tense, I was more or less obliged to own one.

"Would this consultation and decision making on the Patriarch's part be a lengthy process? In your estimation, Brother Ira?"

Again the laugh. "Not necessarily, Mr. Black. I will return your call."

And he hung up. I passed the time after that by fixing myself a letter of accreditation from Cowgate Publishers Ltd. It's not hard to do if you have a desktop publishing programme. Access to the company's website got me their letter heading and I simply endorsed myself as Jack Black, investigative writer, previous publications including 'Doctors' Orders: A Survey of Alternative Medical Therapies in our NHS Hospitals', 'Crystals and Candles: New Age Beliefs in an Old Age Society' and 'What Non-Believers Believe'. I authorised myself to present myself to the Patriarch of the New Dawn at Eden House in Angus to work on my new project, 'Behind Closed Doors'. I attributed the letter to Frank Sexton, Commissioning Editor (Non-Fiction). Next morning, I would get Cho at the Chinese to provide a signature for good old Frank and everything would be as tickety as boo. About as genuine as Liberace as well, of course, but I would worry about that when the time came. Sometimes you've got to brass your case. Shy weans get fuck all.

10

Next morning, there was a voice mail from Keith Young, asking me to phone when I got the chance. As luck would have it, I had a window at that precise moment. I phoned him.

"Keith, you got anything?"

"Yes. That case we mentioned yesterday? There's been no indication of CSA in the care notes."

"CSA?"

"Childhood Sexual Abuse. No record of it. No hint even that the lassie has accused anyone at all, far less her father."

"Ah, right."

"Sorry if that's a dead end for you, Jack, but you're way out there."

"Ach, it was just a thought, Keith. Thanks for the effort. Your blood's worth bottling. I owe you one, buddy."

"Aye, so you say," he snorted and hung up.

The papers were full of Brian Cairns's murder. I had bought three: my regular two intelligent ones and a redtop. The details were identical in them all but the redtop bladder spilt a few columns of drool over the custom of dogging and the fact that the council had taken steps to deter it. There were photos of Brian Cairns and his wife on their wedding day. Predictably. There was a request from Bert Saunders for anyone with information ... the usual. But there was no mention of the lines from the Swan. Standard Saunders. Leave it out and see if anything transpires without it. If not, introduce it and see if it rings a few bells.

I pulled the phone over to me and dialled Livingston piggery.

"Seamus! What news?"

"Well, it's Shakespeare all right."

"Okay."

"You got a pen and paper handy?

"Doin' it now."

"Okay. One's from a play called 'Love's Labour's Lost.'"

"Never heard o' it."

"No, not many have. The other one's from a poem called 'The Rape of Lucrece'."

"Whew!" Bert whistled softly down the phone. "Interestin'. Could that be our motive, I wonder?"

"I don't know, Bert. But that's the dope on your quotes."

"Okay, very useful, Seamus. Thanks. Knew you'd turn up trumps. I'll be in touch, old son. You might be able to help us further."

"Sure thing. Adios."

No point telling him that I had checked out the child abuse/incest angle. Well, checked it out as far as I had done. I had no beef about letting Bert and his detectives slog around doing some footwork for themselves. They might find something I hadn't. They would certainly take more time and expend more manpower. It would be presumptuous of me to tell my old pal how to conduct his investigation. Besides - it would give me time to pursue another line of inquiry. If I could think of one.

11

I did the crossword in half an hour, read *Henry IV Part One* till eleven and then tootled along King Street to Mulholland's. Clem himself was behind the bar. He was looking through a publicans' catalogue of some kind. There were no customers. Maybe he was trying to order some from the catalogue. He looked up as I settled my arse on a bar stool.

"Well, Jack," he said. "How's Bathgate's answer to Humphrey Bogart?"

"No idea, I haven't seen him for some time. Give us a pint, Clem, will you?" As he tipped a glass under the spigot, I said to him casually, "Bobby Shafto come in at all?"

"Bobby? Hardly see him these days. He must be drinkin' elsewhere. Or skint. Or aff it. Naw, that seems unlikely. He'll be skint."

"Still working at St. John's?"

"Far as I know."

Bobby Shafto was an interesting character. His real name was Bobby Shaw. His nickname arose from his reputation of being prodigiously blessed in the trouser department. That and the fact that, for years, he and his woman, Wendy, had been swingers. If that's still the correct expression; I'm a little rusty on the terminology these days. When I was young, it used to be called 'wife-swapping'. I believe that sexual sophisticates these days refer to it as 'the lifestyle'. Whatever you called it, Bobby and Wendy did it. There was a good chance that they'd be doggers nowadays. Bobby was not shy about his hobby. Honey, let me be your salty dog.

He had once, some years back, been lead guitarist of Corundum, one of the finest hard rock bands ever to come out of the county. Still had the rock'n'roll look about him. He was balding, with his remaining hair swept back into a thick ponytail. He sported a bushy and droopy walrus moustache and affected leather jackets, denim jeans and big boots. He liked to wear chains, crosses and chunky bracelets. Wendy went in for black sweaters and tight black leather trousers that she managed to pack attractively with her meaty backside. They looked like swinging, dogging, wife-swapping bikers, though neither of them rode one. In fact, a motor-bike was probably one of the few things they didn't ride. Bobby drove a Skoda. He worked in the mortuary at St. John's, another fact that seemed to fit him well.

My thinking was that, if anybody could give me the juice on this dogging business, it would be Bobby. He was a scornful fucker, mind you, and could just as easily tell me to take the breeze and mind my own business as to provide me with information. But he was the only shot in my locker.

Clem placed the pint in front of me and took my fiver.

"One yourself, Clem?"

"No, ta. Too early for me, Jack." He brought my change. "That's a terrible business, that murder at Bangour," he said.

"Yeah."

"Know anythin' about it?"

"Just what's in the papers, same as you."

"Come off it, Jack. You know a lot more than you let on. You always do."

"And if I keep it that way, I always will."

Clem smiled. "I wonder what that guy was doin' up at Bangour, though? The papers are sayin' it's the place for group sex and that."

"If the papers are saying it, you can be sure it's pure speculation."

"Think it is, though?"

"Think what's what?"

"Bangour – the place for orgies?"

"Jeez, Clem, how would I know? Do I strike you as the kind of guy who indulges in that kind of thing?"

"Nope. In fact, if you don't mind mah sayin' so, Jack, you look like the kind of guy who couldnae get a bird in an aviary."

"Thanks, Clem. But you're right enough. It's some time since I sported with Amaryllis in the shade."

"Wi' who?"

"Never mind."

"Terrible thing, though. Seems he was a decent enough kinda guy, ay? Builder, apparently. Married man wi' two kids.

You wonder why somebody would dae that to him, don't you?"

"There's always a reason, Clem. Always a reason. Bobby Shafto still live up Hillhouse Avenue?"

"Far as I know. Ah! Noo Ah know why you want tae see Bobby. Must be true about Bangour bein' the open-air knockin' shop."

"Not at all," I said. "I just want Bobby to show me the chords for *Purple Haze*." I swung off the stool and tipped the remaining suds down my thrapple. "Cheers, Clem. See you later."

"Aye, be seein' you."

There was still no other customer when I left. I checked my cellphone. No messages. I walked up to the car and drove home. Played the Wolf again. There's evil, evil going on.

There was a message on my landline from Brother Ira, as I'd hoped. It seemed he had spoken with the Patriarch, who had felt initially that MacVicar's article was as much publicity as the community required but, after some discussion with Brother Ira and what he called their 'Archangels' he had acceded to my request. I dialled the number back and, this time, got through comparatively quickly. Brother Ira confirmed that permission to visit Eden had been granted.

"With the following provisos," he said. "The Patriarch wishes to see some written confirmation of your commission…"

"I'll have that faxed to you first thing tomorrow."

"That will not be necessary." (Good, I'd hoped not.) "You will bring it with you when you come."

"Of course."

"You will be allocated accommodation here in Eden. He is anxious that you will respect our way of life and our customs while you are here as our guest."

"I will, of course."

"Finally, he is insistent that there be no photographs taken during your time with us. He made the same demand of Mr. MacVicar. The privacy, dignity and sanctity of our people and our worship is paramount."

"I understand. There will be no question of photography."

"Good. Then, Mr. Black, I am authorised to invite you to stay with us as our guest in Eden for a time."

"Excellent."

"One final thing. The Patriarch wonders if you are kin to a man he once knew at university. A man called Jack Black was a fellow student in Edinburgh."

"I'm his son."

"Then I'm sure your welcome will be the warmer."

Eden is about a hundred miles from Edinburgh; or so Brother Ira told me. If I wanted to get there for the Morning Meet, as he suggested I should, I would have to rise at six – six! – and head off into the morning. The Morning Meet was at ten. I could assist at that and take lunch with the Angels, he told me. The Angels of the New Dawn. He stated his certainty that Brother Gabriel would allow me free access to Eden and all of its activities. In fact Brother Gabriel invited me to stay with the New Dawn for as many days as it took to collect material for my book. Just what I wanted – several days in the company of a bunch of flakes, eating adzuki beans and being washed in the blood of the lamb. But, having more faces than the toun knock, I accepted his offer graciously.

I put the phone down and turned up Howlin' Wolf.

"Devil Satan, you're doggone."

12

Hillhouse Avenue is at the top of Belvedere – a strange name for a housing scheme in an old mining town. A 'belvedere' is a summer-house with a beautiful view. Indeed, the word itself, from Italian, means just that – a beautiful view. The scheme could hardly be less that. It's no more than a few streets of old council housing stock, with no fairer prospect than the houses opposite.

I drove up there around seven o'clock that evening. The sun was starting its descent, and kids were playing about the street.

Wendy answered the door to my knock. She's a big woman, tending to the hefty in fact, and far from conventionally pretty. There is something that attracts there, though, I am forced to admit. Her shoulder-length hair is wavy and dyed suspiciously black. Such a shade is rarely encountered in Nature. I suspect that she is rather more grey than she would like to be, being a rock chick, and has taken steps to remedy it. She wore a baggy jumper and denims. She is blowsy, no doubt about it, but she is attractive, too, in a big fat mama kind of way. At least, a lot of guys would find her so.

"Hello, Wendy," I said. "Is himself at home?"

"Aye," she said and stepped back to let me in. She closed the door and then preceded me through the hall, saying in best couthy Broons jargon, "Come ben."

As ben I went, I could hear an expensive acoustic guitar being played in the living-room. Played very well, although I didn't recognise the riffs and chords.

"Somebody to see you, Bobby," announced Wendy, and I went in.

He stopped playing, looked up and smiled at me. "It's the gumshoe," he said with a sneer. "How you been doing, Jack?" Then he went straight into a flawless rendition of the guitar intro to *Dimples*.

"John Lee Hooker," I smiled, nodding at the accuracy of the playing.

"What can I do for you, Jack?" he asked, stopping abruptly.

"Very impressive, Bobby," I said. "I just wondered if I can pick your brain."

"Do you want coffee?" asked Wendy.

"Sure," I said. "That'd be great. Just black, thanks."

"Bobby?"

"Aye. If Creepin' Jesus here is having one, so will I."

Wendy left. Bobby put the guitar on a stand and smoothed back his lush moustaches with gentle strokes of his thumb and index finger. "I had a premonition I'd see you fairly soon."

"You did?"

"Uh-huh. This is about that Cairns fella, isn't it?"

"Did you know him?"

"It is, isn't it? You working with the polis?"

"No, not this time, Bobby. They're investigating it, right enough, as you would expect. But well, I'm just interested on my own account. Something about it fascinates me."

"Aye? And then you'll work with the Plod when you get the information you want, is that it?"

"I might, aye. But I think, if you can help me out, I can get information that the cops won't be able to, at least for a while longer."

He was sneering again. "And what kind of information would that be?"

"I need to know about dogging."

"Oh aye? – thinking of taking up a new hobby, are you?"

I laughed. "No, Bobby, I'm not the type – you know that. That's why I need the advice of somebody like yourself."

"You'll no flatter me into helping you."

"I didn't mean to. I was being sincere."

"Well ... I don't know. There's plenty of shit on the net about stuff like that. Pictures and everything. You can have a good hand-shandy while you look it up."

A jibe, and not a subtle one. I ignored it. "That's not what I want. I need local knowledge."

"Well... maybe I don't want to get involved."

"A man's been killed, Bobby."

"Aye. That's *why* I maybe don't want to get involved."

"What I thought was, if you could tell me a thing or two about the practice, it might help me formulate a theory about why this man was killed."

"Oh? 'Formulate a theory', is it?" The sneer was so pronounced, he almost had his lip in his ear.

"Did you know the guy, Bobby?"

"I knew him, aye. No that well. But I knew him. We met him a couple of times."

"Was this … dogging? That you met him?"

"Aye."

"And is it right that Old Bangour is the dogging site?"

"It's one. One of a few. You can bet your sweet arse that nobody will go dogging there again."

"That's what I thought. The police are going to find it hard to get somebody to talk."

"Well, I ain't gonna be that somebody, Jack. You can rely on *that*."

"I don't want you to talk to the police, Bobby. I just want to pick your brain, like I said. Just me. No police. You might be able to tell me something that I can use to find who killed Brian Cairns."

Wendy came back in, with two mugs on a tray and a plate of biscuits. "Ah *know*," she said, on a long note like a gossip. "Isn't it damnable?"

"Jack thinks I can help him find the killer," said Bobby, immersing that mustachioed top lip in his coffee.

"Of course," said Wendy earnestly. "Anything we can do to help. Ah mean, we kent that man Cairns, didn't we, Bobby?"

Bobby puffed a silent ironic laugh, then sat back in his chair. "Wendy the snitch," he mocked. Then he looked at me. "None of this goes any further. I don't want my name mentioned outside this room about this. Understood?"

"Understood," I agreed.

"What do you want to know?"

"How well did you know Brian Cairns?"

"Not that well. I told you. We'd met him a couple of times."

"And you had sex with him?"

"Well, no we didn't," interposed Wendy. "Once, he watched us but we didn't invite him to join us."

"Why was that? Was he into kinky stuff?"

Bobby snorted with derisory laughter. "Kinky stuff? Is watching other folk on the job not kinky enough for you stales?"

"Stales? Oh, right. Folk that don't."

"He was kind of a creepy guy, wasn't he, Bobby?" said Wendy.

"Aye. There was something about him that was ... odd. Kinda 'intense', if that's the right word. No like other folk. He couldn't get enough of watching some folk. Drank it in, you know?"

"An' we thought he liked watchin' guys best, sometimes, didn't we?" said Wendy.

Bobby looked at her. "*You* did, aye."

"Did he break any rules, or anything?"

"Well, there arenae actual rules. No as such. I mean there hasnae been a Doggers' Constitution drawn up or anything like that."

"But ... not rules exactly ... there must be some accepted procedures," I suggested.

"Aye," sighed Bobby. "Some couple will start havin' sex in a car. Others will turn up to watch them. You're only supposed to move closer to their car if they ask you..."

"Or if they flash the light," added Wendy.

"Aye," said Bobby. "Sometimes they'll turn their interior light on and off. That means you can stand up close and watch the action."

"Join in?"

"Only if they make it clear that they want you to. Sometimes the voyeurs just stand and play with theirselves."

"So the voyeurs are guys."

"Naw, naw," said Wendy. "Lassies tae. It's a couples thing where we went."

"Okay," I said. "I'm nearly finished. Just one thing - is there *anything* that's verboten?"

"Well," said Bobby. "Obviously, you keep your hands to yourself – or anythin' else to yourself – till somebody gives you permission to dae otherwise."

"And you huv tae respect a woman's right to say naw," said Wendy.

"Aye. Very important. When somebody says 'no' that means 'no'. No argument," endorsed Bobby.

"Do you think this guy maybe didn't observe something like that?"

"Maybe. Who can tell?"

"You see, there's something that indicates that Cairns was killed because somebody disapproved of what he did, or at least disagreed with it."

"What thing?"

"Can't say, Bobby. Sorry – polis would hang, draw and quarter me."

"Well, we cannae say for sure. Really. I mean, we didn't know his name was Cairns or that till we saw the paper. Then we got a fright, eh Wend?"

"Too true."

"But, like we've sais, we didn't really know him at all. We just thought he was kinda creepy, you know?"

It would be a lie to say that I felt unclean when I left Bobby and Wendy's house. But I felt something. Unease, possibly. Being a committed 'stale'. It put my own sex life into perspective, though. 'Vanilla' was way too flavoursome and exciting a word for it. 'Water biscuit' just about summed it up – bland and quickly finished.

Bobby Shafto playing Dimples had put the idea in my head, and I put some John Lee on the player when I got home. Black Jack was curled in a ball on the sofa. I thought things through.

Brian Cairns was murdered because something he did was disgraceful. In somebody's opinion. Maybe rape. The lines from 'Lucrece' and the three L's indicated that much. Originally, I had thought it might be incest. Wrong. But maybe some bloke didn't like the fact that Brian had taken a shine to him at a dogging session, rather than his girl. Shit!

That's what I had meant to ask Bobby – who Brian went to these do's with. His wife? A girlfriend? Fuck it. I would need to get back on the blower to Bobby again. But not tonight. I didn't feel like bothering him again tonight. I had a journey to another world to look forward to, next day. Had Brian Cairns made homosexual overtures to some homophobe at Bangour? Or just some guy who didn't like the implications of the move? And had Brian Cairns paid a heavy price for it? Was that what the Shakespearean tags were meant to tell us?

13

I wrestled my way to the surface, fighting and tearing, heart pounding, sweat streaming from me. With a lung-bursting thrust, I was in the clean air and I ripped great gulps of it into me. My duvet was at my feet. For a moment or two, my heart thumped and I quivered in fright. Then I started to calm down again, breathe less harshly, knew where I was. That fucking Forth Bridge nightmare again. Why couldn't I have been dreaming of Grace McGuire offering me the dime tour of those sumptuous curves? But no, the Forth Bridge again. I let my pulse settle down and then looked at the alarm. Ten to six. I got up.

The morning was a fine one. I hadn't seen six o'clock in the morning for a number of years – and, in those times, I was seeing it as I reeled home, with a head like a drum solo, and a stomach that felt like I'd drunk the entire contents of a dredger. Early morning daylight has a peculiar quality for a drunk, something like the white nights in St. Petersburg. I had a coffee and four fags before my shower, and a coffee and four fags after it. Then I was ready – wheezing, but wired. Speeding like a bullet.

It felt a little like I was going on holiday. Not quite with a song in my heart, for I'm not that kind of guy – the cardiac musical type – but with maybe a manly hum, I ran the electric razor over my bristles, packed one or two things in my holdall and locked the house behind me.

There was no sign of Black Jack. He could fend for himself in the ensuing few days. He knew enough to present himself at Mrs. McDonald's door when I was away. Mrs. McDonald was my neighbour, a sweet old biddy with a house full of her own cats, seven at the last count. There was always a queer old hum off the place when she stood nattering with the front door open. She would feed Black Jack when I was away. In a house full of moggies, what difference does one more make?

My footsteps rang clearly in the gelid morning. The scheme was still asleep. I pulled out of the street and headed for the A89. The road was quiet. The drive was pleasant and, in no time, I was headed for the Forth Road Bridge. Not the one of my dream. The road bridge. The one like Hart Crane's 'rip-tooth of the sky's acetylene'. I don't read Crane any more these days – I have my reasons – but the lines have stayed with me.

Even the Bridge traffic was sparse and, as the Nissan hummed up the incline towards those huge towers, with that fucking railway bridge glinting rust-red in the bright morning sunlight on my right, I got a sudden blast of that scene in *The Graduate* where Ben drives over a bridge in lush countryside on his way to Berkeley. The shot wheels into an aerial swoop and Simon and Garfunkel start to sing *Scarborough Fair*. I started to hum to myself – "deet de-de-de deet dee de-de deet dee de-de dee" – then realised that was a different song and stopped.

The Forth Bridge took seven years to construct. It was opened on the 4th of March, 1890. It cost 57 lives and four and a half million bucks in 1880's prices. It's 2,765 yards long, including the approach viaduct. The length of the cantilever section is a mile and twenty yards. Constructed of 51,000 tons of steel. The height of the steel structure above the mean water level is 370 feet. Above the bottom of the deepest foundation it is 452 feet. The rail level is 156 feet above high water. That's the important bit. Sir John Fowler and Sir Benjamin Baker designed a structure that was built by Sir William Arrol's company between 1883 and 1890. I know that bridge like the back of my hand. Like a lover. Like they say you *should* know your enemy.

Into the Kingdom and the green and golden fields rolled far away. The sun, drawing slowly higher, touched the tips of the trees and the breasts of the fields with a blush of splendour. Colour by colour, the morning opened up to its touch.

The M90 zipped under my tyres and then I was driving along the flat haugh road by the Tay, skirting Dundee and up into Angus where the Aberdeens come from. My intention had been to start with the Tayside Police, but the invitation to assist at Morning Meet had changed all that. I wanted to see the wackos worship. Arbroath, Montrose – sonorous names from Scottish history. I zoomed on past Brechin. Twenty minutes later, I turned off the A90 not far from Edzell and started to keep a watchful eye for Eden.

The air glittered. Conifers, dark and green, cloaked the hillside. The sun sprinkled through the treetops and the river sparkled in the valley. Emerald and silver. Gravel crackled under the tyres. And then, behind walls, trees and a high set of electrically controlled gates, Eden. The trees had leaves. The walls had broken glass.

I parked the car and approached the gates. A sign said:

EDEN

Private House and Grounds
No Admittance Save by Appointment

There was an intercom grille and a CCTV camera high on the right hand post of the gates. I pressed the Call button and waited, humming to myself a scrap of Dylan. There are no truths outside the gates of Eden.

A masculine voice crackled through the squawkbox. "Yes?"

"Brother Ira? It's Jack Black."

"Drive your car through the gates and slowly approach the house. I will be waiting for you at the portal."

Portal, no less.

I got in the car as the gates buzzed and peeled backward. Through and slowly onward. Behind, in the rear-view mirror, I saw the gates smoothly close. The drive was narrow and went in for thick green bushes with crimson and purple blossoms in a big way. A canopy of trees shaded the roadway. And then the house was there at the end of the drive, as if through a telescope: white in the broad sunlight, surrounded by trees. Grey tiled roof, white chimneys and tall windows with bluish grey surrounds. Somewhere among the far treetops a bell clinked.

A massive man was standing by the corner of the building. He was built like a Kodiak bear, bald as a stone gatepost and black as two o'clock in the morning. He indicated that I should pull up by the vehicles that were already parked. One of them was Laura McGuire's maroon Megane. The other was a surprisingly snazzy red sports car. Somebody was a petrolhead. That didn't seem right for a bunch of evangelical bedlamites. I would have thought the chariot of Elijah would have been more apt. Or maybe a donkey, at a push. This seemed much too secular, much more your standard Bright Red Mid-Life Crisis.

The man-mountain was dressed entirely in black: shirt, slacks and shoes. He might have been a roadie for The Four Tops, if looks were anything to go by, rather than an Angel of the New Dawn.

He gripped my hand tightly when I emerged from the car and shook it manfully once. I felt my shoulder give a little as he did it. He had a grip like a lug wrench. "Mr. Black! Brother Ira."

"It's good to meet you, Brother. How are you?"

"I am well, thanks be to God. You got baggage?" he asked.

"No, only a small holdall with a change of clothes and things. Oh, and the laptop, of course."

"Well, brother, that's good because the Patriarch says you have to leave all your baggage behind when you enter into Eden."

He gave an expansive, booming guffaw of laughter. Gold glinted in his mouth. I managed a watery smile. Sky pilots should never try jokes.

"That's what is termed 'symbolic', I believe," he said. "It refers primarily to your spiritual baggage. This here li'l grip should be okay, if it's only clothing and stuff."

"Will I get to speak with Brother Gabriel?"

"That you will, brother, that you will. He is most anxious to meet with you, you being the son of an old friend. He will appoint a time directly. His time, as you might understand, is much taken up." He lifted my holdall and set off, indicating with a jerk of his head that I should follow. "This way. You have a single cabin on the outer ring of the Settlement for the duration of your stay here."

I followed his broad back round the rear of the building and through the flowerbeds of a spacious garden towards a high hedge of conifers that acted as a screen from whatever lay beyond. The Settlement, presumably. The soundtrack was doing the whole serenity number: breeze in treetops and birdsong.

"You made good time?" Brother Ira asked.

"Yes, the drive was peaceful and ... well, beautiful."

He turned and smiled at me, the engaging, affectionate kind of beam that could only come from a holy idiot. He had a gleaming gold cap on one front tooth that made it flash in the sunlight.

"I'm glad of it, brother," he said and turned again.

We passed through a gap in the hedge and there, before us, in a clearing in a valley, was the Settlement. 'Quaint' wasn't the word. But it'll have to do; I can't think of anything better. Tranquil and somehow old-time. With a smack of the frontier about it. Two rings of log cabins lay in the sunlight, grey smoke emerging from one or two chimneys and wavering softly into the blue air. Some cabins were bigger than others. Kids played around in front of some. All had verandas and front stoops, also fashioned from logs. In the centre of the wide circle stood a grander building, constructed like an early American church, of brick and clapboard, with a shingled roof, and a slender belfry on top. A huge stained glass window dominated the side that I could see.

"The Settlement," said Brother Ira. "There is the Meeting House. And the bell you may have heard, as you approached, was the summons to the Morning Meet. The Angels you see are returning from their labours to prepare for the Meet."

From the surrounding forest, by various paths, men and women were heading towards the cabins. All dressed very plainly in drab utility garments, the women wearing bonnets or hats to cover their hair. All walked purposefully, eyes cast modestly down. It was like being on location for a new film version of *The Crucible*.

Brother Ira preceded me down the hill and we entered one of the nearest cabins, a small hut consisting of one room. It was as Spartan as Lysander. There was a bed, a table and a chair. A small, wood-burning stove had been lit earlier and was warming the room pleasantly. The window looked on to the forest and had a pair of light curtains. My companion hefted my holdall on to the table.

"This is your place while you stay with us," said Brother Ira. "It's plain enough, but you got anything you need. Here ..." He opened a door at the back that I hadn't seen before. "... is your washroom."

I looked past him. It wasn't up to Savoy standards but it was better than going into the woods with a shovel and a toilet roll.

"Excellent," I said, not too sarcastically.

"Anything else you want, just ring Room Service," he said and gave another loud guffaw.

"Very good."

"On the bed is a robe. If you want to attend Morning Meet, you will please strip naked and put on the robe. You may keep on your footwear until you come to the Meeting House. You have ten minutes. I will wait for you at the portal."

And he was gone.

The robe was long, white, loose and made of linen, like a priest's alb. It had arms and a simple tie at the neck. I stripped off and donned it. I felt like a Best in Show clown and, no doubt, looked like one: less an Angel of the New Dawn than a slightly bemused, overage Wee Willie Winkie. When I left the cabin, naked except for my alb and my Clarks size 9s, I was conscious of my body beneath the linen. It did not put me into a religious frame of mind.

14

The bell was calling the Angels to the Meet. Brother Ira was there. He, too, was all cherubed-up. He met me at the steps of the Meeting House and took me up and into the building. To the left of the door, in a narrow corridor that seemed to ring the main room, were discarded shoes and sandals. Following Brother Ira's example, I took mine off, hoping that the result wasn't too suggestive of Stinking Bishop. We walked through a second door and into the meeting room.

"While you are with us, I shall stay to the side and keep you company, brother," said Brother Ira.

"Thank you."

"You will stand and observe only. You will not speak. You will not participate."

"Whatever you say, Bro."

Inside, the Meeting House was dim and close. At the far end, as a sort of altar, was a table covered with a white linen cloth. On that, were seven candles in sticks, each bearing an inverted yellow heart of flame. In front of each candlestick, stood a small glass jar with a miniature flame jerking on a wick inside. These jars were of different colours: dark blue, green, red, yellow, lilac, orange and light blue. The huge stained-glass window in the wall of the House was made of lozenges of deeply coloured glass – scarlet, emerald, royal blue, canary yellow, sparkling gold, deep purple – and depicted the coming through the clouds of a meek and beautiful bearded Christ on the Last Day. As the sunlight outside struck it, it threw shapes of coloured light onto the heads of the assembled Angels. Pendants of variously shaped prismatic glass, catching the rays of the sun, scattered rainbows over the walls. At intervals through the room, fine gauzes and voiles in pastel shades were suspended from the ceiling. Spotlights in the rafters, catching their dreamy sway, filled the higher air with drifting clouds of colour. It was a trip, all right.

At one end of the table a young Angel stood, swinging a censer gently from side to side and, at the crest of each swing, heavily incensed white smoke puffed into the air. The room was already stifling with its sweetness.

As if the shifting light and colours, and the sensuality of the incense weren't enough to get you on the first flight to the Land of Cockaygne, Indian music throbbed from speakers hidden high in the roof: a twangling drone on the tambura, over which a sitar played some aimlessly repetitive, though melodic, phrases to the pulse of a tabla.

The Angels, drifting through the second door, wore, besides their linen shifts, the smiles of placid contentment you expect from the sort of brainwipes who are into all this shit. Some were hand-in-hand. Mostly in their late twenties or early thirties, there were some of obvious middle age and one or two plainly teenaged. The men tended to favour beards. Some had shoulder-length hair. The women, now uncapped, all wore their hair long. They all smiled to each other. They all smiled back at each other. Then they smiled into themselves at the thought of smiling to each other. Their smiles were as dippy as dancing Alsatians. Once inside, the gomerels made themselves comfortable, sitting on the fat cushions and bean-bags that were scattered over the wooden floor. Seated, they mostly closed their eyes and swayed almost imperceptibly to the music. Oh yeah, and they cheesed a bit more. Brother Ira and I sat on cushions, to the side of the assembly.

The second door was closed and, after some more light, colour, incense, music and smiling, an Angel ascended the dais by the Table. He had dark, shoulder-length hair and a sculpted black beard. Everybody stood. The taped music stopped and he began to chant in a loud, resonant tenor voice, like a cantor in a synagogue.

He will give the Morning Star …

And the assembled Angels sang:
  … Aurora Nova.

I recognised the tune. It was the plainsong of the old Litany of the Saints in the Catholic church. And the chant proceeded in exactly the same way as a litany, with the cantor singing a description of the Lord or of his deeds and the chorus of Angels singing 'Aurora Nova'.

And there shall be no more night ... Aurora Nova
On His head a golden crown ... Aurora Nova
Alpha He and Omega ... Aurora Nova

There was fully five minutes of this, with the Angels swaying, eyes closed, arms outstretched, palms upwards. It wasn't doing it for me, I have to say. I was aching for some other tune before the cantor came to an end and left the dais. The Angels sat again. Another Angel, a young man with blond hair and beard, now got up and delivered a homily in a measured, paced tone of voice. The content was the kind of apocalyptic rant you can hear from any hellfire preacher any time; that mankind will die in fire and turmoil when the Lord returns and that only the Elect will be saved and taken with Him into His dwelling in Paradise to live there forever. The New Dawn cometh right soon and only the Angels of the New Dawn will be saved when the Lord cometh on the clouds in glory.

But, if the content was predictable, the delivery was remarkable. The speaker's voice kept to the same, measured pulse for the length of his sermon and, though he roared when he spoke of the torments of the Last Day and spoke in soothing tones when he promised eternal bliss to the Angels, his voice kept the same, lulling, deadening beat. The Angels sat like they were hypnotised, drinking in the words.

"Rise now, brothers and sisters," said the speaker.

The Angels stood up slowly. Dreamily, they stood and smiled knowingly to themselves and each other. I guess they knew what was coming.

"Let us love one other, as we are commanded."

They turned and held the person next to them, caressed, stroked hair and cheeks, kissed on the cheeks and lips, then turned again and fondled somebody else. Some huddled in groups, arms around each other, heads bowed, touching together. Some caresses were openly sexual – hips, breasts, groins stroked through the fronts of robes. I almost sniggered. These Holy Joes were really copping a feel. They were swinging like censers. Dogging at the manger. No wonder they smiled so much. After a minute or so, the speaker addressed the congregation again.

"Let us pray."

All stood still and closed their eyes.

"O Lord of Mercy and Might, hear us. We give thee thanks, almighty Lord, for the favour of Thy love; for the gift of the Patriarch, his wisdom and his word; for the light that shines in all of us from Thee. And we ask that, when Thou comest again, to judge the living and the dead, at the end of that day we may be with Thee, forever and ever in Bliss. Amen."

"Amen."

The doors were opened and the Angels began to drift out into the bright sunlight: from what I could see, happy as pigs in shit. Holy, happy and horny.

15

Brother Ira accompanied me to my cabin. On the way, he explained some of the service I had just seen. Those who had spoken and sung were 'Archangels', senior office holders in the New Dawn. Brother Ambrose was the cantor, Brother Enoch the sermoniser.

"What was all that groping about?"

He chuckled tolerantly, like an adult asked a predictable question by a child.

"The body is the gift of the Lord, brother. And sexual gratification is one of the many glimpses He has given us of what Bliss will be like. This idea is, of course, imperfect; only a partial glimpse, a mere hint of perfume compared to the Garden of Bliss."

"And that explains the music and the colours and the incense as well, I suppose."

"You are an insightful man, brother."

"Be not afeard," I said, "the isle is full of noises – sounds and sweet airs that give delight and hurt not."

"I don't know what that is," laughed Brother Ira, "but it sure as salvation sounds pretty."

We had arrived at the cabin.

"I will leave you here for the half hour between now and mealtime. Inside, you may do as you wish, although I have arranged for some reading material to be left for your perusal. I will return and accompany you to mealtime. In the afternoon, I will be at your disposal for an hour to answer any questions you may have."

"When will I see the Patriarch?"

"He has not spoken of it yet."

And he was gone. Major surprise: the reading material was The Bible. And here was me expecting *120 Days of Sodom*. Bible on the table, a bookmark of thin purple silk diagonally across the opening page of the Book of Revelation. I didn't read it. I dressed again and then lay back on the bed and cogitated. For religious zealots, these people sure put a lot of devotion into their fumbling. The world was being washed in waves of sexual desire, it seemed to me. Pity they never quite lapped up to my feet; I was gagging for a paddle. I laughed and then realised that maybe it wasn't all that funny. Grace McGuire's concerns about her daughter falling prey to sexual rites seemed wholly grounded now.

16

Early afternoon and I was sitting in the library of the big house. It was a well appointed room on the ground floor, lit by afternoon sunlight streaming through a wide window topped with a semi-circular fanlight. Outside were the gardens in all their greenery. Inside, there were several bookcases, a huge round table that smelt of beeswax polish, sofas here and there, and two comfortable armchairs on either side of a large fireplace. The fire wasn't lit.

I mooched around, waiting for the next manifestation of Brother Ira. A bookcase held volumes like The Qur'an; Jewish Apocalyptic Literature; The Lives of the Jain Elders; Hindu Sacred Texts; Apocrypha and Pseudepigrapha – very enlightening, if not at all light. Every other bookcase contained similar tomes. There wasn't a Western, a dirty book or a copy of Scottish Field anywhere.

Brother Ira entered and clicked shut the door. He was wearing a black jacket open over his shirt.

"Brother! How are you?" he said, indicating in his usual way that I should sit in one of the easy chairs by the fireside.

"Fine, thanks," I replied, doing so. He sat in the opposite armchair.

"Did you eat well?" he asked.

"Phhh, well enough," I answered, making a wry face.

(An hour before, we had joined the Angels and Archangels as they broke bread in a booming refectory to the rear of the Meeting House. Vegetables, fruit, nuts, seeds and berries. The only slurp was water or milk. I thought I could see Laura McGuire at the back of the crowd, but I couldn't be sure and I didn't want to stare.)

"You are not vegetarian, then?" he asked.

"No."

"Here, in Eden, you will eat and drink only the fruits and the clean water of the earth. Milk from Eden's cows is allowed."

"Yeah, I was kind of afraid of that. Still, when in Eden, and all that. If folks copulate like rabbits, it seems logical they should eat like them too."

He laughed. "Do you have your letter of accreditation with you?"

I passed it over and he placed it, without looking at it, in his inside pocket. "The Patriarch will grant you an interview tomorrow evening after Glory."

"Glory?"

"The main service of our week, taken by Brother Gabriel himself. At Glory, we praise the Lord, we share in the Cup of Salvation and we offer ourselves to each other in Rapture."

"Rapture? Groping again?"

"Sexual contact of whatever nature the individual Angel prefers. I explained earlier our beliefs regarding the human body."

"You did. Brother Ira, maybe if I just read some of your literature... I see you have most of the world's sacred texts here, but I can't see any tracts or publications from the New Dawn."

"There are none. None of our beliefs are written down. They have been brought to us by the Patriarch, Brother Gabriel, Bearer of the Word and Bringer of Light."

"But why nothing written down? Surely you want to spread the Word?"

"Ours is not an evangelical movement, brother. We seek no converts. The Word has been spread for thousands of years. Abraham. Moses. Jesus. Mohammed. Guru Nanak. Brother Gabriel. There is no need to write down what has been written for centuries. Read the Bible, especially the Book of Revelation. Read the Qur'an, especially the sura *Al-Waqi'ah* – That Which is Coming." And he quoted: "'When that which is coming comes – and no soul shall then deny its coming – some shall be abased and others exalted'. The message will be familiar to you, though it comes from the Qur'an?"

"Extremely familiar. I was brought up a Catholic. Eschatology was served three times a day, after meals."

"So it is with the world. The message is out there. These are the Last Days. We are living in Endtime. It is up to each individual how he or she acts upon it. Brother Gabriel has revealed to us that we are the Elect. We will be taken up with the Lord at the New Dawn and live with him forever in

Paradise."

"It surprises me that the New Dawn is not evangelical. You say you seek no converts. I had expected you to refuse my suggestion of a visit. I was surprised you allowed Nairn MacVicar to write a piece on you for the newspaper. Most cults are paranoid about outsiders."

"We have nothing to be paranoid about. We do not consider ourselves a cult, but a holy order."

"But you live in seclusion, behind walls, and electronic security devices."

"We wish to be left by the world to serve the Lord in our labours until He comes again. Outsiders are suspicious, inquisitive, mocking. The Patriarch has served his time in the world. For many years he had a mission in Aberdeen."

"And yet everyone here has been kindness itself to me."

"As one should be to a visitor. 'Be not forgetful to entertain strangers; for thereby some have entertained angels unawares.' The book of Hebrews, Chapter 13."

I smiled at the quotation. He smiled back, that warm and openly sincere grin. "The words make you happy?"

"They do. Sound kinda hippy but beautiful. My father would have liked them."

"It is good."

"Which brings me to one of the first points I want to air with you. I know MacVicar talked about it too, but it's as well to get it out of the way at the start."

"Yes?"

"Is there not some disquiet in the locality about young women becoming Angels? About the sexual customs of the New Dawn? In short, Brother, not to put too fine a point on it, don't some of the local worthies think you're just a bunch of wackos like the Moonies? With added bonking?"

He tipped his head back and laughed loudly.

"I am sure that some of them do. We have been visited from time to time by parents concerned for their sons or their daughters. Concerned that, by devoting themselves to the Lord in the Last Days, they are turning their backs upon the world. They are, brother, they are. And praise the Lord for it. Another soul saved for the Lord. 'For what shall it profit a man if he gain the whole world and lose his own soul?' Matthew Chapter 8."

"You say people have come to collect their loved ones?"

"Indeed."

"And what did you do with them?"

"As we have done with you. Invited them in, shown them our ways. Allowed them to *talk* to their loved ones. If the loved ones wished to return, we did not stop them."

"Did that ever happen?"

"On occasion. Usually, however, the Angel has stayed in Eden."

"Mmm."

I was writing furiously. This guy had to believe that I was a writer. What *I* believed was that Dominic Tweedie, like any other deluded prophet, was not averse to a generous whack of publicity.

"Brother, forgive me. I have tasks to perform," said Brother Ira, rising from his place. "The rest of the day is yours to spend as you will until supper. Wander freely. Talk to whomever you please. Tomorrow, I have leisure in the morning to show you our various labours here in Eden. And tomorrow evening is Glory."

"Thank you, Brother Ira."

"Be at peace, brother."

And he left. I stared at the door after he had closed it. A remarkable man. And this was a remarkable place. And, no doubt, Brother Gabriel would turn out to be even more remarkable. But there was something else. Entertaining angels was all very poetic but … there was something else. What cult ever let its members go, once they had a grip of them? So why would the New Dawn be willing to mollify angry parents? Would it be a simple case of explaining to Brother Gabriel that Laura's mother was unhappy, and then driving her home? Although I could not have said why, I thought, on balance, not.

17

Left to my own devices by Brother Ira, I had returned to my cabin and stretched out on the cot for an hour. Amassing a heap of capital Z's seemed like a good idea. But I couldn't sleep. Lots of things were darting in and out of my mind. Angels and satyrs. Why Brian Cairns was killed, whodunnit, when they dunnit and just precisely how they dunnit. Something had murdered sleep, too. I decided to take Ira at his word, and see a bit of Eden for myself. Maybe even see Laura McGuire.

I came into the gardens again from the track to the Settlement. This time, I noticed a gap in the hedgerow by the gable on the right of the house. It led to a secluded section of the estate, fringed by tall trees and thick bushes. There was a lilypond, a sundial, and a mossed and rain-streaked stone satyr blowing a stone flute. I wondered if he sounded anything like Billy the Buhll and his cronies. A splendid, if dilapidated, gazebo stood on spindly legs.

There was no sign of life in the house, some of which I could still see through the hedge. The wind creaked the branches. Birds flicked across the scene. There was a heavy and sleepy quiet. A frog plopped into the pond. On this side of the house there was a spacious, two-car garage. I walked round to the front of it and tugged on the up-and-over door. Inside, there were two small white vans. Astras. No lettering. Empty. I shut the door again. Still, nobody else around. I might have been the only boy in the world. The warm silence descended again.

A path led down an incline to the fringe of the forest. Halfway to the woods, the Settlement was visible for a short time, over the crest of the brae to the right. There were no adults present but one or two angel cubs were running around the huts. The far sounds of rural activity: the distant whine of a saw; the chug of unseen farm machinery.

"Whose woods these are I think I know;
His house is in the village, though."

I did a course in American Lit at Edinburgh and Frost's words came back to me, as I stepped from the bright sunlight of the late afternoon into the fragrant, green light under the trees.

There were plenty of trees, and they were old. The canopy of their foliage arched over the path on both sides, meeting high in the middle and creating a haven of dark green coolness on a hot afternoon. Blackbirds whistled. Other birds dipped black-and-white tails in flight before me in the gloom.

The sun was now just an intermittent light glimpsed through the mesh of the foliage above, its faint gleams scattered about my feet. Occasionally, away ahead, a bright patch where the crown of leaves above was less luxuriant, and everywhere the calls of birds.

The path itself was fairly well-defined at first, wide enough for two to pass but, farther into the depths of the wood, trickling away progressively into the vestige of a track. Sometimes little side tracks diverged off the main one, tantalising with glimpses of flowery dells, sinister coverts, chequered glades where pillars of sunshine alternated with the trees. Still the leaves rustled and whispered in the wind.

I came to an incline and, at its foot, a broader path ran by the side of a tumbling river that gurgled musically around boulders. I jogged down the brae onto the path then strode over the damp boards of a plank bridge to a path on the far side.

The top of the brae on this side seemed nearer, more accessible, so I climbed up it, to check out the far horizons. More woodland, but also a brick building, a low and long one-storey affair with a flat roof, a few hundred yards away in a circle obviously cleared specifically for it. My nose urged me towards it.

When I got there, I could see a driveway approaching it through the trees in the opposite direction. The door was a solid metal roller, padlocked. No windows. No other means of ingress. A bunker of sorts. Now, what would the Angels be doing with such a building? What would they keep in it, or do in it? I mooched around it for a minute or two and then returned to the top of the hill, and headed home.

When I got back to the shanty, I crashed out on the charpoy and slept the sleep of the just.

18

I woke up, bewildered. There are some who say that's my natural state, but I mean truly bewildered - no idea where I was or, even worse, who I was. It's a feeling not unknown to me, a diluted version of what amnesia must be like. I suspect it's what years of gargle have done to the grey cells. Korsakoff's is probably in the post.

Birds were singing – flocks of them, flights of them, treefuls of them – somewhere not too far away. In fact, it sounded like they were lined up along the roof of the cabin, the doorstep and the window-sill.

Then it came back to me. I was in Eden. And this, I reckoned, was the celebrated dawn chorus. The New Dawn chorus, in fact. I thought birdsong was supposed to be enchanting and musical. Oh, for an evangelical air-rifle.

What's more, the cabin was flooded with light. Sunlight, blasting through those ineffectual thin curtains. Curtains should be made of thick brocaded material; keep all that radiant shit out until a person is ready to face the world of his own accord. I slid my feet out of bed and padded over to the table. My watch said a time that made me cry. It had to be wrong.

I groaned and slouched back to bed. Pulled the covers up around my head, trying to wriggle back into some warmth. Succeeded eventually. Gradually, my consciousness drifted away luxuriously from the birdsong. Till the Meeting House bell started to clink – it seemed, ten minutes later.

"Aw Christ!" I groaned and tried to stuff the pillow down my ear.

But it was no use. That old bell kept on a-clinkin' and a-clankin', callin' the faithful to whatever it was that those deranged bastards did at daft o'clock in the morning. Clink! Clank! Clink! Clank! Then the boards of my door received a heavy thump and the voice of Brother Ira summoned me. "Brother! Arise! Time to break your fast!"

"You fucking jest!"

"Intemperate language, brother! The babble of Satan."

"What time is it?"

"Six o'clock. The day grows late and you lie abed. Time for breakfast. Then the Angels must be about their business. We have the labours to visit today."

"Six o'clock!" This was getting to be a habit.

"I will return momentarily. I expect you to be …"

"Right! Right! I'm awake now anyway."

I didn't wait to hear what he expected me to be. I swung my legs out of bed and sat up. Torture; absolute torture.

I pulled back the curtains. The sky was as blue as Our Lady's robe. The grass was webbed with dew. The forest sparkled in the morning sunlight. The sun was drawing a fine mist upwards from the trees in shreds. A rabbit was squatting on the grass, more like a carving than an animal of flesh and fur and blood. Very seventh heaven. Eden. And this were Paradise enow.

19

Breakfast was more nuts, grains, seeds and fruits. The Angels had arrived dressed for work, the men in heavy check shirts, mostly, and corduroy or denim trousers, with heavy boots or wellingtons. The women wore practical clothes, too, headgear covering up their tresses – woolly caps, broad-brimmed straw hats and even one or two in 19th century style poke bonnets. It was like chewing birdseed in the company of the Pennsylvania Dutch.

When fast was broken, the Angels took a powder in the sunlight to their various labours about Eden. Brother Ira suggested we start our fact-finding tour of the estate with the farm.

Brother Ira explained that they sold all their farm produce, that everything was organic, nothing GM there. They sold eggs, dairy, yoghurt, their own honey.

" It's a hot name in the locality," he said.

"Just the locality?"

"By no means. We trade with a delicatessen chain in Aberdeen. I believe they export some of our foodstuffs. England and the Continent of Europe."

"Mmm. Impressive. A land of milk and honey, eh?"

A bearded angel was tending some pigs. I asked Ira about them. He said Eden reared them and sold them. A local butcher made them into pork, ham and other pig stuff. They also, he said, reared and sold cows and chickens.

I suggested this showed double standards, but he demurred. People who eat animals, he said, would eat them in any case. The animals reared on Eden were cared for and tended with dignity. They fetched many British pounds. A concern the size of Eden had many expenses to defray.

We watched a tractor drag a plough through rich, dark soil. The earth rolled over in glinting furrows. I saw fields planted with cereals; fields of turnips, swedes, potatoes, onions; an orchard of apple trees. In the gardens, I saw herbs, soft fruits and berries. The mill. The dairy store, one of the white vans parked outside and an Angel loading it up with boxes and crates. Everywhere, Angels placidly going about unpretentious tasks in self-absorbed contentment. I asked Brother Ira if I could interview some of them.

"Sure thing. Pick an Angel and ask some questions."

The difficulty was picking one who looked as if he had any time to spare. They were all busy as a cat burying shit. But I stopped a young dude on his knees, trowelling the earth in a herb garden. He had long hair tied back in a loose pony-tail.

Okay. I had a front to throw here, so I guessed I'd best give it my A game. I introduced myself to the young guy, said I was a writer, wondered if I could ask him a few things.

"You have the Patriarch's permission, Brother Thomas," said Ira before moving away to talk to an older Angel tying up some raspberry canes. Brother Thomas stood up and gestured towards a garden seat.

We sat.

I asked him why a young dude like him would want to be spending his days closed off in a religious retreat. He said he had heard the Patriarch preach in Aberdeen and took his message to heart. When I asked him what the message was, he told me it was simply that The New Dawn were the elect, we were living in the Last Days, and that The Lord would soon come again in glory to bear them away with him to Heaven.

I wondered what the precise timetable was on that. Apparently, nobody knew for sure. But, as Conflagration approached, The Patriarch would go from them for a short time and return in the company of the Lord … You're there before me. I had to listen to a fair whack more of this before I asked him to tell me about the sexual side. I'd seen some intimate gropes at Morning Meet, I told him. He parroted the guff that Ira had come out with – one of the few glimpses of Heaven we are vouchsafed on this earth, etc.

I said, ""Is any Sister obliged to have sex with any Brother, whether she likes him or not? What I'm getting at, if some plug-ugly son-of-a-bitch says to a Sister, 'You're for me, tonight' can she say no? If he makes her honk, for example?"

"The situation you describe cannot arise. We are all Angels of the New Dawn. We love and comfort one another as we are commanded."

"What'll happen at Glory tonight? I mean sexually?"

"Tonight we will love the Angel or Angels nearest to us. For the nearest to us on the night is the nearest to us in our hearts on the night."

"Love the one you're with, eh?"

"I do not understand."

"A flippant reference. Thanks very much."

I slipped my notebook back in my pocket and let the young man return beatifically to his trowelling. Later, I interviewed a young female Angel. Sister Martha was in her twenties and extremely pretty. I could see the value of standing nearest to her at Glory. She was tossing hay around in a barn with a pitchfork. Ira stood by me, watched and listened as we spoke. I got almost exactly the same answers about the New Dawn, the Last Days and sexual love as I got from Brother Thomas. Then we got on to the Patriarch.

"What was it that drew you to Eden and the New Dawn?"

"Oh, the Patriarch. I heard him speak of the coming of the Lord and I knew right away that he was the Lord's Prophet."

"Where was this? That you heard him speak?"

"In Aberdeen. A mission in Aberdeen. The Patriarch spent much of his time in Aberdeen, in former days."

She continued to fling hay around in aromatic sheaves as she spoke. All very sensual.

"Tell me about the Patriarch."

"He has the light of goodness shining within him. He has the wisdom of the Lord's chosen. He is the last in a long line of prophets."

"So you revere him, do you? Or is it worship?"

"I love him," she said simply. She said it so simply, in fact so openly, that I felt like a heel for asking.

"You love him?"

"I love him. He has saved me."

"Do you all love him?"

"We do. And he loves us."

It was very clear to me that the Patriarch had a good operation going here. Unlike doggers, these poor bitches didn't have the right to say no. Brother Ira did not interrupt our discussion once, though he watched me scribble in my notebook. Later, he and I took the circle round the grounds in the warm morning sun.

"You have some idea of our work here now?" said Brother Ira. "Earthly work and the work of the Lord?"

"You do any other work?" I said. "Somebody did the lighting and the sounds in the Meeting House."

He smiled. "The Angels do not forget the skills they practised in the outside world. Have you spoken to enough people for the day?"

"What I was thinking, Brother," I said, "was that it might be useful to interview one of the most recent arrivals. You know, somebody nearer to the outside world. Someone who is fresh to Eden and can describe it to me with fresh eyes. Describe what drew them here. You got anybody like that?"

"Yes, I think we can arrange that," smiled Ira, after he looked at me for a second. "There is a young handmaiden lodged with Sister Margaret, one of the older Sisters until the Patriarch has the necessary time to undertake her tuition. She came to us from the world only days ago. Somebody like that, you mean?"

"Sounds ideal," I said.

"They will be working in the Sewing Room."

Made sense, as Nairn MacVicar would have said. Someone would have to launder and to stitch up those robes after they'd been groped so much. A homely and meet activity, being a sempstress.

20

Brother Ira and I clumped up the log stoop and pushed open the Sewing Room door. The cabin was full of garments hung up on a rack. Piles of cloth everywhere. Sister Margaret was a Friday-faced old pill in wire glasses and a hair-bun, like some granny from the Mid West. She was sitting in a wooden chair and pushing a needle through one of the white robes. The new girl was there. To my immense relief, it was Laura. She was sewing a patch on a pair of working breeks. She kept her head down, eyes on her sewing.

"Greetings, Sister!" boomed Ira.

"Greetings, Brother," replied Sister Margaret.

"This man is Jack Black," said Brother Ira.

"The writer," said Sister Margaret, looking at me closely. Her mouth had the disapproving shape of the life-long sooker of lemons.

"He would like to speak to our newcomer, Sister," said Ira.

"She is here, Brother."

Conversationalists, every one.

"Sister Laura!" said Brother Ira. "Will you speak to Mr. Black of your reasons for coming here? Of your desire to join us in the Lord's work?"

Laura looked up from her handwork and gave me an expressionless stare.

"The Patriarch wishes it," said Brother Ira.

"I will, of course," said Laura immediately.

"Thank you, sister," I said. "Maybe we could go out. Take a walk. Get some fresh air. Your eyes must be tired from all that sewing. I won't keep you long."

"My eyes are fine, sir."

"It's a beautiful day..."

"Praise the Lord," said Sister Margaret.

"Praise the Lord indeed," said Brother Ira. "Sister Laura, leave your work and walk a little in God's good clean air with Mr. Black. Sister Margaret and I will sit on the stoop a little and converse. In a half hour it will be time for the Morning Meet."

Meek as a lamb – or maybe even meek as *the* Lamb - Laura stood up and waited. And, when Ira led the way, we all went outside. Ira dragged a couple of chairs with him and he and the old crow settled themselves down in the shade of the verandah to watch us. I stepped slowly down on to the sunlit grass, with Laura by my side.

"I'm interested, Sister," I said when we were still in their hearing, "in how you heard the call of the Lord."

"I awoke one morning," said Laura, "and I knew that the Lord was in my heart and that I should serve Him for ever." She used the same intonation and vocabulary as the rest of them. The Angels of the New Dawn knew how to indoctrinate.

"Tell me how you felt, knowing that the Lord was in your heart," I said.

We strolled out into the sunlight and away from the earshot of the two senior Angels on the terrace. Laura walked slowly, her head facing determinedly forwards. Every so often she would look up at the hills. As she parroted the drivel, I looked at her closely. She was her mother's spit. A younger version, needless to say, but the resemblance was strong.

She wore a light summer dress, smocked below the bust. A full bust, like her mother's. Her complexion was blemish-free and glowed in the sunlight. But, though young and pretty, the expression on her face was of one who did not smile too much. Nor make too many mouths in a glass.

She wittered on. How she felt the call to do something worthwhile. How the knowledge that she should devote her life to the Lord had come like a thunderclap. How she cried with the emotion. How she welcomed the realisation all the same. How the love of the Lord made her feel like she had an inner warmth, an inner light, an inner…

"How far gone are you?" I interrupted her.

"What?" She stopped and looked sharply at me.

"How many weeks pregnant are you?"

"Who *are* you?" she asked. Her tone of daffy devotion had gone completely.

This was it. The crucial moment.

"My name's Jack Black," I told her. "I'm a private investigator. Your mother hired me to find you. To find out whether you were okay."

"My *mother*...?"

She faced me squarely. Brother Ira was facing in our direction, not moving. I could not see his eyes for his sunglasses, but he was obviously watching us intently. Sister Margaret was sewing.

"Look, Laura," I said, "can we sit down? Just sit down as if we're chatting about your vocation. Here on the grass." She looked but said nothing. "Please, Laura?"

She sat modestly down, like she was taking the morning sunlight. Praise the Lord. Her face was chipped from flint.

"Thanks. I don't know for sure but I suspect Brother Ira would be a hard customer if it came to unpleasantness."

"I'm sure he would. Why has my mother sent you here? Does *she* think I'm pregnant? Is that it?"

"No, your mother does not think you're pregnant. I'm here because she cares about you."

"She doesn't care about me. She gives the impression that she does, that she's the doting parent, but it's all a … what's the word? A façade. I'm the last thing she cares about."

"So why would she go to the trouble of hiring someone like me…"

"Because it's all about appearances. She wants people to think she's very respectable. She's a teacher. A decent and upright member of society. Me being here is probably a huge embarrassment to her. That's the last thing she'd want – people asking awkward questions about me. I'm supposed to go to university you see. Something respectable and middle-class."

"Right. She said that."

"Well, this is not what Mrs. Nicely Middle Class would want, is it?"

"I guess not. But is it what *you* want?"

"When did it ever matter what *I* want? I'm not even sure I know what I want. I know what my mother wants for me. University and all that."

"You don't want to go to university? Your mother said you…" I trailed off. Her mother had said nothing of the kind. I chewed this for a spell. If I had been sent up here for a simple case of adolescent existentialism, or for a parent-child squabble, I would be less than stoked about it. There had to be more to it than that. "Don't you want to study modern art?"

"I don't know. I like modern art. But whether I want to study it or not…?" She placed her arms behind her on the grass and leant back, as if soaking up the sun on her face. "I'm not pregnant, by the way," she went on. "Trust my mother to think that, with her nasty cheap little mind."

"I told you, she doesn't think you're pregnant. In fact, she was quite dismissive of the notion."

"Then it's *your* idea that I'm pregnant and your mind that's cheap."

"Oh, mine? Reduced to clear," I said. "Everything must go."

"Are you here to take me back home?"

"Maybe. If you want to go back. Your mother thinks you might be upset because you split up with Billy McPartland. I think she wants to look after you."

Laura snorted derisively. "You obviously don't know my mother. She's only interested in one thing: being a well respected glamourpuss. Don't you think she's good-looking?"

I said I did.

"Lots of men do. She laps it up. But she's got no time for me. I just get in her way. She gives the impression of being all goody-goody; you know - teacher, hard-working single mum – but she cares more about her ability to pull the blokes than she does about her daughter."

I did some creative writing in my notebook, to chuck a good front for Brother Ira.

"Well, you may be right, Laura," I said. "Like you say, you know your mum better than me. Why did she want you to stop seeing Billy?"

"She didn't like him. Thought he was common. Not good enough for her daughter to be going with. But only because it would reflect badly on her."

"Did you love him?"

"Love him?" she snorted. "No, I didn't love him. He's an imbecile, a ned. Only interested in one thing."

"So why did you go with him?"

"Because he was good at it. The one thing he was interested in."

That knocked me back on my metaphorical arse. I hadn't expected that from an 18 year old. "Is that why you're up here? A broken heart?"

"You really do have a cheap mind, don't you? Everything's trite and obvious with you."

"I told you. I got it in the bargain bin at the supermarket."

"Obviously," she sneered.

"I think you're wrong about your mother. I think you need to be back with her," I said. "I think you need to be away from here, and as soon as possible."

"Why?"

"You don't believe a word of this pious claptrap. Why would you want to be among it? I'm telling you, Laura, I believe there's some serious shit going down here, and you don't want to be involved in it. You should come back to Bathgate. Settle it with your mother. Go to university. Meet your own kind of friends. Make your own life that way. Not this way. This is no life."

"No, you're wrong," she said simply. "I know I've not been religious before but I can be now. This is where I belong. This is where I want to be. Be here for my father."

"Your *father*?" I said stupidly. "What's he got to do with it?"

She favoured me with a look of utter scorn. "Not Joe McGuire," she said crushingly. "My real father. My spiritual father. I can start afresh here in Eden and do his will."

Brother Ira was striding out over the grass, his bald head glistening in the sun. Sister Margaret had stood up and was now waiting patiently.

"Find out the information you required?" Brother Ira asked.

"Yes, I believe I have," I said.

"Go to Sister Margaret, Sister," said Brother Ira. "I must prepare for the Meet."

Humbly, Laura obeyed. She stood up and said, "I hope you understand my reasons now, Mr. Black." Then she set off to join Sister Margaret.

Ira said, "Okay. Now I go to the Meet. You got some writing or something you wanna do before lunch?"

I said I had and we set off back in the direction of the Settlement. When we got to my door, he said, "I will call you for lunch." And he was gone, his broad, black-shirted back disappearing among the trees.

I wrote up a wholly fictitious interview with Laura. It might be needed. It also allowed me to mull over what she'd said. What I had here was an angst-ridden teenager. A crazy, mixed-up kid. Common enough. The relationship with her mother was the juice of the matter. There was something about that relationship that nagged – nagged like a wife who's just been given an opened pay packet. I couldn't make up my mind what was wrong, there, but I knew something was. I would leave it to my mojo. It usually turned up something when I got it working.

21

The service of Glory proceeded along the same lines as the Morning Meet: Indian music, incense puffing from censers hooked on brackets, and dim lighting. The Angels gathered as before and sat in their dwam-like trance. Again, Brother Ambrose led the faithful in their chanting. But, when that stopped, a palpable anticipation stirred the congregation, something that had not happened before.

Brother Enoch ascended the dais, with six young Angels, bearing goblets.

"Now, Brothers and Sisters, before Rapture, those who will may come and sip from the Cup of Salvation," he said.

They all sprang up eagerly enough and filed forward to take a slug from one of the holy tankards. I didn't see any who swerved it. Whatever it was, it was obviously a change from the shit they served at mealtimes. Taped music softened the mood. They returned to their places. Then the dais was left bare for several minutes, although the Angels all kept their eyes trained on it.

"What's in the Cup of Salvation?" I asked Brother Ira.

"The elixir of *lurve*," he said with a smile.

Finally, the music approached an orgasmic crescendo and a man walked forward from somewhere behind the Table and stood, surveying the flock. There could be no doubt that this was Brother Gabriel. This was the Patriarch. The wave of joy and love that went forward from the congregation confirmed it. He was handsome and spare with an ascetic look, dressed in a robe so immaculately white it shone. His hair was worn slightly long - not shoulder-length - and was silver-white. His moustaches were sleek and silvered; he wore no beard. Even from where I stood, I could see that his blue eyes were as sharp as a semi-tone over pitch.

But it was his presence that proclaimed his identity. He stood quite still, with an irritating look of benevolence and wisdomtransfiguring his features, and wallowed in the adulation of the room. He was certainly charismatic; of that, there could be no doubt. He was confident of being granted unconditional love. He carried all this with complete poise. It was the man I'd seen in Bangour.

"My children," he said at last, raising his arms as if to embrace them all. "My children."

Voice soft and soothing but carrying all over the hall. The waves of love and joy threatened to capsize this ship of fools.

"My children. We must gird ourselves for the coming of the Lord …"

"Alleluia!"

" … for our lives on this earth are of short duration …"

" … as flashes of lightning in the dark of the night," the congregation murmured.

He looked at them all as fondly as a loving father regards his children.

"As flashes of lightning in the dark of the night," he intoned, nodding as if in agreement with an insightful observation, instead of a learnt response. "Yes, my children, our lives are as the lightning that blazes forth for an instant and then is gone. The void of time is dark and drear and goes on forever. Our life on earth, is a flash of brilliance. And then the darkness swallows it up."

"Alleluia!"

"And the darkness will reign for a time and times and half a time. And then there will be time no longer. For the Lord will smite the sinners of the world and the world of sin. Oh yes, my children, outside here are dragons and devils; scorpions and demons. But the Lord will cause the stars to fall from the sky and the waters of the earth to cover the land. In that time, the mountains will crumble and the continents tear apart. And the sinner will hurl himself to the ground before the awful wrath of the Lord."

"Alleluia!"

"We, too, walk for a space as one in the deep silence of the starless night, walking in darkness, the way obscure. But we will hear the trumpet blast of the Lord, and we will behold coals of fire pitch from the sky. And the world will be washed in waves of flame. And the people of the earth will be robed in fire, passing as torches through city streets; crawling like salamanders in the walls of flame; consumed in a flare to ash and powder."

The Angels hung on his every word. I had to admit it was powerful stuff.

"And Time will be no more. And sin will be no more. For the sinners of the earth, the sinners who scoffed at the word of the Lord, the sinners who continued to sin in defiance, will be no more. And the world will be no more. Fire will destroy the earth and all that was *of* the earth. And the sinners will be ash. Cinders and ash."

He looked around.

"And a New Dawn will come."

The Angels smiled and relaxed. This was going to have a happy ending. They were the goodies, after all.

"A New Dawn will come, my children. And the Angels of the New Dawn will be with the Lord in the Kingdom of Heaven. And the night will be gone forever; gone. The morning will unfold in roses of light. Skies will be blue and the road will be fair as we make our way to the City of Glory. Glorious sunshine will light the road. And Glory will be in our hearts, my children. And Glory will be in our eyes. And our lives will be Glory. Glory, my children. Glory, Glory, Glory."

The Angels smiled, wept tears of joy, said Alleluia, blessed the Patriarch for sharing with them his vision of Glory.

"And now, my children, let us love one another."

Those Angels didn't waste any time. They must have been all holy foreplayed up. Let me make a declaration here. I'm a red-blooded XY man with a full set of working valves and pistons. I like women. I like their different bits from us and I have no particular aversion to them walking around raw. But I had to get out. It was the most reptilian and joyless copulation I had ever seen. Who gets off on watching an orgy of zombies? I noticed, when I looked up again, that the Patriarch had faded. Unless he was under a twitching pile of naked arses.

"I will leave now, Brother," I said to Ira.

"As you wish," he replied, a smirk playing around the corners of his mouth. "I will be at your cabin in twenty minutes to take you to the Patriarch."

I left the Meeting House, walked slowly back to my cabin. The sky was lavender, silver and gold. The trees were scented and the air was fresh.

22

The house stood out against the darkness, a black mass with squares of warm golden light, like a Whistler.

"The Patriarch has a suite of rooms on the upper floor," explained Brother Ira, as we entered.

Ira took the breeze at this point and a young female Angel, dressed simply in a long shift dress with a tabard over it, her auburn hair in slides over her ears, escorted me up the stairs. She was very pretty. She showed me into a sitting room, a ritzier version of the library, softly lit by lamps in brackets. A coal fire burned in an ornate marble fireplace. Above the mantelpiece was a landscape, dark with age, of a mythological scene in a forest. I hadn't read Greek literature for years. But I think it was of Narcissus. They're pretty interchangeable, those Greeks. Mad as fucking badgers and always disguising themselves as swans or showers of gold before they go out on the Olympian pull.

Thick carpet, thick curtains, both crimson. A hi-fi and a cabinet of discs. The hi-fi looked expensive. A TV on, but with the sound down, showing CNN. An old table that looked like it drank polish, with stacks of books and sheaves of paper in a loose circle around a PC. Two extremely comfortable looking armchairs by the fire and, in one of them, the Patriarch.

He was dressed quite normally, in an open-necked shirt and dark trousers, not at all like you would expect the successor to all those prophets to be dressed. He looked like he wasn't exactly shorn of a material comfort or two. No living in the wilderness for him, with only a leather girdle about his loins, eating locusts and wild honey. He looked like a dude who happens to have a big country house relaxing in his own front room.

"Ah, thank you, Sister Mona," he said. "Please sit down, Jack Black."

I sat down in the other easy chair.

"Give Mr. Black a glass of wine, please," said the Patriarch.

I noticed that he had a full glass of superior looking grape in his own hand.

"What is it?" I asked. "Not Communion wine, I hope."

"Not that," he said. "A very special Médoc. You'll like it."

Sister Mona brought me a glass. I liked it all right.

"Thank you, Sister."

Mona left, closing the door with a pleasingly discreet soft thud, and the Patriarch looked at me. Closely. In fact, he looked me over from top to toe. Then he smiled. "You are so like your father, Jack Black," he said.

"So you *are* Dominic Tweedie!"

"I was. Now I am Brother Gabriel, the Lord's representative here in Eden. I was saddened to hear of your father's death, Jack Black. He and I were great intimates in our university days. No doubt he told you stories?"

"Some."

"I am sure of it – wine, women and song, no doubt."

"Wine, maybe. Women, certainly. Song, less so. But plenty of dope."

"Indeed! The days of our youth are few and fleet, Jack Black. And hopefully so is the madness thereof."

I could have done without him calling me 'Jack Black' every time he addressed me. He sounded like my old headmaster. Come to think of it, the set-up was exactly like being hauled before the beak in his office, back in the old days.

"And now you are a writer. And you are writing a book on … on what, precisely, Jack Black?"

"On closed religious societies. Yours is a particularly intriguing one."

He stared at me with those honed blue eyes. I got the feeling he was looking right into where my soul would have been if I'd had one. Part of his qualifications as the Patriarch, no doubt.

"In what way intriguing?"

"You never used to be a prophet or a patriarch. Last I heard, you were making computers."

"Jesus was a carpenter until his ministry began. Mohammed was a shepherd and a merchant before the Lord called him."

"Is that the exalted company you're moving in nowadays? A big change from a bunch of scruffy students in Edinburgh. Or the director of a computer company."

"Long ago and far away."

"For some of us, yeah. This is good stuff, by the way."

"There is an abundance of it. Drink deep."

"So, tell me: what have you been doing since *Flash* computers?"

He shrugged. "Waiting until I heard the call of the Lord."

"Tell me about the call of the Lord."

"You heard my homily tonight. You have spoken to several of the Angels. What have they told you?"

"Oh ... that we're living in the Last Days. Endtime. That here, in Eden, the New Dawn are preparing for Glory. That some day soon, you will blow for a spell and return with the Lord and carry away the Elect to a genuine New Dawn in Paradise. That the world will be consumed by fire and all the rest of us miserable sinners 'will pass as salamanders through the walls of flame and be burnt to powder and ash.'"

"But you are sceptical."

"I am. And salamanders can live in fire."

He dismissed this with a contemptuous wave of his hand.

"An image, an image. You studied Literature. Why else do you disbelieve? Do you doubt my word? My calling? My ... vocation? You think I am in error now?"

"No. Not for a minute. I think you know exactly what you are doing. But I don't believe for a minute that you have heard the word of the Lord. I think you are scamming – these people of the New Dawn primarily, and everyone else who comes into the orbit of your work here."

"Go on."

"These Angels ..."

"Yes?"

"They're brainwashed. They're zombies. It's classic altered consciousness technique."

"What is?"

I counted off on my fingers. "One: isolation. Get a bunch of people away from normality and you can work wonders with them, given the know-how. Two: a charismatic leader who promises them some mystical privileges denied to the rest of humanity. Three: practicalities. Hypnotic and repetitive music, to a beat roughly equivalent to that of the human heart. It induces what is called "alpha state", a much more suggestive state of mind than "beta consciousness", the state of mind we are in at present, alert and aware. For the most part. Along with that, you have suggestive colour and lighting. Your overpowering use of incense is a narcotic, too, of course. Four: a speaker talking like a hypnotist. Five: mindless, repetitive chanting. Six: diet can affect state of mind, too. A diet of fruit and vegetables with nothing else spaces folk out. Seven: long hours of work to fatigue the mind further. Eight: the old reliable "Love Bombing" technique. Create a sense of family and common identity through physical caressing and emotional bonding. The group shagging is just an extension of it. Nine: remove individuality by imposing a dress code. Ten: reject all the old values as being for no-hopers, losers or – in this case – sinners. Eleven: what was in the Cup?"

"The Cup of Salvation? Wine. Not as good as this but good enough."

"Wine? And …?"

He smiled again. "A mild narcotic."

"Exactly as I thought. Eleven: mind-altering substances. And, I suspect now that I think about it, Twelve: encouraging people to commit to the cult by donating financial and property assets. How am I doing?"

"Very well. You have evidently done some extensive research. Is that the 'angle' you will take in your book?"

I thought for a second or two. "No. No, there's little mileage in just another cult. People are fairly aware of the methods used in these set-ups. So … Brother Gabriel," I said, "give me a little more back-story. What made you land up in the Forest of Arden, here?"

"The Dhammapada says that 'Forests are sweet when the world does not enter into them. There, the saint may find his rest.' The forest is a fitting place to retire from the wrongful ways of the earth."

"When did you receive the call, then?"

"I have spent some time sequestered from the world, Jack

Black. In many hospitals around the country, I have wrestled with demons in my mind…"

"Right, so the illness …"

"And then, one day, in the midst of my tribulation, the Lord called me, suffered me to see that I was chosen."

"Chosen. In what way?"

"Chosen to be the Patriarch of the New Dawn. I have been chosen to lead this select band of Angels to Paradise."

"You're either as mad as a stripey snake or you're on the make. My guess is the latter."

The Patriarch looked at me stonily for several seconds.

"You believe in nothing, Jack Black? You have no religious beliefs?"

"Tooth fairies and bogeymen, pal – all of it."

"You don't believe in God?"

I shook my head and sucked in breath through pursed lips: a rejection.

"I'm an adult. I don't need to fantasise about an old pooperoo with a long white beard and a robe. I don't need superstition when I've got reason."

"I would say you certainly need something. You have lost your wife, almost lost your way and it is only by a stroke of goodness on the part of the Lord that you have recovered well enough to make a living. Your addiction to drink cost you dearly. How inadequate is that?"

"Inadequate enough, I agree. But what intrigues me, Brother Gabriel, is how you know so much about me."

"The son of an old and valued friend? I have heard of you across the years."

He looked at me and, flipping it open, passed me a cigar-box. "Here. I think you'll appreciate this, if you are anything like your father."

"What is it?"

"Kif."

"I'm not good with blow," I said. "I tend to whitey. Unlike Dad, I've never been a John Blaze. And I've seen a lot of stoners burnt out like old toasters. I'm not sure I want to risk it."

"You will be fine with this. This is no Oxo cube."

I took one of the small, hand-rolled cigarettes and smelt it.

"Good stuff?"

"Nepalese Temple Ball. The best there is."

"I'll toke to that," I said and sparked up.

By the dead God, it was good stuff. The first puff gave me a sizeable ping. Brother Gabriel lit one, too and sat back in contentment.

"So, tell me what you will write about me. About us."

"Oh, em, the thing that really interests people, of course, is the shagging. Everybody likes to read about a bit of rumpy-pumpy and wish it was them who was doing it, you know?"

"Don't you think they get plenty of that in the Sundays? Suburban housewife orgies and all that?"

"Well, yes, I guess they do, but the angle really isn't about the group humping in the Meeting House. It's about a bit of unpleasantness in the surrounding villages over you spiriting away their young virgins and sacrificing them on the altar of your lust."

The Patriarch smiled. "How parochial."

"Isn't there?"

"No. Not in any real sense. I remember one irate father who came up here, clamouring at the gates to be let in, swearing that I had stolen his daughter from him."

"By spells and medicines bought of mountebanks?"

He laughed briefly at the Shakespearean reference, then he continued. "So we invited him in, showed him round, let him speak to his daughter. She left with him. End of incident. 'This only is the witchcraft I have used.'"

I smiled.

"The only incidence of it?"

"There have been one or two others."

"That's pretty uncommon, isn't it? People leaving places like this?"

"Fairly so, yes. In other communities. But that was what happened. We are not as other communities."

"Had she been one of your bed-partners?"

"Of course."

"What age was she?"

"Sixteen."

"Mmm," I frowned. "Quite a wee seraglio you have here."

"All legal and above reproach, Jack Black."

"So how long does it take for a neophyte to become an Angel? You have one at present, newly arrived. I spoke to her today."

"Ah yes. Sister Laura. Normally I prefer neophytes to study for three months before they are accepted as Angels of the New Dawn.

I looked at him, slightly woozily.

"How do you pay for all this? It must take plenty of the old do-re-mi."

"The estate? Eden? We sell what we produce."

"Naw," I dismissed airily, "you don't run a concern this size on wee tins of honey or pots of Eden yoghurt."

"There are the donations."

"Aah. So new Angels have to pay a tithe of all they possess or something, have they?"

"Not quite as crude as that. Angels are encouraged to donate their worldly goods to the better running of the organisation. They are happy to do so."

"Brainwashed into it."

"They remember the words of Matthew."

"Oh yeah; it is easier for a camel to pass through the eye of a needle; and all that."

"Go and sell that thou hast… and thou shalt have treasure in heaven."

"Yeah. 'Put money in thy purse.'" The Patriarch laughed in appreciation, but I hadn't finished. 'Thus do I ever make my fool my purse, for I mine own gained knowledge should profane, if I would time expend with such a snipe but for my sport – *and* profit.'

He stopped laughing. "Very impressive."

"*Othello* was always my favourite play. I read it several times a year. I find it very Moorish." I giggled sillily. He didn't. I sobered a little. "And I've seen the wee red sports job outside. The Lord moves in mysterious ways but his agents move in Ferraris. Eh?"

"I sometimes have to deal with important worldly people. They are impressed by such trappings. But remember, Jack

Black, that I, like the Angels, may be *in* this world but am not *of* it."

"What's the shed in the woods for?"

"Shed in the woods?"

"Well, more than a shed – a big stone building with no windows and a metal door. Locked up. There's a drive down to it."

"I have no idea, Jack Black. Brother Ira might know. I presume it's a store for farming materials, machinery or whatever."

"Right. How did you get this house? It's a huge bloody place."

"It was given to us by an Angel. Brother Matthew, no longer with us, unfortunately. He was our oldest Angel. His wife had passed on and he had no family. He is with the Blessed now."

"Okay."

I ground the stub of my juju in a huge glass ashtray, big enough for a swimming pool. It took me an awfully long time to put it out. Brother Gabriel offered me the cigar-box again.

"No thanks. Look, Brotherrr…" I was starting to slur. "I think I'm just bout out on my feet. I shd r'lly be 'n bed."

I heard the Patriarch say, "I think so, too, Jack Black. We shall continue this conversation…"

And then the room turned dark and tipped sideways.

23

I came to the surface from a wash of dreams and darkness. The birds were at it again, but showing a little restraint this time. The morning felt more advanced. I sat up and felt a stoun in my head, ignored it and checked the time. Eight thirty. The middle of the day as far as the Angels were concerned. My skull was pounding. Then I realised that at least some of the pounding was coming from the front door.

"Come," I called. Quietly.

Brother Ira came in. "Ah, the sluggard has arisen," he boomed.

"Yeah," I growled. "The dead arose and appeared to many."

"How are you this morning, brother?"

"Dog-rough."

"You were unconscious when we put you to bed."

"I'm sure of it. That shit that Brother Gabriel smokes is powerful stuff. How did I get here?"

"Two of the Brothers and I brought you." He laughed mirthlessly. "You missed breakfast."

"Oh no. I intend to have breakfast. I'm going into town this morning."

"To town. Why would that be?"

"Several reasons, one pressing. I need some medication for my migraine…"

"Shoot, that's just hungover."

"No, it isn't. I know the difference, believe you me. I suffer from migraine. I need something to kill it quick."

"We have medications in Eden. Brother Francis has some skill in medicine."

"What I need is ergotamine tartrate. You haven't got that. But a chemist will."

"The drug store may not be open. It is the Sabbath."

"I'll try, anyway. And, since I missed breakfast, when I'm out I intend to get me a cup of coffee and a croissant. And a newspaper."

"We don't allow newspapers in Eden," he said gruffly. Then, turning it into a lame joke, he said, "We got all the good news we need in the God-spell."

"Then I'll read it in the cafe and leave it there. I'm going out, Brother Ira. And I'll be back in about an hour or so."

"I would recommend you do. The Patriarch enjoyed your conversation so much last night, he wants to complete it today. And he would prefer it if you can stay awake this time."

His laughter rolled like thunder around the cabin.

24

The little town was sleepy, barely awake, not much activity on its clean and sun-washed streets. It might have been the Sabbath effect, of course.

I looked at my watch as I purled along the quiet main drag. Ten past nine. My stomach was reminding me that I had tantalised it earlier with thoughts of a real breakfast. I pulled in by a small stone building. It doubled as café and guest house, if there was any truth in the sign that read, "Rooms". A young woman in a starched apron was washing the plate glass window with a squeaky cloth. A folding wooden notice board, on the pavement outside, advertised, amongst other culinary treats, "All Day Breakfasts." That would do for me. Wrap it up; I'll take it.

"You open yet?" I asked, as I locked the car door and stepped up to her.

"We are," she said. "Go in."

It was a caff from a TV show: little tables with red check PVC tablecloths; frilly lace curtains on the windows; a flower in a glass on each table; nobody in. The girl appeared at my side with a notepad. The name-tag on her apron informed me her name was "Sheena".

"Hi Sheena. I'm Jack."

"Good for you, Jack. What can I get you then?"

"A cooked breakfast, please, Sheena."

"Okay. We can do you: eggs, bacon, sausage, black pudding, hash browns, fried tomato, mushrooms, beans, fried bread …"

"All of the above."

She paused slightly, tipped her head with a wry smile and started to write.

"And to hell with your heart, eh?"

"Well … now you've stolen it away, Sheena …"

"Skip it. Honey doesn't go with fried fat." She held her hand up to show me her wedding ring. "And that isn't just an ornament."

"Fair do's. I am suitably upbraided. Just trying to be friendly."

"That's fine. You want one egg or two? Fried or poached?"

"Two, please. Fried. Sunny side up. Like my disposition."

She shook her head and sighed.

"Toast?"

"Please."

"Tea or coffee?"

"Tea, please. Big white mug with a chipped rim. Milk and four sugars."

"I'll bring you a cup, saucer and teapot. Milk-jug and sugar-bowl are on the table. You can add the tooth-rot yourself."

I laughed. She didn't. I liked her. I'm not sure how she felt about me.

"Anything else?" she asked. "Beta blockers, maybe?"

"Mmm... an ashtray?"

"Light up in here," she said, "and you'll soon know all about it." And she headed off.

I looked around. It was the sort of place I could imagine being busier in the afternoons. Jammed to the tinkling door with old ladies in heather-mixture suits drinking tea very genteelly and nibbling scones. Wiping traces of flour from the corner of their mouths with wee lacy hankies. "Sheena, dear," they would cry, "could I have another wee pat of butter? Thank you, dear." Not too many folk, I thought, would drop in for the belly-banger breakfast.

Sheena brought the tea things.

The tea was wonderful, especially after the water of Eden – strong, thick and brown. You could have tanned hides with it. I drank it with relish and several spoonfuls of sugar. Then Sheena brought me my mountainous breakfast, a breakfast that could have graced the table of Desperate Dan. The plate was the size of a dustbin lid but still the food covered just about every inch of it.

"Enjoy," she said, with the merest hint of irony in her tone, and left.

I tucked in to the working man's banquet. It was *sheer* enjoyment. After two days of grapes, grits, grains and grounds, this repast was worthy of the gods. I had wrapped myself around it and was just mopping up the gravy – a mix of egg yolk, tomato juice, fat and oil – with my soggy toast, when Sheena reappeared. She seemed genuinely surprised.

"My God," she said, half to herself, "he ate it."

"I was hungry," I said simply.

"Unbelievable."

"Don't tell me none of your regular customers ever eat a breakfast like that. What about the working men?"

"Well, now that you mention it, Calum McWilliams used to heck like that."

"Used to?"

"Yeah," she smiled. "Used to. He died last year. Massive heart attack."

I let her have that one. The smile was one of petty triumph but it was worth seeing, anyway.

"Can I get you anything else?" she said, smirking as she cleared up. "How about a laxative?"

"Well, actually, Sheena, you can. I'm looking for some information."

She balanced my breakfast crockery expertly on her arms and rested on one hip. "What kind of information? Directions, is it?"

"No, no. Not directions. What do you know about the New Dawn community up on the Edzell road?"

"The hippies? Not much. They more or less keep themselves to themselves."

"Do they never come into town at all?"

"Very seldom. I've seen the head honcho in a red car once. Well, they told me he was the head honcho; I wouldn't know. Why do you want to know?"

"I'm a journalist. What's the feeling about them, though? Among the townsfolk?"

"Well … we never bothered much about them. They're cranks, aren't they? Jesus freaks or something."

"A religious group, yeah. So far as I know. What about the rumours?"

"What rumours?"

"Well, some say that they're inveigling local lassies up there. And there's sex orgies and all sorts of things going on."

"I wouldn't know about that. I know that Ailish Murray was up there for a wee while and her father drove up and kicked up merry hell. Got her back home again."

"Where does Ailish Murray live?"

"Sheena!"

A grim-faced man with closely-cropped greying hair was standing in the doorway to the kitchen. His white jacket and checked trousers indicated that he was the cook.

"Steve?"

"Get those plates and things in here. You've no time for gossip."

"This man here was asking about the hippies. And where Ailish Murray lives."

The man emerged from the doorway. Tall, with a face like a storm lantern. Serious. Not much given to levity, I should imagine. Certainly not the author of the Crack-a-Joke book for that year. He came up to the table.

"On your way," he said to Sheena.

When she had cleared away my detritus, he looked at me and said, "Why do you want to know about Ailish Murray and the hippies?"

"I'm a journalist."

"Another one? Has something happened then?"

"No, nothing has happened. That I know of. I'm just writing an investigative piece on the New Dawn. Your ... wife? Sheena? ..." He did not react, so I carried on. "... was telling me about Ailish Murray."

"There's nothing to tell about Ailish Murray."

"Sheena seems to think there is. She was up there for a time, wasn't she?"

"You'd best speak to the police. Sergeant McKechnie would know more than we do."

"Yes, that was my intention. And where will I find Sergeant McKechnie?"

"The station is at the end of Main Street here. On the left, next to Razzaq's corner store."

"Thanks," I said. "Much obliged."

"No bother. If you're finished, then, Sheena will take your money."

And with that final scoop of charm, he returned to the kitchen. In a moment, Sheena came bustling prettily back through and took up her place behind the till.

"Let me see… the full breakfast, and one pot of tea …"

"Sorry …"

"That'll be five pounds sixty five, then, please. Sorry for what?"

"Keep the change," I said, handing over a ten pound note. "Sorry if I landed you in the shit."

She rang up the sale. "Thanks. You know what the guy said? Semper in excretum. Sole profundum variat."

I laughed. I like a girl who can talk shit in Latin.

"The Murrays live in a big rambling bungalow about two miles out of here. Just drive along Main Street the way you're headed."

"Thanks. I owe you one."

"You owe me two."

25

There was a paper shop on the street. All it had left was a Sunday redtop. I'm not really an intellectual snob (despite what people think), but I prefer not to read these things. Real people might think I can't manage joined-up news. There was nothing else but a *People's Friend* or one of those magazines full of drivelling gab about soaps and slebs. These things cost several pounds and are too shiny even to make good shit tickets. So I bought the redtop, and read about the Cairns investigation.

Bert's boys were still appealing for anyone with any knowledge of Brian Cairns's movements on the evenings of the previous week to come forward. Hodge had indicated that he thought Cairns was killed two days previous to the body being discovered. Maybe Saturday night, Sunday morning. They had interviewed his wife, Anne. Utterly shocked at the suggestion that he was involved in any shady sexual practices. Right. If she was sincere, that answered one of the questions that had bothered me. No-one who owned up to being a dogger had contacted the police. Cairns's work colleagues and fellow Hibees said what a great guy he was, and how could anybody want to kill him? There was some more background stuff on dogging. And that was that. Still no mention of the treble L quote. That would come soon, if the police were getting nowhere. I skiffed through the rest of the rag and left it in a waste paper basket.

I gunned the bucket along Main Street and then was suddenly out amongst scenery again. Trees, hedges, shrubs and fields – more greenery than the Celtic gift shop. A soft morning. And then, as Sheena had said, a ranch style bungalow, sitting in a blocked yard off a gentle curve of the road. I decelerated and pulled in, just as a young woman came out of the front door, with a dog on a leash. A mongrel with a fair shot of boxer in it. The girl was wearing a blue fleece jacket. She had copper coloured hair spilling out from under a woolly toorie. The dog was straining against the leash, generally giving the girl a hard time as she tried to lock the front door with the hand on the arm that wasn't being wrenched from its socket by the mutt.

I got out the car and that gave Fido an added spurt. Its claws scrabbled on the monoblocks as it fairly launched itself towards me, slavering and attempting to wag the tail off its arse. The girl was spun around by the strain, the leash torn from her grasp and the key left in the lock. "Brandy!" she exclaimed in protest.

"It's all right," I said. "You lock the door. I'll keep a hold of Brandy."

I am not a dog man. I'm very wary of them, especially big ones. But this Brandy was a drooling, jumping, face-licking, tail-thumping heap of canine devotion. The girl looked at me briefly and then took the opportunity of locking the door whilst she could, before accepting the leash from my hand.

"Thanks, mister."

"No problem. I'm looking for the Murrays."

"This is us," she said.

"And you'll be Ailish."

"Will I? It depends on who's asking."

"Good answer. I'm Jack Black. I'm a private investigator."

"Oh aye?" She sounded sceptical until I showed her my ID.

"Dad at home?"

"Why would *your* Dad be in *my* house?"

"Even better answer. I like that. Is *your* Dad at home?"

"He's working. So's Mum. What is it you want?"

"Just some information. I'm working on a case that's brought me up to Eden."

"I'll bet."

"Mind talking to me about it?"

"I don't mind. Just as well my folks aren't about, though. D'you mind if we walk? It's easier with the dog."

I didn't mind at all. It was a fair morning and I could have done with a lungful or two of the finest fresh. We set off along the edge of the road, Brandy tugging like he was pulling a plough. In fifty or so paces we came to a five-bar gate and entered a field where Ailish let Brandy off the leash. He took off for the far blue yonder like a shell. "So. Tell me what you want to know about Eden."

"You were there, weren't you?"

"For a while," she said, her eyes averted to the distance and the rapidly diminishing dog.

"There seems to be a cloak of secrecy about your time there," I said.

"Does there?" she replied. "How did you know about it then?"

I laughed. "Well, what I mean is, nobody's willing to say much more about your stay other than the fact you were there."

"My Dad didn't want too many people to know about it. He's high up in the Forestry and quite an influential guy. That's all."

"Why did you go there?"

She looked at me now, weighed me up as if wondering whether I could be trusted with the answer. "Boredom," she said at last. "Boredom pure and simple. You go nuts up here after a while. There's nothing to do. Read. Drink. Walk the dog. Once in a while go into town. So, I heard about the New Dawn and I thought, I'll check these people out. I hear there's lots of sex and drugs and rock'n'roll. A pastoral existence. Something to occupy the mind and body. I'll give that a try."

"Are you religious at all, Ailish?"

"I believe in God," she said. "I wouldn't say I was Mother Theresa."

"You believe in God, but you're not averse to a little sex and drugs and rock'n'roll?"

"Who is?" she said.

"And did you get that?"

"Not too much rock'n'roll," she said, laughing.

"But the sex and the drugs?"

"Oh there's plenty of that in Eden," she said.

"So I saw."

"Oh, you've been up there? Get any yourself?" she asked with a smirk.

"No," I said. "I made an excuse and left."

"Like in the Sunday papers."

"You got it."

"Well, you sound like you're from somewhere in the Central Belt. You probably get all the sex and drugs and rock'n'roll you need."

"I wouldn't bet on it."

The dog came hurtling back up the slight incline towards us and lay down, panting, in front of Ailish. When she bent down to clap him, he took off again.

"Were you there long?" I asked.

"About a month. My father phoned and complained the first couple of days I was there. But they paid no attention to that. They said I had come to them of my own free will and was staying of my own free will…"

"What age were you then?"

"Oh … sixteen? No, seventeen. Then my father phoned to say he would involve the law if they wouldn't release me. So Brother Gabriel invited him up to see the place and to talk things over."

"And he went up?"

"Oh aye. We met in the library. My mother didn't come up. Just my father. We chewed it over a while and my father said he could make things nasty for the New Dawn if they didn't let me go. Gabriel said they should talk together, man to man. See if they could resolve the problem. I went out for a while. When I got back in, Gabriel said I could go if I pleased, whenever I pleased. My father said he wanted me back with him. So I went."

"Did you want to, though?"

She shrugged her shoulders. "Probably. I was getting bored with it all, anyway."

"Did you have sex?"

"Sure. With the Patriarch when I was working in the house. At Rapture. Sure, I had enough to keep me going."

"I thought they didn't force newcomers to have sex until they were … qualified."

"They'll tell outsiders that. They told my father that. Kept him onside, you know?"

"I wonder what the Patriarch and your father discussed."

"Me too," she said. "Dad wouldn't tell me. But he seemed pleased enough I was coming back."

I nodded quietly, absorbing this information. Ailish called the distant dog in a singsong call – "*Braaan*-dee!" Old Brandy fair came tearing up the hill. Ailish caught him, pulled him to her side and clipped the leash on to his collar. Then we headed back.

"Well, thanks, Ailish. You've been a lot of help."

"Is it another girl you're investigating?"

"Yep."

"Tell them you'll shop them to the police. They come to heel quickly enough when you threaten that – far quicker than *he* ever does," she laughed, nodding towards the pulling, peching dog.

"Why *is* that, do you think?"

She shrugged, then laughed. "That's for you to find out. *You're* the private eye."

I got in the car and reversed out on to the road. Ailish watched me, a quiet smile playing about her lips. Brandy sat by her, his chest heaving and his tongue flopping out, long and pink. He shut his mouth to swallow and had to open it again to resume the peching. Ailish waved to me briefly when I drove off. Then I headed back up the road to Eden.

26

I thought I detected something different in Brother Ira's tone at the gates but it could just as easily have been the fact that I was hearing his voice through the squawkbox. That tends to sieve a voice of any inflection. I drove up the avenue and he was there, waiting, as he had been a couple of days before. He wasn't beaming.

"The Patriarch will speak with you now," he said, as I got out of the car.

"Oh, right. Okay. Is there something wrong?"

"The Patriarch will speak with you now."

That was it. Chitchat interruptus. Something was decidedly not fine or dandy. He was all churned up about something. He accompanied me to the Patriarch's room. Unlike the night before, Brother Gabriel was standing in front of the fire, his hands behind his back. His expression was not hospitable.

"Please sit at the table, Jack Black."

Jack Black sat at the table, in the chair indicated. Ira sat in one of the armchairs by the fire.

"Please take the piece of paper that is on the table."

I slid the sheet of paper towards me. It was my self-penned letter of accreditation.

"That is a bogus document. You are not Jack Black, investigative journalist and writer. You do not have a commission from that publishing firm to write any kind of learned book. You are a lie. I have reason to believe that you are, in fact, Jack Black, Private Investigator, registered office at 38A King Street, Bathgate in West Lothian. Am I correct?"

"You are quite correct. How did you find that out?"

"Brother Ira has some skill in investigative work, himself. Perhaps you would be so good as to explain to me why you are here under false pretences?"

"Be happy to. I'm working on a case for a client."

"You are investigating one of the Angels?"

"I am. In fact, I am investigating the reasons why Laura McGuire is here as a postulant or whatever you guys call it."

Brothers Gabriel and Ira exchanged a glance and the Patriarch nodded in confirmation.

"The reasons for Laura McGuire, or indeed anyone else, being here are not your concern."

"Oh yes, they are. I have been hired to find just that out."

"Then let me rephrase my statement. The reasons for anyone's being here will not be your concern *here*. You have betrayed our trust and our hospitality. You will leave immediately. Brother Ira has removed all of your possessions from the cabin..." Ira stood up with my grip and my laptop. "... and he will escort you from the grounds. Do not make it necessary for any unpleasantness. There has been enough of that already, thanks to your duplicity."

"You mean you haven't entertained angels this time?"

"Goodbye, Jack Black. I will not shake your hand or wish you well."

I said, "Stick, bubbly."

Brother Ira flashed the Patriarch a look of complete mystification. The Patriarch shook his head slightly and, with a sneer, said only, "Goodbye." Ira handed me my things and jerked his head for me to follow him. Dismissed. Goodnight and thanks for playing. Here's your hat; what's your hurry? I followed that broad back down to the hall and out into the sunshine. He watched me unlock the car, sling the holdall and the laptop into the back seat and then slide behind the wheel. He put his hand on the top of my door to prevent me from closing it.

"I will watch you leave," he said. "We don't want to see you or your type back here."

"I'll wager," I replied.

"Hmm?"

"Doesn't it worry you?" I asked. "The possibility of outsiders coming in here and intruding on your little set-up, your little Happy Hunting Ground?"

He looked down on me with a strange smile – almost a sneer – turning up one corner of his mouth. "Now, what kind of intrusion did you have in mind?" he said.

"Me? I have nothing in mind. I just wondered how you would take to some outside influence spoiling things."

"What outside influence would that be?" he asked coldly.

"Nothing specific," I said. "Just – well, you know –

'Nothing Abides' as the Buddhists say."

"You tellin' me you studied the Buddha?"

"No. Hardly. My point is just ..."

"Yeah. What's your point?"

"Just that we make plans and try to live our lives the way we want but there's always somebody trying to make us do things differently."

"You say?"

"Of course. The sinners out there (I nodded in the general direction of 'out there') might try to stop you living the way you do, you know."

"Why is that?"

"Because they don't understand you. And what people don't understand, they fear. And what people fear, they try to change."

He sneered again. "Ain't nobody gonna try and change the New Dawn. We got protection."

"Yeah?"

"Yeah. We got the Lord and the word of the Patriarch." Here he smiled that angelic smile, the gold filling glinting in his mouth. "An' nobody – nobody – fucks wit dis nigga; I is always rollin' deep."

He laughed, and shut my car door, stood back from the vehicle. I put her in first, turned her round on the gravel, and pouted Brother Ira a kiss as I pulled off down the drive. He stood and watched the car all the way until a bend and the trees obscured him. When I got to the gates, they backed open. I rolled down the window and gave a cheery wave into the lens of the CCTV before leaving the precincts of Eden. I was slightly disappointed at the low-key nature of my dismissal. No cherubim. No flaming sword turning every way. Maybe atheists don't merit the full expulsion.

27

The estimable Sergeant McKechnie was not at all the burly, beef-witted Teuchter I had imagined him to be – garrulous and credulous: ochone, ochone, how do you take your tea now, Misster Black, would that be three lumpss of shoogar or five?

Quite the reverse. He was thin, hawk-featured, well-spoken and intelligent. Probably an Oxbridge graduate into the bargain. He graciously welcomed me into the office, and allotted me a short span of his precious time, but he did not offer me any refreshments. Nor did he vouchsafe me much information when I asked about Ailish Murray.

"Well now, Mr. Black," he considered thoughtfully, "I think the Murrays had enough nuisance at the time without yourself – saving your presence, of course – raking all that back up. It would serve no purpose other than to distress the family. Mr. MacVicar of the Scotsman was sniffing around the Murrays not so long ago, and Dugald got a little irate about it. They're a very private family. I suspect you know as much of the story as is relevant."

"Well, the people at Eden told me one or two things but I can hardly credit that they told me the whole story."

"What exactly did they tell you?"

"That Ailish was a candidate Angel of the New Dawn for a short while; that her father came calling, extremely angry that his ewe lamb should have been spirited away by a bunch of beardie weirdies; that they admitted him to the estate and allowed him to speak to Ailish; that he had a private chinwag with Brother Gabriel, and that Ailish left with her father after that. That was all there was to it. *They* said."

"That's about as much as there was to it, in fact," said Sergeant McKechnie.

I shook my head. "More complicated than that. Didn't Mr. Murray press charges?"

"What kind of charges?"

"I don't know – statutory rape? Corruption of a minor? Unlawful intercourse?"

The sergeant meshed his fingers together over the broad blue chest of his uniform. He looked at me, and a smile played over his lips. I was beginning to resent that expression. "No," he said at last. "Nothing like that."

"Didn't he suggest that your boys should go up there and investigate the goings on in Eden?"

"He didn't, no. What goings on are you referring to?"

"Why wouldn't he do that, do you think?"

"I have no idea."

"How do you think the New Dawn pay for the upkeep of that estate?"

"I don't know. By selling what they grow?"

"Really, Sergeant? By selling a few dozen eggs and the odd cow? You think this is Jack and the Beanstalk? You think they bankroll the big house, the cabins and the furnishings, the electricity, the vehicles, the gadgetry, the God alone knows what else that they have there by flogging double cream? Come on, Sergeant. You're an intelligent man. All that takes a fair bit of scratch."

"Well, how do *you* suggest they pay for it?"

"Drugs."

"Drugs?"

"Drugs. I think Brother Gabriel and his cohort of angels are drug dealers. And I don't think they are small time operators. Maybe Dugald Murray got cut in on the action to keep his mouth shut."

The Sergeant sat up erect in his chair and looked interested. "Have you any evidence of drug misuse on the estate?"

"Just last night I was offered Nepalese Temple Ball marijuana. The finest shit a man can git. I have witnessed several of their religious ceremonies. It was evident to me that mind-altering substances were being misused in the course of them. I think they kick the gong around a fair bit up in Eden. They must get their stash from somewhere. Wouldn't surprise me if Brother Gabriel is running the biggest drugs operation in the North East."

"Have you met Brother Gabriel?"

"Yes."

"A fascinating man. And an educated one."

"He is. He is one of the most charismatic human beings I

have ever met. He was a friend of my father's. Was at university in the 60's with him. Did you know he is clinically insane? Oh yes. Been inside the booby-hatch on several occasions, getting his nuts tightened. He's zooming. And now he thinks he is the last prophet of God before the Conflagration comes. Ever noticed how often madmen are attracted to the Bible? The notion of good and evil? It's nicely black and white for them: goodies and baddies. Their minds are not usually capable of subtler concepts. They think they're God. Or the Devil. That's the Bible for you. Maybe they should widen their reading a little. No madman ever thinks he's Mr. Darcy or Leopold Bloom."

"This man, Brother Gabriel, was a friend of your fathers?"

"Absolutely. At one time, his friend … and dealer."

"So why should you accuse him of what you do?"

I considered carefully before I said, "Because all his life he's been a bastard. A self-centred, egotistical bastard. And as mad as a tuppenny watch. He's a dangerous individual, Sergeant."

The policeman looked at me. Was that distaste on his face, or just bafflement?

"How do you suggest he traffics in drugs?"

"There are two white vans that ostensibly ferry Eden's produce to the shops. They're missing at night and back in the morning."

"Mmm."

"They call at Aberdeen harbour. Obviously at night time. They're supposed to be carrying produce for loading on boats going to the continent. The drugs are brought into the country there. How the New Dawn distributes them will be the same, I suspect. The vans run too often to be carrying only milk and honey. It should be a piece of piss for your boys to check."

Sergeant McKechnie sat forward and said, "Would you be prepared to make a statement?"

I returned his gaze. "I would at that," I said.

28

It was good to be back in the world of sinners. I felt a distinct waft of Vanity Fair as I left Christian and Faithful behind. Give us Barabbas! I felt at ease negotiating the hairpin bends and rough roads of the countryside. The serenity of the trees and hills was getting on my nerves. I wanted streets, houses, betting shops, Chinese takeaways, lamp-posts, tanning salons, traffic lights, idiot youths yelling obscenities in the streets, pretty office girls walking and giggling in pairs. I wanted the city. Well, Bathgate.

Soon enough, the main road gave promise of it – zipping traffic heading both ways, fast and futile. It came on to rain as I drove south: big, fat drops that splattered on the windscreen at first and then turned to lashing sheets of rain that were whipped across the dark green backdrop of the trees in drifting shrouds. But the old radials kept sizzling through the wash on the road surface, taking me back home. Sonny Boy on the player.

After the morning I'd had, my blood pressure had been up in the face cards, but the wipers' regular pulse did wonders for it. That and the prospect of being back in familiar surroundings. By the time I was driving over the Road Bridge, the sun was out again and drying up the rain.

Armadale is the next town west of Bathgate on the A89. It had originally been called 'Barbauchlaw'. Apart from being as hard to pronounce as the Xhosa for 'catarrh', this had something to do with this whole area being part of the boar-hunting lands of the Stewart kings when they lived in Edinburgh. This part of West Lothian still has a hangdog air about it. Never the seat of anything royal or important, always the site of necessary but essentially dull activities, it's been called 'Corridor County'. About sums it up. Mining towns were strung out along the A89, the old main road from Edinburgh to Glasgow, only now they're ex-mining towns. An added patina of dreariness. The original West Lothian question was '*Where...?*" Armadale is all that, only more so. The town is full of those drab, between-the-wars council houses that you get in every town in the county. But there are some estates of private housing going up these days, too, and it was to one of the most recent that I drove first.

Grace McGuire's place was on a corner. A big front garden and a six-foot high fence around the side and back. The roof of a hexagonal conservatory. The sun was warm again when I got out the car. She answered the door, wearing a blue top and a pair of shorts.

"Mr. Black!" she said with a winning smile that allowed me to scrutinize her crockery again. "Come in. I was just enjoying the sunshine out in the conservatory. I'm back to school next week so I'm taking advantage of things while I can. Come through."

She closed the door behind me and brushed past me again to lead the way. Close enough for me to smell her hair and the rose-water that she probably used as a facial cleanser. "Through here," she said and headed off along the hall. The shorts took a trick as she sashayed ahead.

The conservatory had cane garden furniture, a glass-topped table with a tray of tea-things on it, and a pile of newspapers on the floor by one of the seats. There was also a lingering aroma that had nothing to do with rose-water. I sniffed. It wasn't air freshener.

"Would you like some iced tea, Mr. Black?"

"No thanks. I see you were expecting me, though."

There were two cups along with the teapot, that flowery china stuff, what's it called… Royal Doulton, maybe. A plate of hard-looking biscuits.

"Ha," she laughed shortly.

"Mr. McPartland can come in or stay out," I said. "It makes no difference to what I have to say. But it does perhaps explain things better."

"He can stay out," Grace said shortly. "And you're wrong. It explains nothing. Did you see Laura?"

"I did," I said, sitting down in a cane chair and helping myself to a biscuit. "I fact, I spoke to her."

"What did she say? How did she look?"

"She looked fine. She said she was where she belonged. She doesn't seem at all interested in coming back."

"She said she *belonged* there?"

"That's what she said. Jeez, what are these – *dog* biscuits?"

"Don't eat it if you don't like it. Why would she say she belonged in a religious cult?"

"Why not? Especially if her old lady's knocking off the guy who used to be her boy friend."

"Laura doesn't know about Billy and me."

"Laura knows a lot more than you give her credit for. I can't think of a better reason for her wanting to up sticks and live with the Last Day Loonies. Your Ma's shagging your boyfriend? 'Goodbye, cruel world' every time."

Grace stood up and crossed to the door, called into the house, "Billy!" In a moment, the handsome hunk stood in the doorway, a glossy ad cliché in a white T-shirt and jeans, stinking of that after-shave. He had his hair gelled up in the modern spiky fashion, like straw sticking out of a pig's arse. Stop press: Carriage trade dame has a weakness for the boy polloi.

"Aw right?" he nodded, then added to Grace, "Why'd you tell 'im Ah wis here?"

"I didn't. He knew."

"Two cups on the table, Billy, and that fly-spray you insist on hosing over yourself."

"That's fuckin' Joop," the hunk snapped. "Tasteless prick."

"Well... maybe it's best experienced as a subtle hint rather than something you bathe in," I said. "Whatever, it kinda announces your presence, Billy. I could smell you on a pig farm."

"What's he want?" he asked Grace.

"Tell him," she answered. "Did Laura know about us?"

"Nup. Hadn't a scooby."

"Why'd she chuck you then?"

"Because Grace here kept on about me no' bein' right for her, eh? Grace thought it aw oot. Very clever."

"Grace is, yeah," I answered. "But you're only assuming that's why Laura finished it up. In my opinion, neither of you is as clever as you think you are. I think Laura knew about you. And I think it scunnered her so much, she took off."

There was a silence. Then Lothario growled, "Is that it?

Ah'm away back tae watch Big Brother."

I said, "See you, stud."

He snarled at me and left. Grace sat down and poured herself more iced tea and said, "Tell me about your meeting with Laura."

"You want the whole story, complete and unexpurgated, or just the Janet and John version?"

"The whole thing, please."

I told her in detail: how she looked when I'd first seen her in the Sewing Room; what she'd said in the sunshine that morning, and how she'd been as she said it.

"What happened after that?"

"Well, the Angels kinda blew my cover. There's a hotshot guy there called Brother Ira. He chased up the false ID I'd given myself. They didn't take too kindly to my deceiving them. They gave me the bum's rush, in short. I've just come down this morning. I thought it right to report to you first. I was going to ask where you want to take it from here, but now I'm not so sure. This has just fitted in the last piece in the jigsaw for me."

Grace smiled. "Don't be too sure."

"Do you want me to go back and try to spring her?"

"I thought you said they gave you the Order of the Boot? How can you go back? And Laura said she thinks she belongs there."

"I think if I went back – on the square this time – and said that Laura's folks are kicking up a stink about her being there, they'd let her go. They've done that before. I checked with the local Plod and he says that's true. Sure, they got narked about me trying to slip one by them but I don't think they'd want bad publicity, or the police calling for elevenses. In fact, I'm sure they wouldn't." The reasons for my certainty I kept to myself.

"But," said Grace thoughtfully, "if she says she wants to stay there. Well," she went on quickly, seeing me about to interrupt, "at least if she says she *belongs* there… Do you think she'll come to any harm, there Mr. Black? Any actual harm?"

"If you mean, will she be physically hurt, no. If you mean,

will she be involved in ritual sex, then I'd have to say 'Probably'. I've seen them indulge in it in their Meeting House."

"What? Sex? Group sex? In front of you?"

"Yeah," I said slowly – there was something about the way her eyes lit up. "As yet, I'm not sure Laura's been involved. She's not a full member of the community yet, and apparently only fully paid up, card-carrying members get involved. But, if she stays, she will, for sure."

"Well…"

"And that doesn't take into account any mental harm she might incur, just listening to that shite, day in and day out. She's being brain-washed, all right."

"I don't know that there's any point in *forcing* her to come back. Against her will. Do you? Isn't that liable to do her mental damage, too? Maybe we should just wait and see if this all blows over."

"Meanwhile there's nothing to stop you and the walking cock from doing just what you like, eh?"

Her face closed. "You've no right to take that tone with me, Mr. Black. I employed you to do a job of work for me, not to speak to me like that. I now consider the job done."

"In that case," I said, standing up, "I owe you some money. Something in the region…"

"Keep the money, Mr. Black. You have done as I asked and you have been paid in full. That ends the matter."

The kid had been right all along – no love lost there. I didn't care for Grace half so much as I had only half an hour previously. Brushing her soft verges by me at the door; putting some ball-race motion into her hipsway as she walked; smiling a torch at me – bitch. In fact, I felt so chewed at her that, as I followed her back through the house, I didn't even ogle her hurdies. She said, "Goodbye, Mr. Black – and thank you." Then she shut the door.

29

I was mightily hacked off with her. With the whole situation, in fact. Playing me for a dummy, her and Romeo. I wondered. Why did Grace McGuire come to my office, asking me to make sure that her daughter was all right, when she knew where she was, how she was and why she was there? Some easing of her conscience, maybe. Surely Laura knew about McPartland and her mother. Surely that was why she was in Eden. I felt like getting in the car, heading back up there and freeing her myself. If she would come. Then a better idea struck me.

It wasn't hard to find where Joe McGuire lived. Blackburn isn't a big place and there's always somebody in a wateringhole who'll have the information you require. I stopped at the pub that is officially known as The Happy Valley but is still called 'The Jolly' or 'The Roger' having once been called a combination of those names. It was mid-afternoon and there was a scattering of men around the bar. Zip jackets and baseball caps abounded. Two men sat by the window, in earnest discussion about football. One small, bald-headed man, nattily dressed, checked out the racing section of a newspaper. An elderly gent in a bunnet, and with a walking stick leaning against his leg, sat away from the others with a nip of whisky and a half pint of beer in front of him. I sat opposite him.

"Can I get you a drink?" I asked.

He looked at me. "Eether you're a gay boy or you wahnt somethin'. Ah cannae see me bein' the answer tae a jessie's prayer. So whut is it ye wahnt?"

"An address."

"10 Downin' Street. Ah'll take a Grouse an' a half pint a heavy."

I smiled at the sassy old bastard. "Not that address, but I'll get you the drink if you can tell me where Joe McGuire lives."

"Oh, I can tell ye that, all right."

I crossed to the bar where a woman with a nippy sweetie face was watching me closely. Maybe not accustomed to passing trade, nor to entertaining angels unawares, she looked at me as if I'd just fallen out of a dog's arse.

"A large Grouse and a half of heavy, please."

"Fur Bill?"

"If Bill's the old codger with the stick," I said.

She chewed on her tongue behind thin wee lips and then turned, gave two dunts of the Grouse optic into a glass and slid it before me. Then she filled a half pint of beer, with which she did likewise. "Oanhin yersel'?" Which is the local pig-Latin for 'would you care for anything for your own consumption?'

"Thank you, no," I replied. "I prefer to imbibe in more congenial company."

"Three pound dead."

"Done with warmth and panache," I said and carried the drinks over to Bill. She watched me all the way.

"There you go, Bill," I said. "Now, Joe McGuire."

"Aye. What is it ye wahnt wae Joe? Ah mean, he's a quiet, respectable block, Joe."

"Nothing bad."

"Ah mean, if ye're 'is long-lost natural son come tae tell 'im that 'e's a millionaire, Ah'll be glad tae tell ye where he lives. Bit ye could be a debt collector gaun tae kick seven diff'rent colours a shite oot ae 'im, couldn't ye?"

"I'm not that, Bill. I'm a private investigator. I want to talk to him about his daughter."

"A private investigator? By Christ, ye don't look like wan, son. You look mair like a schoolteacher, or someth'n' lik' that."

"Do I? Right."

"But mibbies that's aw tae the guid. Cos then ye kin go undercover, like, an' nae cunt'll ken whae ye are. What's wrang wae 'is lassie?"

"Nothing's wrong with her. I just want to talk to Joe about her."

"Whit's she done? Been shopliftin' or someth'n'?"

I was beginning to regret picking Bill.

"Up the duff, is she? Eywis oan the cairds wae the young yins the wey they are nooadays."

122

"Bill. I can't discuss his daughter with you. But there's nothing wrong. I just need to know where he lives. So that I can talk to him about her."

"Fucksake, son. Ye don't give much away. Here a man here," he said, lifting his voice to everyone else in the bar, "says he's a private investigator. Wahnts tae talk tae Joe McGuire."

A few heads turned. Some earnest discussion was started by Bill's revelation. One wag called, "Disnae look much like Jimmy Cagney tae me."

"Can you tell me where he lives, Bill?" I pleaded.

"Aye. In the Spam Valley hooses. Rattray Gardens. Doon on the Main Street."

"What number in Rattray Gardens?"

"Nae idea."

"Thanks," I said, standing up and sighing. I had been thinking of having 'Discretion a Speciality' added to my business card. Now I wasn't so sure.

"I don't know the number," said Bill, "but it's the wan wae the wa'er feature in the gairden. Wae a' the wee gairden gnomes in it. There's gnomes fishin', gnomes weedin', gnomes pushin' a barra, gnomes daein' everythin' but makin' *wee* gnomes."

"Thanks, Bill," I said and moved towards the door.

"Whit ye wahnt'n' Joe McGuire fur? Whae hus *he* murdert?" chortled a big-faced man near the door.

I smiled wanly and left.

30

Bill's jibe about Rattray Gardens being a 'Spam Valley' was almost as old as he was. The estate was Blackburn's first private development, four-roomed bungalows built in 1969. Till then, all housing that was private had consisted of old buildings. The rest was council stock. Blackburn folk sneered at the Rattray Gardens houses as being for toffee-nosed social climbers. But things change slowly. Well, slow things change slowly. Nowadays, plenty of Blackburn people bought their houses. The Conservative government of the 80's under a certain blonde harpy put the policies in place that lubricated the buying of council houses and encouraged working folk to buy rather than rent. Most Blackburn folk wouldn't thank you for mentioning that, though. There are more Tories in the Kremlin.

You couldn't miss Joe McGuire's house. Gnomes? There was a multitude of the rubicund little fuckers in their primary coloured togs, some ceramic, some porcelain, some plastic, some resin: gnomes raking, gnomes digging, gnomes sweeping, gnomes reading, smoking pipes, carrying lanterns, fishing, drinking beer, and, right at the back, under a jaggy bush, my favourite – a gnome standing with one hand in his pocket and the other holding his pecker as he had a whizz.

I strode past them towards the front door. There was something vaguely unsettling about them. No, something a great deal unsettling about them.

The door was opened by Joe's missis. I didn't know if they were married, and I cared even less. 'Partner' always seems to me to be a term better associated with the worlds of business and the law than romance. Whatever the precise nature of their legal status, she was some kind of missis. She seemed very pleasant.

"Hello," I said, "my name is Jack Black. I'm a private investigator. I wonder if I could speak to Joe McGuire."

"I'm Joe McGuire," said a man's voice behind her. He had just come through from the back of the house. "Come in."

We went through to the living-room. The woman offered me a coffee and I accepted. Iced tea!

"Sit down, please," said Joe.

"That's quite a platoon you've got out front," I said, sitting on an extremely comfortable armchair.

"The gnomes?" Joe laughed. "They're repellent, aren't they? A hobby of Pat's. She has a mania for collecting certain things. Gnomes happens to be one."

"I like the one taking a leak."

"Yeah, that was my contribution to the casting. I said if she wanted all of that lot, I got to pick a joke one."

"Good choice," I said.

Pat brought in some real coffee in a big cafetiere and then left us to it. Joe sat and listened as I told him the story. He was a stereotypical teacher – balding and bespectacled. He said nothing until I'd finished.

"Grace *isn't* a typical mother," he said. "Never has been. She does like her gentleman friends. That was the reason I got out of it. But the suggestion that there's little love lost between them is, frankly, a nonsense. Grace is devoted to Laura. And Laura? All for her mother. The sun shines... as they say. Her mother can do no wrong in Laura's eyes. They're devoted to each other."

"That's not the impression that either of them gave to me."

"Then they've been misleading you, Mr. Black. I can't imagine why. But they have."

"How do *you* and Laura get on?"

"Fine. We have a very affectionate and warm relationship. But it's nothing compared to what Laura and Grace have."

"And you and your ex-wife?"

"We can be civil to each other when the need arises. Thankfully, it arises very seldom. I'm sure, to be fair, that Grace feels the same way. But I'm greatly concerned about this religious cult. It does not sound like Laura at all. Not at all."

"So, when her mother said she was not a religious girl, she was telling the truth?"

"Absolutely. She's *not* a religious girl. In spades."

"And you have no particular religious beliefs, Mr. McGuire?"

"Oh, I have strong beliefs, Mr. Black. Strong beliefs *about* religion. But I'm an infidel, I'm afraid. A science man."

"Right, so Mrs. McGuire was telling me the truth about that, then."

"Certainly, if that's what she said."

"Then Laura's change of mind is beyond you, too? You can think of no reason why she'd do this?"

"None. I'm worried, frankly."

"Well, you should know your own daughter, even if she doesn't live with you."

"You may be labouring under a misapprehension, Mr. Black," he said to me very precisely.

"I wouldn't be at all surprised," I said.

"Laura is not my daughter. Not my biological daughter. She's my step-daughter."

"Step-daughter?"

"Yes. I am not her natural father. Although I love her and brought her up as my daughter, she is another man's child. I married Grace when she was four months pregnant with the baby. Somebody else's baby. I had loved her for years. But she was daft about this other fellow. I thought I had no chance with her. And then I heard that she was pregnant and the father of the child had done a bunk. Left her to it. So I told her I would marry her. Give the child a name. I reminded her that I'd loved her for ages. I would be pleased to marry her and bring the child up as my own. Even though it was somebody else's."

"Did you know who the father was?"

"Yes."

"Who?"

"That's not my secret to divulge to you. It's Grace's secret. I did tell Laura, though."

"Yes?"

"Yes. Pat and I took her for dinner for her 18th. And the subject of her natural father came up. I said she should ask her mother, if she wanted to know. I thought the girl had a right to know."

"But you won't tell me?"

"No, Mr. Black, I won't. I think Grace has been a heartless and hot-arsed bitch all her life, but I won't do that to her.

You'll need to ask her that yourself."

"Mr. McGuire, I've asked your ex-wife this question. Now I want to ask *you* it. I'll be interested to see if your answer tallies with hers."

"Yes?"

"As far as you know, was Laura in any kind of trouble?"

"No."

"Could she have been pregnant? I don't mean to be offensive …"

"I understand. Any girl *could* be pregnant, Mr. Black. Laura…? I don't think so. She's far too serious. But that's just my impression."

"Understood. Did you know of any boyfriends?"

"I'm not sure she's had any. Not serious ones. I think she has been out on dates with the odd one, but none that has meant anything to her. She's not a great one for the boys. She spends more time at the gym and her ju-jitsu, or judo or whatever it is."

"Really? Interesting. I didn't know she worked out. Do you know her current boyfriend? A lad from Broxburn. Uphall way, somewhere like that. Billy something?"

He wrinkled his brow. He was bald. It took a lot of wrinkling.

"No, I know nothing about any Billy from Broxburn."

"Do you know who she pals about with, Mr. McGuire?"

He considered. "There's a lassie from Armadale. Hell of a nice lassie. Charlene. Don't know her second name. Pat! What's that lassie Charlene's second name?"

"McRobb!" Pat shouted through from the scullery.

I drove home in weak evening sunlight. I was all out. The last three days had squeezed me dry. Sleep rocked my brain; oh for the azure-lidded sleep, the everlasting sleep, the season of all natures that knits up the ravelled sleeve of care. To sleep, perchance to dream … What the fuck were Grace and Laura McGuire up to? I couldn't fathom it. No matter what way I turned it to the light, I could see no sense in it. I was being played for a fool, that much I knew. But why? And, more to the point, how? My mojo was dead on this one. Not a kick from it. Got my mojo working but it just don't work on you. Static on all channels.

31

The Cairns case was still nagging away at my thoughts. Now I put it on the front burner. Abuse ruled out. It seemed. Homosexuality – maybe. But the kind of wonks who indulged in activities like dogging are not liable to be scandalised by a man's being attracted to other men. No, that didn't ring true either. I was missing something. Despite what the Shaws had said about there being no hard and fast regulations in swinging or dogging, there had to be some rules of engagement, something that the guy had infringed. Something that had cost him his life. I wondered what.

And then there was those damned quotations from Shakespeare. Factor that in. Who would go to the bother of finding fairly recherché quotations from almost unknown works and then stick it in the pocket of the man they had murdered? Too baroque to be true. What kind of mind would think of that? Think it up? Had to be somebody educated. Nobody without an education and a certain cast of mind could do that. To a builder. For example, would a builder have thought that up? …

And then it came to me all at once, like the second way of looking at an optical illusion suddenly jumps out at you after you've stared at it for ages. The answer was 'Yes'. Nobody had placed that quotation in Brian Cairns's wallet. It was *in* his wallet when he was murdered. Far from putting it there to puzzle the police, the murderer had been unaware of its presence. Cairns had looked up the lines, just as I had, in some reference book and had been intending to use it himself. But he had never got the chance.

So what had he been intending to use it for? Blackmail, was the obvious answer. But against whom? Somebody he knew from his al fresco aerobics sessions, no doubt. Who, though? Time to get in touch with the Shaws once more.

Bobby Shafto was less welcoming this time round. The possibility of entertaining angels did not count for too much with him. He opened the door himself and almost shut it in my face immediately. It cost me a sore foot to keep it open.

"What the *fuck* do you want? I told you I wanted nae mair

to do with this carry on."

"Can I talk to you, Bobby? It's important. Something's just occurred to me. I promise, the police know nothing about our wee chat and they never will."

"It's no just the police," growled Bobby. "The fuckin' neighbours can see you coming to my door. Get in, you useless cunt!"

He threw the door open and jerked his head. I obeyed quickly and went through to the living-room. Wendy was sitting back in an armchair, with her feet up on a stool, a box of chocolates on a table by her side, and a magazine in her grasp. "Oh, hiya," she said. 'You want a coffee?"

"Naw he disnae," Bobby growled. "He's no steyin' – are ye?"

"No. Not long."

"Well, sit doon onywey," invited Wendy, swinging her legs down and making to stand up.

"Thanks," I said, sitting. "Sit tight. I'm fine."

"What is it you want?" said Bobby, sitting too.

"Right. The police found a bit of paper in Cairns's pocket, with a quote from a play on it."

"Aye. I read it in the paper."

"Oh. Right. I haven't seen that. They're assuming – well, everybody's assuming – that the murderer put it there as a kind of justification. Right?"

"Aye."

"Well, I thought that, too, up until just the day. But I don't think that's what it's all about. I think Brian Cairns had the quote to use against somebody else."

"What for?"

"Blackmail, maybe."

"Blackmail?" Bobby and Wendy said together. "Blackmail who?" Bobby said himself.

"Do you mind the last time we spoke? You described Cairns as 'creepy'?"

"Aye," said Wendy.

"You said he fancied some of the men as much or more than some of the women?"

"He liked to watch the men more than the women,

sometimes," said Bobby.

"Right. So, is there one particular man that he took a shine to? Somebody maybe who didnae love him back? Somebody that he knew? Somebody who wouldn't want what they did to be common knowledge?"

Bobby took his chin in his hand and breathed heavily through his nose.

"I cannae think …" he murmured.

"Bobby," said Wendy quietly and, when he looked up, said, "it's that wumman, intit? That posh wumman."

"What posh wumman?" said Bobby testily.

"You know… he was ey lookin' in at their windae, aye wantin' tae take part wi' theym, mind?"

"Oh aye," said Bobby. "Aye, it could be. Could be."

"Come on," said Wendy, "it *hus* tae be. Mind her man was gonnae kick the shite out of him wan night? He suggested swappin' partners an' gaun tae diff'rent cars."

"Aye, aye," said Bobby hurriedly, as if Wendy had already said too much. "It could be, it could be."

"Posh woman?" I said. "What's she like?"

"Proper spoken, mair than posh, I would say," said Bobby. "Good-lookin' woman, right enough, Forties, maybe. Long broon hair. Good body."

"Any names?"

"Naw,' sneered Bobby. "Nae names, nae packdrill. Know what I mean?"

"But what would he be tryin' tae blackmail 'er fur?" mused Wendy.

"Could be any reason," I suggested. "This sort of activity is considered scandalous by most of society. Even if *you* think that view's as behind the times as an old colonel sleeping under his paper. Most folk think it's perverted. I imagine many of the folk who take part do so because they enjoy the thrill of doing something that's scandalous. The risk is half the kick, I would think."

"Some folk, aye," said Bobby.

"So, some folk obviously have a lot to lose if they're found out. This woman might be married to somebody else, for example. It's obvious now that Cairns didn't come along with his wife."

"No," said Bobby. "The girl was too young for that. Only a lassie."

"So, maybe the woman that Cairns was fixated on was married to another man."

"Maybe. I don't know," said Bobby. "We don't know their names or anythin', you see."

There was a pause.

"Is that it?" said Bobby. "Because if it is, I'd like you tae fuck off. And no tae come back."

"Would you take me to a doggin' session, Bobby?"

"Whit?!"

"Take me to one. I need to talk to some folk."

Bobby stood up. "Right. Oot!" and he jerked his thumb towards the door.

"Bobby!" shouted Wendy. "For God's sake! Mind yer manners."

"It's oot ae the question," said Bobby. "Come on, Gumshoe, on yer way."

"Bobby! Stop right there!"

Bobby stopped. He had his fist closed tight around my right arm and was dragging me to the door. "What!?"

"Let that man go. Let him go." He let me go. "Noo, come back in here, Mr. Black, and sit doon." I looked at Bobby. "Never mind him. I sais tae come back an' sit doon."

I obeyed. With a face like thunder, but saying nothing, Bobby returned too, though he stood by his seat rather than sitting on it.

"Why dae ye wahnt tae go doggin', Mr. Black?" said Wendy.

"I don't actually want to do any dogging," I said. "But it's the only way I can meet and talk to doggers."

"Oot of the question," Bobby spluttered. "I'm no takin' a man up tae… wherever… and then him askin' folk questions like the polis. I'd get lynched."

"Better me than the police," I said to Bobby.

"They'd still string me up for bringin' a snoop intae the meet."

"Naw, they widnae," said Wendy. "And mind – a man's

deid. Maist ae the group will be scandalised. Aw bar wan, Ah suppose."

"Well, exactly right, Wendy," I said. "I have no interest in what folk do with their sex lives. But I do have an interest in catching a killer. And I think most of your acquaintances will feel the same. And another thing – how safe do they feel they are themselves, if one of the group is a killer?"

"No that safe," said Bobby quietly, sitting down. "But I cannae take you, Gumshoe."

"Well, tell me where to go and I'll go myself."

"You cannae go yersel' because it's couples," said Wendy.

I clicked my tongue.

"Ah'll go wi' ye," said Wendy simply.

Bobby looked at her and said, "Och, fucksake…"

"Bobby, I'm not going for sex. I won't even look at folk. I just want to find out who killed Brian Cairns," I said.

"But Wendy!…" protested Bobby.

"Ah'll drive the man there. Wance he's there, it's up tae him."

"What wan wid ye go tae?" snarled Bobby.

"Broxburn prob'ly."

Bobby breathed very heavily through his nostrils for a moment or two. "I knew I should never have got involved," he said. "Right, if ye wahnt tae take 'im, Broxburn's probably the best."

"Thanks very much, folks. I appreciate it."

"You dae *exactly* what Wendy tells ye, hear me? Exactly. I don't want any shit comin' oor way because of this."

"I'll do nothing at all unless Wendy says it's okay."

"You better not. Fucksake, I don't know…"

Bobby relaxed a bit and even allowed himself a wry smile. Then he opened a tobacco tin, removed a suspicious cigarette, lit it and inhaled deeply. Then he offered it to me.

"No dagga for me," I said. "I get the twinks. But you bash on."

He passed it to Wendy.

"Why'd they dae it, Mr. Black?" asked Wendy.

"Do what?"

"Murder the boay."

"Blackmail, the man said, didn't he?" Bobby said.

"Aye," I agreed. "But, you know, with all due respect to your good selves, there's very little that produces such powerful emotions as sex. Desire. Jealousy. Resentment. Humiliation. Insecurity. Revenge. These are all powerful feelings. And sometimes people can't master them. And if *you* can't master *them*, *they* master *you*."

"Aye. We're lucky that way, aren't we, Wendy? It's just sport for us. We're quite secure in oor relationship."

"Yes, I think you are. But not everyone can separate love and the sexual act, like you can."

"No ev'rybody would wahnt tae," said Wendy.

She was right. As always, Shakey had the line. "Dangerous conceits are, in their natures, poisons which, at the first, are scarce found to distaste; but, with a little act upon the blood, burn like the mines of sulphur…"

32

Almondell Country Park was, at one time, the estate of the Erskine family, which included the Earls of Buchan. The Lords of Torphichen owned it at one time too. The grounds are now used for the most part in daytime as a rural walk, the location for ramblers and twitchers. It's full of beauty spots. They flicked past the car in a succession of images: fields, open grassland, narrow lanes overgrown by leafy trees, stone bridges, a lodge. And then a gravel circle in the evening light, one or two parked cars.

I drew the car up opposite the vehicles already there. A grey Passat had its interior light on. Two couples stood by it, one on either side. The couple on the right hand side were craned over, hands on the roof, watching what was going on inside. On the other side, the couple were also watching but their hands were beginning to wander all over each other whilst they did. I found it all as cheesy as a Stilton sandwich.

The agreement was for Wendy to go out, if the opportunity arose – for example, if she recognised a couple, a couple that would know her – mention my presence and why I was there. Maybe somebody would talk. I had no intention of getting out of the vehicle before it was absolutely necessary. Not my kind of thing. I had already found the drive quite stressful, possibly because of the prospect before me. Wendy, smelling like a joss warehouse and with more stick on her pan than a Kabuki actor, had treated the excursion like any trip to off-the-wall jollies. Her appearance had alarmed me more than somewhat. I feared she might use the occasion to acquire herself a few shudders anyway, hubby or not. But no, she was simply made up for going out. She had burbled on the journey, giving me directions in between stories of Bobby's heyday in the rock scene and how they used to like Benidorm as a holiday destination but now it was all cheap and vulgar unless you stayed in the old part of town which was almost unchanged, remarkably. Sexual experimentation had featured not at all in her torrent of babble.

Two more cars arrived. The couples inside got out and meandered hand-in-hand over to the Passat, where they joined in the spectating.

"I ken that couple," said Wendy, when the second car pulled up. "If you want, I could try them."

"Yeah. Okay. Maybe give it five minutes or whatever, eh?"

"Yeah, whatever you want. They're sound, like. It would be nae bother."

And she used the intervening time to touch up her pancake. I don't know why; she already looked like Madame Butterfly. A minute or so later, a vehicle pulled up that I recognised myself. The helio Suzuki arrived quickly and parked in a slither of gravel. When the couple stepped out, I said to Wendy, "That's fine. Let's go home. I know those people. Now I've got a contact."

"Theym?" said Wendy. "She's the one we were talkin' aboot. The one that the Cairns fella was daft aboot."

Things were clicking together like Lego. I drove out of the park and back down the narrow, winding country roads.

I dropped Wendy back at Hillhouse Avenue and drove home in a brown study. Which is a trick you don't see very often. I wondered if it was time to get Bert Saunders further into the picture. If Cairns had been bothering Grace McGuire, who else but McPartland would be the man who had threatened to empty him of manure by foot? Was McPartland capable of murdering him? Hard to say. Capable of giving him a good tanking, certainly, which might have gone wrong in the donation.

I ignored the scatter of mail behind the door. There was never anything I wanted to read.. I left the holdall in the hall and the laptop on the desk by the window in the living-room, then let Black Jack in from the kitchen window-sill. What I required was some quality flying time. And at last I pulled the bedroom curtains across – unlike the gauze efforts in the cabin in Eden, these ones provided a satisfactory black-out – stripped to my junglies, clambered into bed and dived straightaway into a fathomless well of sleep.

33

The moon was a slender crescent of pearl. The stars were a scattering of diamond points, sown through the velvet blue of the desert sky. In the harem, the air was fragrant with sweet-smelling gums. My divan was soft and luxurious. Girls of bewitching beauty attended to my every whim. One fed me plump Muscat grapes and cubes of opaque jelly flavoured with rose water. Another hand-rolled my Old Holborn in liquorice Rizlas. In a corner, sucking on a hubble-bubble pipe, in Arab robes and headgear, curly slippers on his feet, was Gabriel Ben Mustafa-Shandy Hochmagandy Cockie-Bendie Tweedie Effendi. His hand toyed idly with the jewelled hilt of the scimitar through his cummerbund of many colours and he chanted in a voice as honeyed as syrup the melody of "Fry's Turkish Delight…"

Then he stood, with a sudden movement, a supercilious sneer playing around his Valentino lips and kohl black eyes. "Come with me to the Kasbah," he said. "I give you many camel; many women; many ounce of mary-jane." He clapped his hands and disappeared in a puff of brimstone smoke.

The fine voile drapes around the seraglio parted and Grace was there with her opulent curves. The other odalisques disappeared. Grace's eyes were green and deep as oasis pools. Her lips were kissing comfits. There was poetry in the way she walked, a sonnet in the tinkle of her voice and several quatrains rhyming ABAB in the way she slunk up to me like a cat. She ran a fingertip around my craggy chin and rugged cheek. "It is I, O Stallion of the Sands," she whispered and ran her hands through my raven locks, "with my lotus as wet as the figs in the poem: glittering, rosy, moist, heavy-petalled. What exquisite pleasures can I bring you, my Bronco of the Dunes?"

"You can bring …"

BRING! BRING! BRING! BRING!

What was I? Is this where? Isn't it why not at work was when?

The phone drilled me from sleep. I sat up, my eyes trying to bore through the darkness, with my heart going round the kit and my hard-on as hard as a chisel. Sweat was cooling unpleasantly on my forehead and chest.

BRING! BRING!

Phone.

BRING! BRING!

Where? Oh Jesus, yeah. Fell asleep. Home from where was it…? Fuck, Grace's gone. Phone. Yeah …

BRING! BRING!

Phone. Can't remember the number….

BRING! BRING!

"Hello?"

"Are you pissed?"

"Pissed? No. I was asleep. Who is this?"

"It's Nairn MacVicar."

"Nairn …?"

"From *The Scotsman*."

"Oh. Right! No, I fell asleep…"

"Makes sense. Put your telly on."

"Eh?"

"Put your telly on. Any round-the-clock news channel."

"Erm … yeah."

"Put it on. Now!"

"What? Why?"

"You'll see. Put it on. Hang up now and put it on. I'll ring you back in five minutes."

Stumbling over to the set, bleary-eyed, yawning, detumescent, finding the 'On' switch, pressing it. As usual, it came on to Morons' TV, the default channel with the ads and the shows for people who like loud brainless things. It took me a minute or two to locate the remote, inexplicably lying where it ought to be, on the arm of the chair I usually sit in. I zapped the channel to the News station.

After a few seconds, I sagged down on the floor, chittering in the cold room, and watched the set with my jaw on my chest.

The picture showed a fire storming through black night. It was difficult to discern exactly what was burning, other than the fact that it was a substantial stone building. Sheets of flame, scarlet and orange, surged into the dark sky. The camera seemed to be on an eminence some hundreds of yards away, for the scene was sometimes shown in long shot, sometimes in relative close-up. In long shot, it looked surrealistically beautiful, surrounded by ghostly canopies of trees. There was the unmistakable sound of a helicopter's blades battering the air and, now and then, the ludicrously childlike distant 'pops' that firearms make in reality, as opposed to in movies.

A red strap along the bottom of the screen screamed in yellow lettering SCOTTISH SIEGE. Moving slowly along past it were tags like: *Police Raid Scottish Cult; Fatalities As Police Force Way Into Cult Estate in Scotland; Drug Raid Ends in Inferno; At Least Two Policemen Among Dead; Total Number of Casualties Unknown.*

And "Our Scottish Correspondent" was yelling his report in the teeth of a howling wind and the beating helicopter: "Tayside Police, including their Armed Response Unit, have thrown a cordon around the Eden estate in Angus-shire and are slowly closing in on the New Dawn religious community. Unconfirmed reports indicate that the Army Bomb Disposal Unit are present as well. The fire you can see on-screen at the moment is a blaze at the headquarters of the commune, formerly known as Scriddan House and presented to the commune by one of its former members. The house, like the estate, has been renamed Eden, in accordance with the New Dawn's religious principles. The fire is not thought to be the result of action by Police but is believed to have been started by New Dawn members themselves. Officers from Tayside's Armed Response Unit joined their colleagues earlier this evening when one officer was shot dead during a routine ..."

The picture flicked to an aerial shot. The correspondent's voice rose another semi-tone in excitement. "And there you can see the overhead pictures from the helicopter as it flies over the sprawling estate in the heart of the rural Highlands of Scotland ..."

The picture showed not only that the big house was engulfed in flames but also that the double ring of cabins in the Settlement were alight. They burned like an eye of fire in the night. Tiny figures sometimes moved across the glare of the fires. The scene yawed across the TV as the helicopter swivelled over the Settlement until it showed both the burning cabins and a rear view of the big house, now a screeching ball of fire. Sparks and drifts of fire showered across the darkness. Sporadic outbursts of gunfire crackled over the soundtrack under the screaming halfwit reporter.

"It is not known how many 'Angels', as members of the New Dawn cult are known, may be on the Eden estate, but there are unsubstantiated reports of gunfire from several sites on the ground. The Firearms Unit of Tayside Police are in the grounds of Eden now, but exactly what the plan of action is, is impossible to tell at the moment."

The picture slanted to the side and a companion shot of an elegant female anchor in the studio took its place beside it. She spoke down the line to her correspondent. "Jeremy, fill us in on some detail of what has caused these incredible scenes. What set the whole thing off?"

"Well, Tanya. The story is that members of Tayside Police Drugs Unit, acting on a tip-off from a member of the public, called at Eden in the late afternoon. Now, there are impressive security measures in place at Eden. The estate is surrounded by high stone walls topped with really rather vicious shards of broken glass or equally fearsome coils of razor wire. There are electronically controlled gates at the entrance to the estate, gates some twelve feet high, and monitored by electronic surveillance – close circuit television cameras amongst other things. There may be guard dogs on the estate; we don't know. But it seems that the Drugs Squad called at the gates of the estate this afternoon and were initially refused entrance. When entry was forced, there was some gunfire from the grounds. One officer was killed at the scene and two others received gunshot wounds. It is believed that the police then retired from the scene to regroup and were joined by the Armed Response Unit a little after nine o'clock. The forced gates at the entrance to the estate were then demolished by an armed response vehicle and the forces of law and order started to advance through the grounds. They were met by gunfire and were forced to take cover in the trees and undergrowth of the estate."

"And what is happening now?"

"Tanya, the New Dawn members have retreated through the estate, it is believed, pursuing a scorched earth policy as they go, setting fire to everything. The mansion house is a raging inferno – you can see the pictures on your screen as I speak. And it now seems that the Angels have set fire to their dwelling places, an encampment of wooden cabins behind the mansion house, and are firing on the police as they retreat. So it seems reasonable to assume that the police are advancing on the members of the cult."

"What do you know about fatalities … er, or casualties?"

"As I said, at least two officers of the police team are known to have been shot dead, one in the initial foray into the grounds, and one in the opening salvo the second time around. Some other policemen have suffered gunshot wounds, I'm not sure how many. And, of course, nobody yet knows about any casualties amongst the Angels."

"What is known about this cult – the New Dawn?"

The correspondent gave a slight laugh.

"Well, not much, to be frank. They are a Christian movement, who believe that Christ will come again soon to judge the living and the dead and they are preparing for that day. They believe that they are the Elect and that they will be spared when the world ends. Their leader is one Brother Gabriel. Not much is known about him other than the fact that he is a typically charismatic figure who has gathered this flock around him here in the beautiful old Scriddan estate by force of his personality. The members of the flock pursue pastoral activities on the estate – farming and such like - and live a life of labour and prayer. Until now, it was assumed that they were a harmless New Age phenomenon, tilling the fields and waiting for the end. Now, of course, it is evident that they are anything but pacifists and are prepared to fight to the death to protect their way of life here."

"Jeremy, tell us …"

But what the anchor wanted Jeremy to tell her was left unasked. There was a tremendous report and the upper section of Eden house collapsed. I could see it fold into the flames.

"Tanya!" shrieked Jeremy, "the house has just collapsed.

The mansion house has just crumpled under a huge explosion. I don't know if you could hear it where you are, but there was the sound of an explosion and the upper storey of the house fell in. I don't know if it was an explosive device or if the intense heat caused the explosion but ..."

The screen flicked to black for a second or two and then the studio image was reinstated, complete with eye-linered and lip-glossed anchor.

"Dramatic pictures there from Angus in Scotland," she said, slowly, a half-gone look in her eye as she listened to instructions in her ear-piece from the producer. "Police are laying siege to a religious commune in Angus after two policemen were shot dead earlier in the day as they ... attempted ... to operate a drugs bust. We will resume with pictures as soon as we get them. But to repeat the headlines. Two policemen have been killed in a raid on a commune in Scotland. Police units are involved in exchanges of gunfire with the residents of the estate at the moment. Now other news making the headlines, with ..."

I zapped the remote to mute and sat for a moment. What a turn-oot. The phone rang. I had it with me this time. It was MacVicar.

"Well...?"

"I don't know what to say."

"Were you up there?"

"Just back."

"When did you get back?"

"Uh, this morning." I thought. "*This* morning? Uh, yeah. This morning."

"I'm going back up now, for the paper. Want to come?"

"Yep."

"Meet me at the Bridge in an hour. The filling station on your road in from South Queensferry. I'm in a green BMW."

Then the line went dead.

34

The moon was up, though not a slender crescent of pearl. The stars were a scattering of diamond points, sown through the velvet blue of the sky. It was a fine night for a drive up to Angus. The roads were almost deserted and we made excellent time. MacVicar's car was comfortable. I'd left mine parked in the 'Ferry.

"So, did you see the girl you were after?" asked MacVicar.

"I did, aye. Not sure about whether I can get her out of there, though."

"She's hooked, huh?"

"Something like it," I conceded. "There may be a bit more to it than just that, though. I've found out one or two interesting pieces of information that may have a bearing."

"Okay. How'd you find the Angels? Gabriel?"

"Oh, pretty much as you described it. Your piece got it all, really. I see what you mean about Gabriel being a charismatic fucker."

"Isn't he, though?"

A pause followed, during the course of which I lit up two fags and passed him one. I inhaled and felt the bite, revolved the smoke around my puddings for a moment or two before releasing it again in a slow plume.

"So, what'll be happening up here?" asked MacVicar. He was keeping his eyes on the corridor being hollowed out of the darkness by his headlights.

"You've seen the footage, same as me."

"No, I don't mean that. I mean – what are we going to come across when we get up there? Police-wise. Cordons? Exclusion zones? What?"

I took another drag and said, "You're the fuckin' journalist. Don't you know these things?"

"Hell, I'm a features writer, a columnist. I'm no newshound. This is the first news thing I've been on since I used to do council reports in Haddington when I was a cub. I'm only coming up because I did the splash on the fuckers. There's a team on the night desk working from base. It's my job to add the *actualité*," he laughed.

I laughed too, just to keep him company. "Well, if things follow the usual pattern, there'll be a cordon all right. There'll be two, in fact. There'll be an outer cordon, well out of range of any danger to the public. That'll be the uniforms keeping Joe Cunt well away. Keeping the area sterile, they call it. But there'll be an inner cordon as well. Round the walls of the house and grounds. That'll be the armed guys. They're there to stop any danger getting out and to prevent any injuries to innocent parties and so on."

"Will *we* get inside the cordon?"

I thought for a second, rolled down my window and flicked my dowt out into the night, then rolled the window back up. "We might. Ordinarily, there would be no chance of it. You guys usually set up outside the cordon, don't you? Overlooking hills, say. Or buildings out the line of fire. Some fuckers have got the helicopter going, satellite or somebody. But! *We* know Eden. We know the layout of the place. We know the wheres and whereabouts. That might be to our advantage. For the simple reason that it might be to the cops' advantage."

"Right. I take it there'll be a guy with scrambled egg on his hat in charge of all this."

"There's normally an inspector in charge on the ground. What they call a Bronze Commander. He's answerable to a dedicated Control Room run by a Superintendent – the Silver Commander. And, of course, there's a Gold Commander somewhere, overseeing all armed operations, some Assistant Chief Constable or other. That's if Tayside polis are like everybody else."

"So we won't be meeting Gold Top?"

"Nope. No milk or scrambled eggs for us. We'll get Bronze - if we get among the medals at all."

More silent driving.

"What made you take this game up?" Nairn asked me.

"What made me take it *up*? It's all I've ever wanted to do. Ever since I was a kid."

"Seriously?"

"Seriously. It was Sherlock Holmes at first. I loved those stories. You know, all the observation and deduction stuff. 'I observe, sir that you have recently arrived in these shores from the Zuider Zee, that you once kept wicket for Northants Second XI and that your grandfather was a short man with a hare lip and a plum-coloured waistcoat.' All that shit. Loved it. Couldn't get enough of it. Read every sentence of it."

"Elementary, my dear Watson…"

"Never says it," I said. "'Elementary my dear Watson'. Never says it. It's a bit like 'Play it again, Sam'. Bogart never says that either."

"Sorry, I'm sure."

"After Holmes, in my teens I got into the Chandler novels. Philip Marlowe, Private Investigator. I loved them even more. All that hard-boiled, 'down these mean streets' school of writing. Chandler, Hammett, Mickey Spillane. So, once I'd been to university, like I promised my folks I would, and got my degree, I set about becoming a private detective. I started with Flying Horse, in Livingston, and, after a while, set up on my own."

"What's your degree in?"

"English."

"Seems a waste."

"Why? I studied at Edinburgh Uni, like my father wanted me to. I read a lot of good books. I had a ball. I got a degree. But I never wanted to be a teacher or work in the Civil Service. Never wanted a … *vanilla* job like that. I promised myself I'd give it a go as a sleuth for five years. If it didn't work out, fair enough. But at least I could say I'd tried. Then it might be time to go into the classroom or whatever. Well, I'm still doing it. And still liking it."

"Yeah? Does it pay?"

"Enough for me to drive a Nissan and do without holidays."

MacVicar tutted a bemused laugh. "You a married man, Jack?"

"Not any more," I said simply.

"You too, eh?"

"Yep. Marriage was something I shouldn't have done. Tried it on for size. Found it nipped my head a bit after the first six months."

"Another woman?"

"Not at the time. And not that often since, I have to say." He laughed. I went on. "No. Penny and I just weren't made for each other. Not a marriage made in heaven. We both agreed it would be best to lob it into the Divorce bucket and move on from there."

"No kids, then."

"No. Nothing to stop us splitting up and being single again. What about you?"

"Nothing so colourful. Ten years. Two kids. Too many nights on the ran-dan. I came in from a session one night and found a note on the dresser. 'Going back home to mother.' Or words to that effect."

"Mmm."

A supportive silence.

"Turn the radio on, Nairn," I said.

He flicked on to a news programme for an update from Eden.

"Reports from the besieged estate of Scriddan in Angus indicate that there have been no more exchanges of gunfire between police and the members of the New Dawn movement. Cult members have set alight the wooden chalets in which they lived and it is now believed that they have barricaded themselves in a larger building in the midst of the grounds. Police marksmen have surrounded the area and police are attempting to set up negotiations with the Angels of the New Dawn, as they have called themselves. The old Scriddan mansion house has been totally destroyed by fire, started by the Angels to prevent it falling into police hands. The drama began in the late afternoon, when officers from Tayside's ...."

I was glad when MacVicar switched it off. This was an alarming development. If I knew anything about the collective mindset of the New Dawn – and few knew more about it than myself and Nairn MacVicar – negotiations were a waste of time and effort. They would not have any truck with unredeemed sinners – the enemy, in fact. Much more likely was that they would see this as the opening skirmishes in the last great battle: the forces of good versus the forces of evil. In a match like this, there were no replays. It was strictly extra time and then penalties if required. There would have to be a result. The war to end war. The final conflict. Armageddon.

I wondered what part in all of this Dominic Tweedie was playing. Was he rallying the Angels for one final onslaught against the baddies? Gabriel's last stand? Was Ira marshalling the troops to smite the Amalekites, hip and thigh? He certainly had the look of one who knew a thing or two about guns and smiting. But maybe that was lookism on my part. Fuck it; it's generally right. Ira certainly didn't look like he collected butterflies. What about all those gentle people tending herbs and tossing hay? Had That Which is Coming finally arrived? Was it Kingdom Come? Tribulation before Rapture? What about Laura McGuire?

And what part had I played in all of this?

I put that uncomfortable thought to the back of my mind as we drove on through cavernous glades of moonlight.

35

Soon enough, we pulled off on to country roads again. Life is old there, older than the trees. The sky in the distance ahead was glowing pink and orange as if a localised sunrise was happening. We chugged slowly around the tight corners, keeping an eye on the glow as it drew nearer. My nostrils started to prickle with the acrid hint of smoke. I found myself wishing that the Angels could win this struggle, even although I knew that they had been doomed from the outset. Before that, in fact.

Then we came upon a road block, a simple one, consisting of two police cars parked broadwise across the road, their blue lights revolving shadows in the trees. A policeman emerged from the driver's seat of the nearer one. MacVicar rolled down his window as the cop leaned in.

"Where you headed, sir?"

"Eden."

He shook his head. "Nobody else allowed up that way, tonight, sir."

"But I'm a journalist." He flashed his ID.

"So I see, sir. I'm sorry I can't allow anyone else up past the Scriddan estate tonight. Who is the other gentleman in the car?"

"My name is Jack Black," I said, craning forward to let him see me. "I'm a private investigator. I'm working on a case up here."

"My orders are to ensure that no-one gets up to the estate for the moment. I'm sorry, sir."

He was a pleasant young man and his apologetic manner seemed genuine enough. At that moment the walkie-talkie on his lapel crackled and a voice spoke. Although I was not listening to the message, I did pick up a reference to a name I knew.

"Is Sergeant McKechnie up there?" I asked.

"Yes. Why? Do you know him?"

"Please. Do me a favour. Get on the blower to Sergeant McKechnie for me and tell him I'm here. Jack Black. He'll want to talk to me. I can assure you of that."

"Why would Sergeant McKechnie want to talk to *you*? If you don't mind my asking, sir?"

"No, I don't mind your asking at all. Nairn and I know the layout of the place. And I think I am the man who may have started all this. I spoke to Sergeant McKechnie early this morning ... well, early yesterday morning now ... about the fact that I thought there was drug-dealing going on at the Eden estate. "

When I said this, MacVicar's head jerked round in my direction so fast I could hear it click.

"Hold on a minute, sir, please."

"Of course."

The young policeman went back to his own vehicle and hung in the driver's window of that for a minute or two. Then he straightened up and I could see him operating his walkie-talkie.

"You didn't tell me about the drugs," said MacVicar.

"It was only a theory," I said. "I'm pretty sure I was right, though. How else would they bankroll that place?"

"Selling their..."

"Oh for fucksake, Nairn," I said. "Think about it."

The policeman came back. "Okay, sir. You were right. Sergeant McKechnie does want to talk to you. Leave your vehicle locked sir. We'll take you up."

Nairn and I accompanied the policeman to his car and slid into the back seat. His companion did not even turn his head to look at us. The car slid smoothly off into the night.

"So you were on the estate recently, were you?" the driver said into the rear-view mirror.

"Yes," said Nairn. "I did a piece in *The Scotsman* on it a few weeks back."

"I left yesterday," I said. "I'm trying to get a girl out of there."

"Right. The Sergeant thinks you should have a good idea of the layout of the place."

"Fairly good," I qualified. "I was only there a couple of days. I wouldn't say I know the precise whereabouts of everything but, yeah, I have a reasonable idea of it."

"Right. And *you* wrote a piece on the hippies, did you?"

"Yeah," said Nairn. "Just a features piece on them. You know – lifestyle, customs, beliefs, that kind of thing. Nothing too exciting really. At least that's what I thought until tonight."

"Yeah."

"Yeah," Nairn said. "Funny the way things work out."

"Hysterical," said the copper in the passenger seat without looking round.

We drove up the way a little and passed a news encampment, all lit up like a war zone itself. Cars, vans. A well-known BBC Scotland reporter was standing by a police-car with the glow in the background, doing a piece to camera.

36

Eden House was still burning although the flames had died down considerably from when I watched the scene on TV. The wind was blowing the smoke and smell away from the direction of the gates, but both were still powerful enough to bring tears to my eyes and a cough to my throat.

Emergency vehicles were in the drive and around the house: police cars, two fire engines and a fleet of ambulances, their blue and orange lights adding to the shifting, phantasmagoric quality of the scene. All around, the crackle of radios. The massive, pulsating throb of the helicopter overhead. Sergeant McKechnie came striding through the parked vehicles. He held his gloved hand towards me and I shook it cordially. There was an inspector with him. Old Bronzey, no doubt.

"Mr. Black. This is DCI Baird, officer in charge here. I've told him about your involvement with the New Dawn."

"Mr. Black." I got to feel some more glove leather. "You must know the geography of this place."

"To some degree. Both Nairn and myself do. This is Nairn MacVicar," I said. "He wrote a piece in *The Scotsman* some weeks past. He's been in here before, too."

"Excellent. Mr. MacVicar – Sergeant, take Mr. MacVicar to DI Madison – Mr. MacVicar, if you wouldn't mind consulting with Inspector Madison?"

"Uh, no, of course…" said Nairn and he disappeared into the throng of the police, his biro primed and ready to flow.

Baird turned to me again. "What's this place they are holed up in? Do you know anything about its layout?"

"It's the Meeting House, I think. I only heard a description on the radio news as I drove up here. But it sounds like that. Are there any casualties among the commune?"

"We don't know," he said, ushering me up the drive. "We had to ensure that there were no snipers around the house before we could get the fire brigade in. And, by the time we were sure, the house was gone."

"Was there anybody in it?"

"We don't know. But we need to make sure that it's safe around the cabins before we can let the other engines in. I'm afraid the cabins are gone, too."

We had reached the top of the drive and McKechnie was back with us. Two fire engines were in attendance on the house, jets of water playing over the flames. Helmeted firemen, yellow-clad. Policemen in riot gear. Nightmare knights of the futuristic kind.

"Have you established communications with the Meeting House?" I asked.

"Not yet. That's where I thought you might be useful."

"What!?"

"No, what I mean is: it's tricky getting near for the heat. We don't know if there are guns in there. So we're trying to talk to them through a loudhailer. No joy so far, though. There's also the risk that this Meeting House will catch fire. A spark's all it needs. Is there some other way into it? Underground or anything?"

"Not that I know of."

"Damn. Did you *know* these people were armed?"

"No, I didn't. That was the last thing I expected. I thought they were farmers and poets."

"Mmm. Would you talk to them through the loudhailer?"

"Me?"

"They might listen to you. They've been ignoring us for the last hour."

"I suspect there's a good reason for that."

"What's that?"

"I think they're all dead."

Baird stopped and looked at me, a grimace of anguish contorting one side of his face. "And why do you think that?"

"Because this is their time. They think that they've fought the good fight and now it's time for them to go to heaven. We are the enemy, the beast, whatever it is that the book of Revelation calls the baddies. We have defiled Eden. They have this last chance to thwart us and all the legions of hell. They'll take it."

He looked at the ground. "Yes. That's what we were worried about – some fundamentalist stance. I wonder if John Madison has had the same thought."

"Madison?"

"Our man from the Firearms Unit. We should speak to him. He will want to storm the Meeting House. For sure."

"It's too late for that, now. When was the last time your officers were under fire?"

"Whhh. A couple of hours ago, anyway."

"No, they're dead."

I knew the Angels were dead, as sure as I knew Elvis was. Dead as mutton; dead as mackerel; dead as music-hall. It was what they'd been building up to, what they'd been preparing for, what would give their lives here on earth some meaning. They would have been convinced that they were on their way to paradise, bound for glory, about to be gathered to the Lord. Game Over. Sign here.

The Settlement was an inferno. A firestorm raged through the night air and showed no signs of abating. No gunfire had been heard for hours. Eventually, Baird made his men fall back. He suggested that I catch a few hours' kip at McKechnie's place and then we would return in the morning. MacVicar arrived, his notebook stuffed with purple. The police arranged a gaff for him in the town – with Steve and Sheena, who ran the café. I had to smile. Once again, God – or whoever depped for him in these secular days – had pissed in my soup.

37

In the smoky rose light of morning, Eden was a heap of smouldering stones and charred rafters. The stink of smoke was everywhere. The red sports car, now a blackened hull, creaked and smoked beside it. The Megane was gone. I had spent a wide-eyed couple of hours on a Put-U-Up in McKechnie's spare room before breaking my fast on a mug of tarry black java and half a dozen weeds. Fire officers informed us that they had found four sets of human remains, burnt beyond recognition even as to gender, in the ruins. There was no sign of MacVicar. Presumably he was still fast in the arms of Somnus, or enjoying one of Sheena's All Day Specials. How I envied him. McKechnie spoke to the officers who had been there all night.

"And what about the compound?"

"Fires are out there, now, Sergeant."

"And the Meeting House?"

"Piles of bodies, there, Sarge," said a policeman. "Looks like suicide. Poisoning, most likely. Aye. Place never even took a spark," he added. "Amazing."

"Forensics and medical teams down there now, sir."

Dead beat and depressed beyond expression, I followed McKechnie and several policemen and firemen down the incline to the Settlement. All that remained of the cabins was a smoking circle of ash and embers. The Meeting House was surrounded by vehicles and activity.

"Morning, Sergeant."

"Ah, morning, sir."

"Mass suicide pact, by the looks of it," said Baird the Bronze, beckoning him up the steps. "Do you think you could possibly ID the head of this outfit for us, Black?"

"I don't know, sir," I said. "Possibly. Perhaps better than your officers. I don't know."

"Seen dead bodies before, Black?"

"One or two."

"Do you want to see this? I don't know if your friend is among the dead."

"I don't know either. But I should imagine he will be. And he was actually my father's friend."

"Well, up to you," he said curtly and ascended the steps with McKechnie. "Get this man a paper suit if he wants one."

Unhappily, I followed. An armed uniformed officer was keeping a log of everyone entering and leaving the scene.

"Put him down as J. Black, civilian, assisting DCI Baird with ID."

"Sir."

I was fitted with a white forensics suit, given overshoes and gloves and then, accompanied by McKechnie and the others, similarly attired, I went into the hall.

The Angels had fallen about the floor. The features of some were as rosy as if they'd just run the mile. There was a stink of vomit and faeces in the air. Touchingly, one or two couples lay in each other's arms or held hands. Here and there, a face was contorted in the rictus of agonising death, but most wore expressions of peace and contentment. At my feet, as I stood and stared at the carnage, lay Brother Enoch. What got to me was the kids. I'd only ever seen the kids playing around the cabins. But there was no sign that I could see of Tweedie. And certainly none of Laura. I was extremely painstaking in examining the young female faces. I saw the once very pretty Sister Martha. She was now very dead. She would be forking no more hay around lofts. Ruby, too. Dead as earth. But no Laura. The Scene of Crime wallahs were passing among them, examining, commenting, photographing, videoing, gathering and bagging evidence. I don't know all they were doing. The stained glass window cast coloured lights on the grim scene. The Meeting House had become the Charnel House. McKechnie came to stand by me.

"Cyanide poisoning, the pathology people reckon. One or two found with capsules in their mouths. Salts of hydrogen cyanide. Smell the almond smell? Scent of bitter almonds?"

It was the old Nevada Gas, all right. Under the smells of puke and shit, there was a strong whiff of almonds. Death by marzipan.

"Yeah," I said, ready to leave.

"I'm sorry, Mr. Black," said Inspector Baird. "Is your father's friend here?"

"No," I said. "No. But he never really was."

"And the girl you were investigating…?"

"No sign."

"Sure?"

"Absolutely."

"Can you help with any identifications?"

I ID'd Enoch, Martha, Ruby, Margaret and maybe half a dozen others. All dead as last week. No Gabriel; no Laura. And no Ira. Then I spoke to Baird and McKechnie away from the others. "I'm really concerned for the girl McGuire," I said. "She came here in a maroon Megane. It was here beside that burnt-out sports job the first time I came. Now it's gone. I don't know if that means that Laura has driven it away or whether anyone else has. But someone has for sure, or it would be doing the old burnt-out creakeroo as well. What bugs me is the fear that she might have gone away with the Patriarch. The man's fucking insane. Sex-obsessed and dangerous. Just what a lassie that age doesn't need."

"We share your concern, Mr. Black," said Baird. "And we'll do all we can to find her."

"It occurs to me," I went on, "… has anyone checked whether the two vans are in the grounds?"

"Yes," answered McKechnie. "Both of them are. In the double garage."

"Okay. So if anyone drove out of here, they drove in the Megane."

"Gabriel might have left in it," said Baird, thoughtfully.

"Yes, he might," I said. "So might Laura. But then, so might anyone who survived this inferno. There's another major player unaccounted for, so far as I can see – Brother Ira. Ira is a black Jew from Chicago and as hard as lignum vitae. He might have taken it on the lam in the Megane too. You won't miss him if he's around. He's as big as a house and black as three feet up the chimney."

"Any of the people you've mentioned might have died in the house," pointed out Baird.

"They might, sir. I agree," I answered. "But I felt the absence of the car was something your guys would need to know about."

"Mmm," said Sergeant McKechnie. "Why take the Megane rather than the sporty one?"

"Because Brother Gabriel is known in it," I said. "It would stick in people's memories more readily than the Megane."

"Good thinking, Black," said Baird. "We need ID on those bodies in the house as soon as possible. But, we can put the word out now about the Megane. Circulate descriptions of Gabriel and the others."

When I got out into the air that only stank of smoke, MacVicar was hanging around in a huff. They hadn't allowed him access.

"I've got all the details you'll need," I told him.

38

I left contact details with McKechnie. Then I gave MacVicar all the gen he needed as he drove us back south. He'd filed copy overnight, simply telling the story as related by McKechnie, adding one or two dabs of on-the-spot actuality. He was barely communicative on the drive south, having been up most of the night working. Not even Sheena or her hash browns had cheered him up. So we sat shtum for most of the car ride. At the Bridge, we parted. I told him I looked forward to reading his in-depth piece on Eden.

I stopped off at the office, checked the answer machine. One call. I was headed to Armadale anyway.

She met me at the door again, only there was no archness and no arse-wiggling this time. "Come in, Mr. Black, I've been trying to contact you. Is there any word? Is Laura all right?"

"I don't know."

"Have you been up there?"

"Yes, I have."

She led me through to the lounge. Big fireplace, no fire. Plasma TV. Glass-topped coffee table with magazines. I looked around and sniffed theatrically. I knew it was a cheap shot. Fuck it, so was she.

"No, Billy's not here. Did you see her?" She sat down and invited me to do likewise.

"No I didn't. But I'm glad about that, actually. I saw a lot of her fellow worshippers, and they weren't pretty at all."

"How do you mean?"

"I mean they were dead, Mrs. McGuire. Cyanide poisoning. Mass suicide."

"Oh God!" she sniffled. "Laura!"

"Save it," I said. "You don't believe in God, remember. And you don't believe Laura is dead."

"But she might be …"

"She might be, but I'm beginning to think it highly unlikely. Her car was gone. It was there on my first visit and this time it wasn't. I looked very carefully, Mrs. McGuire.

158

Laura was not among the dead in that hall. And neither was her father."

Grace McGuire stopped sniffling and looked at me.

"That's why she's there, isn't it, Mrs. McGuire? Because Dominic Tweedie is her natural father."

"Have you been speaking to Joe?"

"I've been speaking to a lot of people. But yes, Joe told me that he'd told Laura that he was only her step-father. And she asked you to tell her who her biological father was."

"It's true," she said. "Laura asked me who her father was, ages ago. Trust Joe to think she never knew. He's such a bloody ... innocent! Not a worldly man, Mr. Black. Decent enough, but not a worldly man. Laura has known for a while that her father's name was Dominic Tweedie. I knew him when he had *Flash* computers. We met at a going-away do. Somebody from the school. PT Computer Studies. He must have invited Tweedie along. I was wild about him. But it was hardly an affair. A two or three week thing, more like. But he managed to get me pregnant. Just what I needed, with my career starting to take off. I would have been Principal Teacher by now if that hadn't happened. But there – what's done is done. You can't go back. Isn't that what they say? And then – that piece in the paper about the nutjobs up in Angus. And who was their leader? I'd no idea whether Tweedie was alive or dead. But then I saw that thing about the Holy Joes, and Tweedie's photograph was in it. I'd have recognised him anywhere. He was a bit more hippified, a bit more Jesused up. But it was still Tweedie."

She sat, licked her lips once, was miles away.

"So Laura went to see her father?'

"Yes. You're wondering now why I came to ask you to investigate it?"

"Not really. I might have been before. Now I have something of an idea. I'll need you to confirm it of course. But I'm pretty much there, I suspect."

"Really? You intrigue me."

"I wonder if I do, Mrs. McGuire. I wonder if anybody intrigues you nearly as much as you intrigue yourself. Do you mind if I smoke?" She shrugged. I lit up. "Before I move on," I said, exhaling, "I want you to know that I think you've put your daughter into a position of extreme danger. She has probably gone away with her father, and the man is psychotic. And a sexual predator. Think about it. You said when you first hired me that you were frightened she might find herself under some sexual threat. I know now that you were spinning me a line, Mrs. McGuire. But the irony is, that she very well might be."

"Not with Tweedie," she said.

I let her sit smug for a second.

"How long have you been a swinger?" I asked.

"A what?" Her reply hung in the air, frosted and sparkling.

"All right. How long have you enjoyed dogging as one of your leisure pursuits? Open-air sex."

She looked at me steadily. You could have used her arse to freeze ice-cubes now. "What makes you think I do?"

"I saw you. Last night. In the country park at Almondell. With your young friend, Mr. McPartland. It was the car I recognised first. But when the two of you emerged from it, there was the proof."

"Ah. You were the time-waster in the Nissan."

"In the Nissan, yes. Wasting my time, no. Seeing you and 'the Buhll' brought one or two matters quite sharply into focus for me."

"And you weren't there for the cheap thrill."

"No, *I* wasn't. But you were. How long have you been dogging?"

"About a year. There's no law against it, Mr. Black. However much it might strike you and people like you as *outré* behaviour."

"*Outré*? I'm not sure I know what that means. But you are not quite correct in your analysis. There are laws to protect the public at large from being unwilling witnesses to sexual activity and to protect them in their legitimate right to use common ground without being scandalised."

"Perhaps. I have infringed none of them, in any case."

"You're probably right there. But that's not my interest in the matter. How well did you know Brian Cairns? The man who died?"

"I didn't know him at all."

"That's not the information I have, Mrs. McGuire."

"Information from whom?" Her tone was developing the hardness of permafrost.

"I'm not at liberty to divulge that. But my information is that you not only knew Mr. Cairns but that you knew him quite well. Didn't you have sex with him at one point?"

"Quite possibly."

"You know you did. And did he not develop a fascination for you? A *fix*ation, in fact. Not to put too fine a point on it, he began to stalk you, didn't he?"

"Did he?"

"I'm asking you, Mrs. McGuire. Did he?"

"Yes, he did."

"He suggested swapping, didn't he? You and Cairns to have sex together whilst his partner and Billy McPartland would do the same."

"Yes."

"And Billy lost the plot, didn't he? Threatened him with violence?"

"Oh, I see what you're driving at. Because the man became a pest at a meet and because Billy threatened to punch him on the nose, you think that Billy somehow killed him, do you?"

"It's at least a possibility."

She smiled a superior sort of smile, a pitying put-down of a Grade A stale. "No. Not if you knew Billy. He is not at all a violent young man. He was protecting me, that's all. And let me assure you, Mr. Black, men becoming nuisances at meets is hardly a rarity. Most men are led by the prick. Mr. Cairns was no exception. He got slightly out of hand one night, and Billy frightened him off. It's quite common for other men present to police the meet. They don't want their chance of no-strings sex with a beautiful woman wasted. Like I say, led by the ..."

"Yes, I get it. 'As tenderly led by the ass as nosies are'. As Iago nearly says." She gave a wry puff of laughter.
"But he did start to stalk you, didn't he?"

"Och, I'd hardly dignify it with a word like 'stalking'. He was a bit of a pest is all."

"Mmmm. And now he's a dead pest."

"Sadly, yes."

"Do you see why thinking Billy might have done it is a logical step?"

"I can see why *you* might consider it a logical step. But the fact that B follows A is no evidence that B is caused by A."

"Ah, yes. 'Post hoc ergo propter hoc'. The False Cause fallacy."

She smiled that condescending smile again. "Mmm. I forgot you do have some education, Mr. Black. Have you passed on your Post Hoc theory to the police?"

"Not yet."

"I suggest that you don't bother, for your own reputation."

"And what about *your* reputation, Mrs. McGuire? Was there some threat of blackmail from Mr. Cairns? If he couldn't have you, then your reputation would suffer? A respectable, middle-class woman with a good job and a place in society? Although, as Iago tells us again – 'reputation is an idle and most false imposition, oft got without merit and lost without deserving'."

"Spare me the Shakespeare, Mr. Black. I'm getting sick of it. You seem to me a man who lives in a fictional world, and who gets his ideas from fiction. You need to spend more time in the real world. And now, if you'll excuse me, please... I'm tired of this interview."

I stood up.

"I'll go now, Mrs. McGuire. But think about what I've said. I certainly will. And I notice that you've lost all concern for Laura. I believe you *know* her to be safe, as I certainly *believe* her to be. I also believe that you sent her to her father for a specific reason. And when I've got that worked out, then I might just go and have a word with my old pal, D.I. Bert Saunders. Good morning, Mrs. McGuire."

39

For some reason that's still not a hundred per cent clear to me, after I left Grace McGuire I went to see my mother. She's in a nursing home in Whitburn. If she's anywhere. The body that once housed my mother is there, but the person has long since left. Dementia is a pitiless illness. It's hard to watch someone you love fade away like breath off a mirror. I don't often go these days. For one thing, my mother has no idea who I am. She looks through me most of the time I'm there. For a while, I actually frightened her. She would look in alarm at this stranger who sat down beside her and took her hand. I stopped going for a long time. Now, though, she just looks at me like she looks at everybody else. I speak to her and once in a while she says something that makes sense. I'll ask, maybe, 'All right, Mum?' and she'll say 'Oh yes,' but it's just a reflex response, one of the few left. If I say something else like 'It's a nice day today', she'll start to talk Chinese. It's hard. But she's the husk of my mother, one of the last things to connect me to my past, so I go once in a while.

Mad father dead, alive mother mad. Get you to my lady's chamber. Tell her, let her paint an inch thick, to this favour she must come. Make her laugh at that.

I sat with her for half an hour. I'd taken her a bar of chocolate and I fed her squares of that, like you would a bairn. She's always had a sweet tooth. Now she has a sweet gum. She mumbled the chocolate and looked out the window in silence at the view of fields and trees. So, while my mother gazed absently at the view and slurped Dairy Milk, I told her all about my week.

"I've been up and down the road to the Highlands twice this week, mother," I said.

"Oh yes."

And I told her of my having to checkout Laura McGuire; of her stay with the New Dawn; of Dominic Tweedie being both the head of the cult and the father of the girl; of how Laura's mother's toyboy had once been Laura's boyfriend; of how he and Grace were now into experimental sex; of the murder of Brian Cairns; and of how I wondered whether that fact, and the related fact that Cairns was also into dogging, was the reason for Cairns's murder; and whether there was a connection to all of that and Laura's presence in Eden. Well, it helped me think, and let me pass some time with my mother.

My mother looked directly at me and said "Oh yes!" very emphatically. Which was encouraging. Then she didn't say anything else. The chocolate was finished and she had no further interest in my being there. So I kissed her on the cheek and left.

40

My pal, the janitor with the carious choppers, was picking up papers in the playground. I dream of janny with the pea-green teeth. He had one of those paper picker-uppers, a pincer thing on a stick, and a big white recycling sack in which to deposit the crisp pokes and similar that he weeded from the yard. He looked up when he heard my car door shut and stopped picking up paper to give me a winning flash of mush. That smile didn't get any better. It still looked like a burnt-out fusebox.

"Back again, eh?" he said as I strolled over to him.

"Just can't stay away," I said. "Lot of cars in the yard. I thought term didn't start till next week."

He looked at the dozen or so vehicles in the playground as if they'd just materialised out of thin air. "Oh aye. Right. Naw, what it is, you see, the exam results are oot an' some ae the teachers are in, checkin' oan how their weans done. Know what Ah mean? There some a them right keen bastards onywey. Never oot the place, know? You'd think when four o'clock came they'd be anxious tae git tae fuck hame. But naw. No some a them."

"Right."

"Well, sir, what kin we dae ye fur this time?"

"Any idea where Billy McPartland works?"

"The Buhll? Aye. Up the iron works at Livvy."

"Cameron Iron Works?"

"Aye. 'Course, it's no cawed that noo. It's eh, whit is it again? Wyman Gordon, that's it. How? Hus he been up tae somethin' right enough? Here – is this aw a dae wi' thon boay that wis kilt?"

"No, no. That's a police job. I'm on a different tack."

"Right. Well, that's where he works. Wyman Gordon. He bides in Uphall, though. Wyndford Avenue. Ken where that is? Up by the ceemetry?"

"I know, yeah. I've been there. Just come from there in fact. Nobody home."

"He might be at 'is mother's. Stewartfield."

"No. Thanks. I won't bother his mother."

"He's maybe ridin' some bit a stuff somewhere, of course."

"Well, that's another possibility," I said. "Well, nice to see you again. Thanks for the info."

"Nae bother. See you around."

I got back in the yoke and pulled away. He gave me a sad kind of wave. When I looked in the rear view mirror as I drove through the gates, he was still standing watching me go. I think he was missing me already.

41

First thing, back in the office, I called Sergeant McKechnie and broke the news – stale news, granted – that Laura was Tweedie's biological daughter. He agreed with me that that added a little vinegar to the sauce and that the Tayside guys should probably be looking for them travelling together. Then he told me about the drugs they'd found on the Eden estate. I think 'vindicated' is the word for the way I felt. Like old schoolmates after a reunion, we promised we'd keep in touch. Then I looked at the paper.

Nairn MacVicar's piece was impressive: four pages in the magazine section, including the centre spread. The headline – THIS OTHER EDEN – appealed to me. I like to have it confirmed every so often that it's not just me who reads Shakespeare. The teaser impressed me less: "Nairn MacVicar spent three days in the company of the Angels of the New Dawn. He made a few new friends. Two months after he left Eden, the Angels all died in a mass suicide pact ..."

There was an inset photograph of MacVicar, looking suitably contemplative and bohemian. Also deceptively young and unfat. The text was embellished with a full-page Victorian photograph of the main building, in the days when it was Scriddan House. There were smaller snaps of the ruined house, and the miraculously untouched Meeting House standing in a circle of charred remains. Plus they reprinted the photograph of Brother Gabriel, along with an older one their researchers had dug up, of him at University, looking wild-eyed and hairy, with a necker and shades, a nineteen-year-old Edinburgh version of Ché.

The writing was downright purple in places. Where it wasn't, it was at least lavender in some parts and definitely mauve everywhere else. But it had an elegiac quality that half appealed to me as I skiffed through it.

Eden is no more. In the smoky light, where once it stood, is smouldering rubble, ash and cinders. The stench of burning thickens the air, tears like regret at the eyes and throat. Every breath is a rasping sigh; the wind in the trees a lamentation.

Now, with the destruction of Eden, this place knows death and devastation, and the wail of mourning that will not be comforted. How silent and empty is the New Dawn, now; how hollow and worthless all its promise...

I wasn't sure what much of it meant. I wasn't sure if it was the same Eden that I'd known. But it took the interest. There wasn't so much about Tweedie, though, and that was a disappointment. He interested me. A social chameleon. Such depths, so many layers.

But then, I thought, giving free rein to the deep and philosophical side of my personality, hasn't everyone? Doesn't everyone have so many sides to them; aren't there so many aspects to a human personality, that we can never truly say we know anybody? I must have read that somewhere; I wouldn't have thought that up by myself. It's not like me to come over all Captain Kirk. I don't do deep much, these days.

Now I would have to take Bert Saunders and his team into the loop. It was becoming much too hot for me to handle on my own. The law needed to know that Laura McGuire was almost certainly alive and had decamped with her father from Eden, in the Megane presumably. Dominic Tweedie would be wanted for questioning with regard to drug dealing and the mass deaths of the New Dawn. He was responsible, however indirectly; that was a certainty. They also needed to know, as a matter of urgency now, that Grace McGuire and Billy McPartland were habitual doggers and that the murdered man had been stalking Grace, if 'stalking' was not overstating the case. Dizzy on her, at least. Maybe the Buhll was a murderer. But first I wanted to talk to McPartland alone.

I left the office and walked up the street. I bought myself a salad in Witherspoon's – a few curly leaves of lettuce, two or three cherry tomatoes, half a dozen coins of cucumber, a shredding of cheese and a couple of hard-boiled humpty dumpties. It filled a hole. I walked back down the street to the Steelyard. There was always an assortment of oddballs around the centre of town, and two of my favourites were there.

Jim Dandy is a dwarf who stands at less than five feet and dresses like he was at the races: brown trilby hat, camelhair coat with dark brown reveres and soft brown shoes. As far as appearance goes, he might be a bookie's runner or a pox-doctor's clerk. In miniature. He likes to stand around, smoking cigarillos and passing guttural comments on the passing scene in his grumbling rumble.

Sky Blue Green acquired his nickname as a result of an unfortunate affliction. Macular degeneration is a progressive wasting of the centre spot of the retina, which results in the gradual blurring and eventual loss of central vision. Peripheral vision is often good, though, and a lot of sufferers can see from the edges of their eyes. Sky Blue can only see what is in front of him if he tips his head back and stares at the sky, peering from the bottom edge of his eyes. Hence, the name Sky Blue, the chromatic contrast with his surname adding to the appeal of it.

I was somewhat in awe of Sky Blue when I first met him, but I quickly grew to like him and once quizzed him about his singular way of looking at the world. "Doesn't it bother you, having to look up at the sky, to see what's under your nose?"

"No. Maist folk cannae see what's under their noses anyway. And sometimes you have to look in a different place from what you thought, to see what you want."

"You might be right."

"Like when you were a wean. D' you never lie on your back when you were a wean and look up at the ceilin' and imagine it was a flair?"

"Aye, I did."

"Well, then."

Unlike Jim Dandy, who hasn't enough brains to grease a door-hinge, Sky Blue has the reputation of being something of a wise old man of the Steelyard because of this kind of gnomic utterance. He tends to ask you questions rather than answer any and, when you reply, he finishes off the exchange with a tag like "Right you are," or "Well, then". Which gives the impression that he has just solved a very big problem in a very straightforward way. He lives on benefit and spends most of his time mooching around the Steelyard or drinking in one of the pubs, supping at a pint of lager and looking at the ceiling when he wants to ogle the barmaid.

Sky Blue and Dandy were taking the air in the Steelyard, sitting together on a bench facing the Edinburgh Road. I sat down beside them.

"Aw right?" said Jim Dandy.

"Oh, it's you, son," said Sky Blue, after fixing his gaze on the region of the Pole Star to see who it was. "You goat onyhin to do wae the murder enquiry?"

"Naw, that's the police, Sky Blue," I said. "I've been on my own case, though, the last couple of days. Trying to find somebody that's got themselves cloistered up in a religious community."

"No easy," ventured Jim Dandy.

"Not easy at all, Dandy," I replied. "In fact, difficult. Try telling somebody religious what to think."

"Still," said Jim Dandy, "Ah sometimes envy theym that's goat religion. It must be a great comfort at times. Mah mother was a Cath'lic. Devout, ken? Chapel every week fur what d'ye cry it?... Mass. Mah faither noo, he could take it or leave it. Religion. But mah mother? Pious as fuck."

"Well," I said, "I'm very suspicious of people who believe in all that stuff these days."

"Naw, ken, don't git me wrong," he said. "It's no jist Cath'lics. Ye've goat yer Jews tae. Yer Jew's a religious man." He sat back in comfort, like the Grand Turk, and puffed a mist of cigarillo smoke around himself. "Then there's yer Muslins. They're religious tae. That's what aw yer Paki grocers are. They worship Allah. Allah be praised an' aw that. That's yer Muslin religion. They're awfy religious folk."

The conversation had veered off a ways from where I had intended it to go. Conversations with Sky Blue and Jim Dandy had a habit of going like the buzzer-round. But Sky Blue managed to haul it back to the general locality where I had last seen it.

"Ye were sayin', son, that it wis hard tae get through tae religious folk. The thing is, you see, that religious folk are kinda unwaverin' in what they believe. And that's where the problem lies. Kin ye argue wi' a mind that's closed? Kin ye tell onyhin' tae someb'dy that kens it a'? Kin ye?"

"No."

"There ye are, well."

That was as good as it would get. So I gave them good day, in fact I gave them one each, and ankled on out of there.

There was something nagging at my mind. I didn't know what it was but I was sure that, when I did, I would have solved the case. I couldn't be arsed with going back to the office, so I drove home and put my feet up. I dug out a favourite album – one of my father's LPs from the 60's – 'East West' by the Butterfield Blues Band. I closed my eyes and let my mind wander.

42

Uphall and Broxburn were originally quite separate communities but nowadays only the locals can tell where one ends and the other begins. Only the locals would care. It used to amuse me that strangers to Uphall occasionally mispronounced its name as 'Yoofal' when it was blindingly obvious to me that it was 'Up-hall'. Anyway, I drove to Uphall that evening, to Wyndford Avenue to be precise, and found young Mr. McPartland pushing a flymo over a square patch of lawn no bigger than a hanky. The joke was obvious but McPartland was a ned, so I cracked it anyway. I leant on the fence and watched him until he stopped and looked at me.

"Bit of a change for you, Billy, isn't it?"

"Whut is?"

"Cutting your own grass. You're used to cutting other folks', I hear."

"Whut the fuck dae you want?"

"A wee blether. It won't take long."

"Come in, then. But it better no take long."

I went in, but not without some trepidation. The Buhll was a dangerous individual – and here I was venturing into his hidey hole. Won't you walk into my parlour, said the spider to the fly. It was the living-room I expected. King Billy on the wall, Rangers on the mantelpiece, a couple of posters of that kind of art that young stags like – highly mannered shite with bikes and skulls and big-breasted women in tight leather clothes. All strictly out of the 'Bat Out of Hell' school. Comic book art. Mind you, I hadn't pegged him for a lover of De Stijl.

"You wahnt a cup a coffee or somethin'?"

"No thanks. I won't be staying that long."

"Right," he said, sitting down, "get bletherin'."

"Tell me what happened between you and Brian Cairns."

"Whae's Brian Cairns when he's at hame?"

"Well, unfortunately, he won't be at home now, ever again. He's the man found dead in Old Bangour last week."

"Oh aye? What makes you think Ah kent 'im?"

"The fact you like to go dogging. And so did he. The fact

that you have a thing for Grace McGuire. And so did he. The fact that you threatened to give him a bleaching if he didn't stop trying to hit on her. Wee things like that."

He sniffed. "Think you're a smart cunt, don't you?"

He was the second man from that area to accuse me of being one. Maybe there was a chronic shortage of them in Yoofal. "Do I?"

"Grace tell you aw that?"

"No. As a matter of fact, she didn't. Somebody else told me. But Grace did confirm that…"

"Ah ken what Grace confirmed. She phoned me, eh?"

"Of course."

"An' Ah ken what you think aboot me, tae. You think Ah kilt that Cairns boy, don't ye?"

"And did you?"

"Naw. Ah didnae. Ah didnae hurt Laura an' Ah didnae kill Cairns." I'd certainly hit a nerve that time I spoke to him about Laura.

"What were you doing in the evenings last week?"

"Last week? Ah was night shift last week."

"I take it that can be confirmed?"

"Phone the plant."

"You go dogging with Grace last week?"

"Naw."

"But you did last night."

"Aye. Grace tellt you that. Hell, you said ye seen us."

"And you didn't attack Brian Cairns?"

"Ye ken that story tae. He got to pervin' on Grace. He suggested a straight swap wan night. Him tae go aff wi' Grace an' me tae go aff wi' the young thing that he was wi'. Ah tellt 'im. Ah sayed if he didnae git 'issel' tae fuck, Ah wid sparkle the cunt." I inclined my head, and breathed in. But he continued. "But that disnae mean tae say that Ah kilt 'im."

"Okay."

"That you done?"

"Pretty much. I'm going to the police with all I know about this set-up now, Billy. So, if you have anything on your mind that you need to get off it, now's the time."

"Ah tellt ye. Ah didnae kill 'im."

"You know, Billy," I said. "I think I believe you."

"So fuck off and leave us in peace."

When I fucked off and left him in peace, he was standing at the window, watching me go. They obviously hate you to leave, in that part of the world.

43

I took the notion for a jar before I went home. I had a spit as heavy as mercury. So I drove to Bathgate and parked just behind Mulholland's. There were about a dozen guys in and the craic was 90, so I stayed for a while and had two pints. Good, tangy stuff, just the very dab to quench a private eye's thirst. Talk ranged over several topics, including football, the government and the inevitable Cairns case. They speired the arse out of me but I gave nothing away.

"Come on, sir," said Rough Hugh. "You must be involved somewhere along the line."

"He is," said Clem from behind the bar. "He was off to interview Bobby Shafto the other day."

"Bobby? How? Did Bobby club the boy tae death wi' that big tadger o' his?"

Laughter.

"Bobby involved in this business, Jack?" asked Rough Hugh, when the sniggers had abated.

"Listen. I told Clem here I just wanted Bobby to give me a bit guitar tuition."

"Ach, there nae use tryin' tae pump Jack there for information," said Davie Walker. "That's why he can make a livin' at that gemme. He's one ae the few that can keep 'is trap shut."

"I don't know that I would call it a living, Davie," I said.

"You dae aw right," said Davie. "You're mibbies no rollin' in it but you've goat yer ain office, ye make yer ain 'oors, it's an int'restin' joab an' ye don't exactly look like yer starvin' tae me!"

I finished my second pint and reluctantly refused a third. I distributed adieux among them and left the bar. The jalopy was only twenty yards or so away. I pulled my keys from my pocket. As I passed the back door of one of the shops and stooped to insert the key in the lock, I caught a movement from the corner of my eye. But that was all I had time for. Somebody pulled a coat or something over my head and pinioned my arms. Somebody else punched me several times in the gut and I puked up my beer. Then there was an almighty thump to my skull. A shape like a bat zoomed through my head and then nothing.

44

I woke up, lying on the cold ground by the car. My head throbbed. Tentatively, I put my fingers up and had an exploratory feel. I had a lump, but the skin wasn't broken. My throat felt raw from retching and my stomach was sore. I was shivering with cold and shock. But that was all. Fuck, I've had worse after a night on the piss. I looked at my watch. I'd been out about ten minutes. I swithered briefly about going back into Mulholland's but that would have involved telling them about it, their wondering who did it and why, and other shit that I couldn't be bothered with. I knew who did it. I don't suppose that only one guy in West Lothian wears Joop, but only one that I know swims in it.

It was boneyard silent. Aching, stinking of puke and shaking like a dog having a shit, I opened the car door and got in. I sat with the heater on until I warmed up and till the Charlie Drakes subsided a little. Then, with no other sinner in sight, I turned on the engine and drove slowly home.

I washed my face, examined the goose-egg on my skull in the mirror extremely carefully, and then poured myself a coffee. I sat in the armchair, stretched my feet out on a little stool, sparked up and relaxed. Black Jack flicked up on the arm of the chair, stilted about a second or two, then curled round himself and settled down looking at me.

"Well, Jack old son," I said to him, "I've had a doing tonight. From Billy the Buhll and accomplice, or accomplices, unknown. But you would think that, if he wanted to give me a serious going over, and if he wanted to stay anonymous, he would have done without immersing himself in that perfume he uses. You would think that, wouldn't you? Anybody with a glimpse of intelligence would. But he didn't. He was stinking of it, as usual. It's almost as if he wanted me to know who it was that was handing out the battering."

Black Jack fixed those green eyes on me, little slits of green in an otherwise featureless face.

"Well, of course he did. He wanted it obvious that it was him."

I dragged deep on the fag.

"But why? I was out there at Uphall tonight, grilling him about the Cairns murder. He wasn't any too pleased with me, but to get me as soon as he did, and as obviously as he did...? I mean, it looks so obvious that he's got something to hide. A lot to hide, by his carryings-on."

I got up and put some sounds on low. Sonny Boy's finest moment – Help Me, a few short minutes of blues heaven, the old wizard's harp wheezing over the Green Onions riff in F and his sly, insinuating leer on the lyrics.

I told myself, "Look at it objectively. You first hear about him from Grace McGuire as her daughter's ex-boyfriend. Her most recent ex. She paints a picture of him as a brainless dork in the flute band, somebody not remotely worthy enough for her wee lassie. Then you meet him. He's dense and charmless and vaguely threatening. A neanderthal. He says he chucked Laura because she was the possessive type. Grace McGuire wanted the relationship stopped because of the religious difference. But there is no religious difference. Confusion number 1. The janitor tells you he's got a one-track mind. Next time he's mentioned, it's Laura McGuire, talking about him. And what does she say about him? That he's an imbecile, a yobbo but good at the old hochmagandy. That her mother didn't think the relationship a suitable one. Fits right into the picture, doesn't it? Handily so. But! – Laura gives the strong impression that she and her mother have barely any time for each other, something her mother also suggested on her visit to the office. Whereas, her stepfather, the good and worthy Joe McGuire, tells you that they adore each other. Confusion number 2."

"So, two good confusing elements up to now. All silk so far. You find out that Grace and Mr. McPartland are an item. Is this why Laura has hied herself off to the Highlands? Confusion number 3. Grace and the Buhll go dogging, where they come across – if that's the right expression – a man called Brian Cairns, who develops a fixation for Grace and who is threatened by Billy the Buhll for getting just a wee bit too close to his woman. And then your man is found on a path at Old Bangour with his head stove in. Poor old Cairns takes the dirt sleep. Meanwhile, it transpires that the leader of the religious cult that Laura has buggered off to join, is her natural father. And her stepfather says she has hardly any time for boys. Let alone the Buhll. Confusion number – 4, is it? 4 or 5. And the cult is a front for drug running. The night after you get back from Angus, the whole place goes up in flames. Laura and her father nowhere to be seen. Gone. Done a bunk. Conveniently. But, where it gets even muddier," I said after it was over, "is that McPartland yokes on me a couple of hours after I've interviewed him and made it plain that the next step is the police, with all this information. Why would he do that? Why would he incriminate himself so obviously?"

The music moved on to the next cut on the album.

"The short and obvious answer is that he *wants* to incriminate himself. He wants to be the number one suspect for the murder of Brian Cairns. He's protecting someone else. And could that someone else be his leman, Mrs. Grace McGuire? Upon my word, this is some Chinese angle on the old game where a tart lures a guy into bother with her gorilla of a boyfriend. Cherchez la femme, Jack old boy. Cherchez la fucking femme."

Pleased, I lay back and glugged heartily from my glass.

"But that still doesn't explain why Grace and Laura McGuire, mother and daughter as close as a dead heat, pretend that they can barely stick the sight of each other, does it? Or why Laura McGuire took herself up to Angus and joined a cult. Or why her mother came to the office and asked you to investigate Laura's presence there in Edzell. If her mother *knew* that Laura was there to be with her biological father, why would she want you to find out?"

Maybe there was an inside play on this that I'd been missing. I smelt a device.

45

Next morning I drove to the cop shop in Almondell. They told me that DI Saunders was at a funeral. Brian Cairns was being buried. I asked one of the girls on the desk if she knew where the funeral was taking place. I had to undergo a snatch of dialogue from a revue sketch as she, whilst 90% of her attention was being taken up typing on a PC, tried to elicit this information from the other girl on the desk, who was taking a phone call at the same time.

"El'nur, d'you know where that funeral is this mornin'?"

"Funeral?"

"Aye."

"Trying to put you through now, madam. Funeral?"

"Aye. That boy that was murdered. What was 'is name again?"

"Cairns," I suggested.

"Connecting you now, madam. What funeral was this, Marion?" said Eleanor.

"The one that DI Saunders is away tae."

"Oh aye. That was the man that was murdered at Bangour. Cairns, I think."

"That's the one," I said.

"Oh, eh, East Calder, I think," said Eleanor. "That's where the man belonged, anyway."

"Yes, but some folk from East Calder get buried elsewhere," I said. "Lots of people do. The fact that you live in East Calder doesn't mean that you *have* to get buried ..." I stopped. They were both looking at me. "I knew a man from East Calder once, got buried in Mid Calder," I said lamely.

Eleanor stood and walked to a table behind her. There was a large Page-A-Day diary lying on it, and this she consulted. "DI Saunders. Funeral St. Theresa's RC Church, East Calder, 9.30. East Calder cemetery afterwards." She looked at me haughtily. "That the information you require, Mr. Black?"

"It is, thank you," I said.

"You could wait until he returns," suggested Marion.

I looked at my watch. It was only 9.55 then. "No, I'll go and meet him there."

"The cemetery in East Calder's at the start of Main Street," said Marion helpfully, "as you drive in from the Mid Calder side."

"Yes," added Eleanor, "and remember St. Theresa's is the one on the way out of East Calder on the Edinburgh Road. The one in the middle of town's the Church of Scotland."

"Thanks."

It was a big funeral. Cairns had got 'a guid turn-oot', as locals would have said. There were cars parked all along Main Street and out along the Edinburgh Road, too. I tooled the rustbucket slowly along and noted the grimly humorous fact that the church was not a lightyear away from the East Calder driveway into Almondell Country Park. I turned in the forecourt of the big filling-station there and parked on the church side of the street, facing back towards Livingston and Mid Calder. Then I got out and walked along to the church.

I slid open the door and squeezed myself in. The wee church was packed to the Stations of the Cross with mourners. All pews were occupied and a number of people stood at the back. I could see the coffin dimly, resting on its trestles away at the top of the aisle. The priest was distributing Holy Communion, so there was not long to go. I slipped back out of the church and crossed to the other side of the road. I mooched about here, smoking, until the church doors were opened by the undertakers in readiness for Cairns taking his final journey.

Presently, the coffin was carried out by six men, one of them presumably Cairns's son, and slid into the back of the hearse. The immediate family followed. Cairns's wife was petite and blonde, in a black veil. Their daughter hung on her mother's arm and looked out of it. Sedated to the max. A couple of awkward looking breezes in make-do mourning stood to the side, watching the daughter. Her nurses, I guessed. It all went off without any problems. The congregation started to file out and some shook hands with Mrs. Cairns and her kids. Then Bert Saunders came out and made his condolences with the family before moving off. I caught his eye and he nodded. We walked off briskly towards the cars.

"Well, Seamus."

"You going to the cemetery, Bert?"

"Aye."

"I'll come with you, if you'll drop me back for my own car before you go back to work."

"Okay. Got something for me?"

"Yep. I believe I have."

I climbed into the passenger seat of Bert's police car. We sparked up and watched the mourners exit the church, speak to the family, mill around the cars.

"Don't like your paint job," I said. "The whole white, blue and dayglo yellow thing is *so* passé."

"It's aw the crack in law enforcement circles."

"How's the wife taking it?" I asked.

"Devastated," said Bert. "Aboot the murder *and* the sexual thing."

"Mmm."

"See the young thing, there?" Bert indicated a young woman in a black suit. She was shapely and the weeds did nothing to detract from her collection of shapes. Mourning becomes Electra.

"Yes."

"Cairns's secretary. Or receptionist. Or typist. Whatever the fuck she is."

"Yeah?"

"Yeah. *And* his partner in the old communal hanky-panky."

"Ah! Now *that's* interesting."

"Oh? How?"

"I made a few inquiries about Mr. Cairns and his sexual shenanigans. I found out that the woman he brought to the meets was young and attractive – I presumed not his wife, no insult intended to her – but nobody was sure who she was."

"Well, that's her."

"What did she say?"

"Bricked it when it was obvious that we kent what they'd been up tae. But I told her that her private life is only of interest if it has anythin' to dae wi' Cairns and his death. She kent nothin' about why he was at Old Bangour. She said they went to…"

"Almondell."

"Right first time. She hadn't been to Bangour with him. She stays with her old mother. Had been in every night last week. Alibi tight as a duck's arse. I don't think she'll be flauntin' her wares in public any more, though."

"No, I don't suppose so." I chuckled. "It's laughable, isn't it? Knocking off your secretary isn't daring enough any more. You have to take her along to swingers' do's."

They were closing the back of the hearse now. The immediate family moved into the funeral cars. We'd be moving off soon.

"So what have you to share with me, Seamus?"

"You want to pull in two folk for questioning. Names are Grace McGuire and Billy McPartland."

"Doggy doers, too?"

"Oh yes. But there's better than that. Mr. Cairns, whom we are about to follow to his last long home, had a thing for this Grace McGuire. A crush as big as steel rollers."

"Did he now?" Bert indicated and pulled smoothly out into the cortège. We purled along slowly. "Keep talkin'."

"Well, just that. He'd obviously seen them at a meet, got involved in some of the old Hancus Pancus and taken a wee notion to 'issel' about the lovely Grace."

"Oh, and is she lovely?"

"Do bears wear a big hat? But here's the rub, to coin a phrase. He got so cranked about it he wanted a dose of Grace on his own and suggested as much. I think the deal was that Cairns would have a session with Grace toot sell, and her beau, the appositely named Billy the Buhll, could have the same time in the arms of the Rt. Hon Sec, there."

"And Billy the Buhll didn't like it."

"Not one wee toaty bit. He jumped salty on him."

"He what?"

"Jumped salty. Blues talk for got in a towering huff."

"Fucksake Seamus, between Shakespeare and that fuckin' plantation music you're into, it's a wonder I can make you out at all."

"Yeah, right. He took the rue at him, as they say. In fact, he threatened to rearrange Mr. Cairns's features for him. If not worse."

"So you think this Billy ... whatever his name is ..."

"McPartland."

"... McPartland is oor man?"

"Strangely enough, no I don't. Not now. I did. But not now."

We'd pulled into a parking space for the cemetery. Bert cut the engine and looked at me. "Go on."

"I think he *wants* me to think it was him. I think he wants me to think that enough to pass it on to you. I think he wants *you* to think it was him. But I also think that..."

"Fucksake, Seamus, you're doin' a hell of a lot of thinkin'."

"Aye. I also think when you and your guys investigate him thoroughly, you'll find he has cast iron alibis for any time that Cairns might have been murdered."

"So who is he protectin'? This Grace McGuire woman?"

"Ah! Maybe. Maybe not. Give me till this time tomorrow on that, Bert. I think I might be able to give you a killer."

"So why pick up these two?"

"You'll want to hear them. It might *still* be McPartland. He *might* still be protecting Grace McGuire. I could be wrong. You'll find out. But just give me another 24 hours and I might be able to help you a bit more."

He looked at me, considered for a second and then nodded. "Okay, Seamus. I'll go for that. Sounds like you've turned up the real deal. The Dick done good."

We watched Cairns being lowered, watched his relict throw a fistful of clay in after him. To my mind, it looked like she was wondering if she'd ever really known her husband, but maybe that's because I'm a hopeless romantic. Maybe she was wondering if she'd left the gas on. You can never really tell. I remember Jim McGravey's wife, Betty. Day of the funeral, she had to be prised off the coffin. Two weeks later, she was down the Masonic in a mini skirt and a lurex boob-tube. Poor Jim was pushing up the daisies and she was pouring brandy and Babycham down her neck like it was going out of fashion. They tell me you couldn't have filled her with a hose. Then she was up on the dance floor, giving it plenty at the Slosh. Now there's some tattooed skinhead wearing poor Jim's slippers and taking the piss out of his Tartan Lads LP's. It's not right.

Bert ran me back to the far end of East Calder. He jotted their details down in his notebook. "Right. Mrs. Grace McGuire and Mr. William McPartland. Good. Where are you headed now?"

"Goin' where the Southern cross the Dog," I replied.

"Okay, Seamus, if you're gonnae start talkin' piss again, get your scrawny arse out of my wagon and I'll get this show on the road. Phone me tomorrow."

"You got it."

He drove off into where the sunset would be in about ten hours' time. I slid behind the wheel of my little dooce coop and sparked up a weed. I rummaged through the discs in the glove compartment. (I wonder if anyone ever kept gloves in there.) Somewhere I had the one I needed. Eventually I dug it out. Butterfield again, some lost tracks from before his eponymous first album, one of them a version of a song by the first Sonny Boy Williamson. John Lee Williamson, the original Sonny Boy, was the blues harp's first great virtuoso and the man who made it into a lead instrument. He had a stuttering, almost tongue-tied style of singing but, boy, could he blow that old mouth piano. At the age of 34, he was beaten to death in a mugging in Chicago in 1948, as he walked the block and a half home from a gig. His wife, Lacey Belle, opened the door to find him, collapsed in a bloody heap, murmuring "Lord have mercy." As I drove down Main Street, Butterfield's band started going like a printing press.

Good morning, little schoolgirl...

46

Charlene McRobb lived in Baird Road in Armadale, a council street on the north side of the town near the glen that the Barbauchlaw Burn runs through. I drove there and knocked on the front door. Somebody loved their flowers. The garden was small but that somebody tended the botany in it with a skilful hand. The path was swept and lined with white painted stones. The lady of the house evidently kept the knocker and letterbox well Brassoed. I wouldn't have been surprised if she stoned the step and cleaned the mirror with newspaper, too. There weren't many miners left in West Lothian – in fact, there were more private investigators – but their traditions hadn't died out. Somebody somewhere in the vicinity kept pigeons as well. A squadron of them were flying in formation around the rooftops in a tight, magnetic square. Their dookit was somewhere hard by, for sure.

The door was opened by a teenage girl. Too young a teenage girl.

"I'm looking for Charlene McRobb," I explained to her.

"She's at work," the teenager replied curtly.

"Oh. Right. Where does she work?" I asked.

"Who is it, Marlene?" asked an older female voice, before an older female person replaced the teenager in the doorway.

"Mrs. McRobb?" I ventured. It was a reasonable venture.

"Yes." She was wearing a pinny. I hadn't seen one of them since the Pope was an altar boy.

"I'm looking for Charlene, your daughter Charlene."

"Why are you looking for Charlene?"

"I'm a private investigator, Mrs. McRobb. I'd like to speak to her about a friend of hers."

"Laura McGuire?"

"Well…"

"Come in, Mr…?"

"Black. Jack Black. Thank you."

I followed her along the lobby and into the living-room. Clean. Bright. Spotless. Airy. Nicely furnished. A smell of baking that was utterly irresistible was coming through the door from the kitchen. I could feel myself start to slaver like a bulldog.

"Sit down, Mr. Black."

"Thank you. Here's my ID." I flashed my card but for all the notice she paid it, it could have been a Global Video membership.

"Would you like a cup of tea?"

"Black coffee would be nice."

"I only have Nescafe, I'm afraid. We're none of us great coffee hands in this house."

"Nescafe's fine," I said.

"Do you like home baking, Mr. Black?"

"Do koalas like eucalyptus leaves, Mrs. McRobb?"

"I've no idea," she laughed. "Do they?"

"About as much as I love home baking."

"Well, you bide a wee, and I'll bring you something nice."

She went out to the kitchen and I bidit a wee. Strictly speaking, this was holding me up but it was years since I'd tasted home baking as good as this smelt. Half an hour in this pleasant woman's company could hardly be described as time wasted. The teenager had dematerialised, in the way that teenagers have. In no time at all, Mrs. McRobb was back with a cup of coffee and a slice of something crumbly and golden on a plate. There was even a wee spoonful of cream with it.

"There you go, Mr. Black. Home made rhubarb tart. I hope you like it."

I liked it. I liked it immensely. I liked it enough to have a second helping of it. It's a pity this woman was married already. Forbye being a Black Belt baker, Ninth Dan, she was plump and jolly, with an engaging smile and an easy manner. She would be great to have on your arm at the theatre or the cinema. And, I suspected, a whole lot of fun to be with when she took her corsets off after News at Ten. Best of all, if the man was worth it, she'd be as loyal as a Labrador for the rest of her life.

"I'm afraid Charlene's working just now," she said, settling herself down on the settee with a cup of tea. "She's got a summer job, you know? In Tesco in Bathgate."

"Okay. I'm sorry I've missed Charlene but I would have been sorrier to miss her Mum's baking."

"Charmer," she said, blushing slightly. "You could always try her work. She works on the checkout. If they're slack, she helps out with other things. Stocking shelves and helping out on some of the counters – that kind of thing."

"Fine. I will."

"Is it about Laura McGuire, if you don't mind my asking?" she said.

"It is, aye," I replied, putting down my plate reluctantly. "Do you know her at all, Mrs. McRobb?"

"Oh ... I know the lassie. I wouldn't say that I knew her that awfy *well*. But she's been here once or twice, with Charlene."

"And what was your impression of her?"

"Of Laura? Oh well. She struck me as a dour kind of a lassie. Oh, polite enough; don't get me wrong. But awfy... what's the word? ... sombre. Aye, that's it. Sombre. She didn't seem to me to have a lot of fun. No for a lassie of seventeen or eighteen, anyway. You know what I mean?"

"I do, yes. Did she ever stay over?"

"Sleepover, kind of a thing? No, never. Her and Charlene went out a couple of nights – to the dancing and parties, and that. She came here to collect Charlene. She had a car, you see. One night, they got ready here together. But that was about all."

"Okay. Did Charlene ever talk about her to you?"

"Not much. She wasn't her biggest pal, or anything. I don't know that Laura had many pals, anyway. I think Charlene felt a wee bit sorry for her, to tell you the truth. She's bright, right enough. Probably the cleverest in the class, Charlene told me. But a wee bitty ... what's the word, when it comes to social things? Gauche. That's it. Gauche."

I tore myself away from Mrs. McRobb. The conversation was pleasant and she was, too. But I had only limited time to work in before I reported back to Bert so, eventually, I took my leave and drove back to Bathgate.

47

Tesco started in 1924 as a single store. Now it's taking over the planet. It's the Japanese knotweed of the supermarket world. It bought the chain of Willie Low's stores in Scotland and established a foothold that way. Now it's so ubiquitous that Inverness, which has three huge stores, is called Tescotown. By unimaginative people like tabloid reporters, granted, but nonetheless, the point is made. The Bathgate branch is on the Blackburn Road, just off the Toll, where Car Collection used to be, but there's talk of them constructing a huge fuck-off one out by Livingston, big enough to have several government departments, a football stadium and a shipbuilding yard.

I parked at the far end of the car park from the store and walked there. It's not that I distrust supermarkets. Well, it is. Especially when you've got a loyalty card. Use that when you buy your frozen fajitas and your toffee-flavoured yoghurts and they know everything about you in a matter of weeks: whether you're married or single, what income bracket you're in, where you keep your spare fuse-wire and who you summon from the depths of your mind when you feel a little lonely at night.

I spoke to an important looking woman. She had a name-tag on her waistcoat that told me her name was Eileen Norris.

"Hello, Eileen," I said.

"Hello?" She looked at me as if trying to place me – someone who would address her by her first name.

"Your name's on your badge," I pointed out. "I always use people's names if they're labelled like that, in case it hurts their feelings if I don't."

She looked at me as if she was swithering whether to call the local bughouse and see if any nutters had absconded.

"I'm actually looking for a girl called Charlene McRobb who works here, Eileen," I said.

"Oh Charlene. She's serving on the fish counter today."

"Right," I said. "Ta."

The girl on the fish counter wore a white coat and a fairly incongruous looking boater. She had a piece of fish in a square of cellophane in her hand and was plonking it on the scales when I drew alongside. She told her customer that that was three pounds, and the customer said 'Fine', and she wrapped it up, then stuck an adhesive price label on it and handed it over, and the customer went away with her fish. Then she turned her attention to me. "Hi. Can I help you?" she asked in that bright and corky way kids have.

"You can, Charlene," I said, "but I don't want any fish today."

She looked puzzled, as well she might, for here she was behind a counter heaped high with ice chips on which lay trays of mottled and marbled fish, piles of slimy grey prawns, medallions of bivalves, white kites of fish fillets and the garish orange sand of fish-dressing through which to drag them. All manner of fruits of the sea to tempt the most jaded of palates, and here was I looking for something else.

"I'd like a wee word with you about Laura McGuire," I explained.

"Oh," she said in sudden realisation. "Are you the police? Is it true she's run away and become a nun?"

"No. And no. My name's Black and I am a private detective." I did the shtick with the ID card again. "I've been out to your house in Armadale and your mum said you were working here."

"Oh, you've been at the house?"

"I have. And your mum's an excellent baker, by the way," I added, as a clincher.

The lassie beamed. "She is, isn't she?"

"Well, can we have a wee chat?"

"It's kinda awkward the now. But I've got a break in ten minutes. I'll meet you outside then."

"Great. I'll be at the far end of the building," (I indicated which end I meant) "having a puff. Okay?"

"Yes. I'll see you then."

There was a wee pepperpot of a woman standing next to me now, looking very meaningfully in my direction. What her look meant was 'Buy some fish or stop chatting the wee lassie up, you sad old fuck'. I smiled at her and she looked at me like she was sniffing shite at a distance. So I left.

48

I was on my second gasper when Charlene came round the gable end of the building for smoko, turning her back to the wind and lowering her face into her cupped hands to light one for herself. "Hi," she said.

"Hello again."

"So what's Laura done wi' herself, if she's not run away to join a convent? That's what they're saying in Armadale."

"Well, she is missing, that's for sure. But she's not likely to become a Little Sister of the Assumption, I don't think."

"Are you trying to find her?"

"I am, hen, aye. Your mum said you kind of palled about with her."

"Well I do and I don't. Laura's a bit funny sometimes. A bit of a loner. She's as clever as anythin', like, and some of the others don't like that. They think she's a swot and a smart arse."

"How does Laura take that?"

She snorted. "She couldn't care less. Thinks they're all morons. 'Morons, neds, chavs and tramps' she calls them. They don't like that either."

"I can imagine. Does she ever flare up at them? Have a real slanging match, say?"

"No. I've never seen that. The only thing, once or twice when somebody's said something that's really got under her skin, you know, she gives them this look. It's chilling, it really is. Scary. She looks like she could knock hell out of them. They tend to get out of her way when she's like that."

"Right. But that's not very often?"

"No. Most of the time, she keeps herself to herself. Once in a blue moon, she'll hang out wi' me and bitch about classmates or teachers. Studies really hard. She's top in everything, just about, bar maybe Maths."

"You've been to one or two dances and things with her?"

"Oh yeah. One or two. When she bothers to come along."

"And how does she get on with the boys? Is she flirty or

anything?"

"Laura! No chance. She despises guys. Despises them! I don't mean she's the other way or anything..." she added hurriedly.

"No, I didn't think..."

"She just thinks guys are dopey and slow and only interested in one thing, you know?"

"I know." I knew all right. This reminded me of two conversations I'd had not too long before. "Does she even think that about the ones she goes out with?"

"Goes out with? I think she's been out with two – and both of them were one-nighters. The two best looking guys in the school, certainly, but I think she agreed to go out with them just because it would show the rest of us that she could get these guys. Not that she was interested in them much. One date each, I think."

"What about the guy Billy from Broxburn?"

"What guy Billy from Broxburn?"

"Didn't she have a relationship with an older boy from Broxburn? Billy McPartland? He's in the flute band...?"

"Not that I know of."

"Would she tell you, if she had?"

"Aye. I'm certain she would. Just to get at the others, if for no other reason."

"Would she confide in anyone else?"

"Never."

The last pieces in the jigsaw were falling into place with audible snaps and clicks.

"Does she speak highly of anyone?"

"Her mother?"

"Okay, Charlene, you've been very helpful. I want to ask you one last question. And think about it seriously. Okay?"

"Sure."

"In your opinion, as the one who probably knows her best, is she capable of hurting someone? I don't mean hurting their feelings. I mean, could she *hurt* somebody who crossed her?"

Charlene did me the honour of thinking extremely seriously about my question. She pondered it for all of five seconds. "I think Laura is capable of just about anything," she said. "You've never seen these looks she gives folk. She just has a snidey kind of smile. She doesn't seem to have a lot of emotions, do you know what I mean? She doesn't throw hissy fits or scream the place down. She just gives these looks. There was one time some of the girls were talking about that rape case last year – you remember? The lassie from the Job Centre?"

"I remember."

"Well, the lassies were talking about that guy that did it, saying he should be castrated and all that kind of thing. And then one of us, Kirsty I think, said 'it's all very well saying we should cut his balls off but none of us would actually do it.' And Laura said 'Give me the blade and I'd do it in the Steelyard.' But it was the way she said it – very quiet and composed, very calm. 'Give me the blade'. That was fucking scary – oh! sorry!" I shook my head; the swearing was irrelevant. The feeling was not. "But it was. Nobody laughed after that. Or even smirked. We just changed the subject as quick as we could. She meant it." Charlene paused for a second. "Is that any use to you?"

"Charlene, you're a star!" I said. "Thanks a million, Probably saved me a week's leg work."

She beamed. "Glad to have been of help."

"You know," I said, "you're a really nice kid."

"Thanks."

"And your wee sister seems a nice kid. And your mum's a lovely person. Your dad is one lucky guy."

"My father died about five years ago, Mr. Black. It's just Mum, me and Marlene."

"Oh, shit," I said, prising my size 9 from my mouth. "I'm sorry."

"No, no. You meant it as a compliment. That was nice. Thanks."

"Trust me, uh? Sorry."

"Don't worry about it."

"Okay, Charlene. See you. Oh, tell your mum I loved the rhubarb tart, eh?"

"I will. Cheerio, Mr. Black."

I felt as sensitive as a commode, having mentioned her

father when there had been no necessity to do it, but why was I so interested in the little item of news it had elicited?

49

I drove back to the office. I'd just got in and unwrapped my sandwich when the phone rang. I pulled it over the desk, lifted the receiver and told it, "Jack Black." A familiar voice purred in my ear.

"You are a meddlesome man, Jack Black. You have cost me a great deal of money and caused me a comparable amount of inconvenience."

"Ah, Tweedie," I said, none too politely. "Where are you?"

"Somewhere far from you and your meddling, Jack Black."

"Have you got Laura with you?"

"Not currently. Not as we speak. Although I am travelling with her. She claims to be my natural daughter."

"I know."

"I saw MacVicar's piece. It was interesting. He was fairer than I expected him to be."

"Fairer than you deserved," I said.

"He hardly mentions the drugs in it. Or your part in it."

"No."

"You were right, of course. The store in the woods."

"Yep. I spoke to Sergeant McKechnie. Poppy gum and stuff like that."

"That. Heroin. Cocaine. Lysergic Acid. Cyanide, for that matter."

"In the vans going to Aberdeen?"

"Aberdeen and all points south, Jack Black."

"How did you get away with it?"

"Harmless hippies selling eggs and honey. Religious people. Responsible. Respectable."

"But didn't you risk being seen, even at night, in harbours and places?"

"Containers are forty feet long, Jack Black. They are full of stuff like sports tops, canned lychees, trainers, seafood, machine parts. All on pallets stacked with cardboard cartons. Right in the heart of all that, is the stuff you're after."

"Poppy gum."

"Among other things. Blocks of compressed powder. Canisters of oil. There are a myriad ways."

"And you process it later."

"You do." There was a slight pause before he went on. "You have a seriously big mouth, Jack Black."

It was obvious he wanted to talk. Megalomaniacs – bedlamites of all kinds – often do. Usually about themselves. The last thing I wanted was to spend any more time listening to him. I found his discourse by no means uplifting or entertaining. But I let him ramble. Some of it was to satisfy my own curiosity. Most of it was because there was just the faintest chance that he'd let slip something that would lead me to where he was earthed. He touched on various topics, but just that. Touched on them and then abandoned them, like a housewife in a rummage sale. Now and again, I held him to a point. I kept it going for as long as I could, in the hope of gleaning that one ear of corn I wanted.

He said he held me personally responsible for everything that happened. No surprises there, then. When I pointed out that I thought *he* was the one responsible, especially for the deaths of the Angels, he lifted his peever. Said they'd got what they wanted. Which was Glory. He'd built them up to it, told them that Rapture and the Conflagration was coming. They supped it off a spoon, those poor lunkheads, and look where it got them. I asked him if Ira was with him and he snorted contemptuously, dismissed him as a dangerous hoodlum from the projects until Brother Gabriel converted him.

"At least," he said, "he was handy with guns."

I asked him how he'd managed to be away from Eden when the porkers came a-calling. He said he knew I'd blab to somebody; it was time to truck on out of there. He didn't see it as deserting the Angels. He'd merely told them that he was leaving for a short time and they assumed it was the start of the Conflagration. The rest, if not actually history, was at least a Features piece in the magazine section. How did he get the guns? One two three; if he could get drugs, he could get guns.

He was starting to sound like he was winding down, so I jazzed him up a bit. I asked him – and he would love this – how he managed it. Not just the guns or the drugs but the whole fucking thing. How, I asked him, even with all his charisma and charm and all that guano, how could he con people on such a massive scale? I wasn't just talking about smooth-talking some fox into bed, or impressing wee laddies with an image. How did he persuade people to join a movement, give away all their worldly possessions, swallow all that mantic crap about the end of the world and, ultimately, do away with themselves? How the fuck could he do that?

The unctuous bastard purred. This was what he wanted most: to talk about how clever he was. I could almost hear him preening at the other end. He was so much his own cup of tea that it was entirely unstrained. He said what I had to understand was that the vast majority of people are easily influenced. Easily led. Too frightened of life to try and work it out for themselves. They listen to other people. Let other people do the worrying and the working out, and just follow them. But most of all they let *religion* do the thinking for them. Priests, ministers, rabbis, imams, shamans – they do all the meaning of life for most folk, because they claim to be hip to what God wants. What we have to do to get to heaven. Most folk let these people tell them how to live because most folk are inadequate. Not confident enough to think for themselves; terrified of the process, or of what the process might throw up.

He paused and, down the line, I could feel his smirk oil my ear. I said, "Go on."

The frightening thing, Tweedie said, is that you can do *anything* with these kind of people, if you mould them the right way. You can make them the kind of fanatics who will gladly die for the cause, or even kill for the cause. Fanatics. Animal Rights. Anti-Abortionists. The Bible Belt. Hezbollah. Zionists. UDA. IRA. There are fanatics everywhere. Hitler said people will believe any lie if you just make it big enough.

The light outside was thickening.

"Does that nauseate you?" Tweedie asked.

"No. It just depresses me. I can see that you're right and it's what I've always thought. But, unlike you, I never thought it right through."

"Well, there you are. Existentialism versus Fanaticism. Or Fundamentalism."

"Why have you phoned me, Tweedie? Not to lecture me on fundamentalism, I'm sure."

"I phoned you, Jack Black, to tell you that I hold you culpable for the losses I have incurred in the last few days. And to inform you that we shall meet again in the future, I am sure. I need not remind you that we did not part on amicable terms in Eden. Be wary, Jack Black, be wary."

"A threat?"

"A piece of friendly advice. From an old friend of your father's. I miss your father, you know."

"Yeah?"

"Oh yes. An admirable man in so many ways. You are aware that the herd consider suicide to be 'the coward's way out'? I disagree profoundly. To take one's own life requires an act of stunning bravery. To take your own life in the way your father did was not only courageous; it was an act of artistry. Truly creative. From the Forth Bridge, no less! Significant. And artistic. Such a pity that his son should have none of these qualities. Such a shame that he should be only a prying imbecile. Goodbye, Jack Black, until we meet again."

I put the phone down. Frustration and anger simmered in me. Having to listen to all that smug flatulence and not even a hint of where he was. I was fizzing. I checked 141. Mobile phone. Of course.

50

For once, the music playing was not Chicago blues, nor nostalgic psychedelia but quiet piano music – a CD of classical piano pieces. Reflective. Calm. Tranquil. Like myself. Chopin's 'Tristesse' in E major tinkled through the room. Black Jack was gone, out on the tiles with a lady friend. I had no light burning. Twilight settled quietly in the room, flattening colours, deepening shadows, intensifying sorrow. The television set sat unregarded in the corner, a glaucous glass eye staring back at nothing. A car drove up the road, meshed its gears and turned into the next street. The light, which had slowly been creeping skywards for the last hour, was trembling there now, like a screen just switched off.

I was steadily putting myself outside of a few bottles and thinking of my father. I rarely allowed myself the indulgence. 'Stunning bravery'! 'Significant' and 'artistic'! What a cargo of spherical objects. My father leapt from the Forth Bridge, from the parapet of the permanent way, 156 feet to his death below. Stupidity. Insanity. Fuck all to do with bravery or artistry. No doubt my father imagined it would be a graceful and airy way to end his days, taking off into the blue and joining the angels. It was not. He might as well have jumped 156 feet on to a tarmac road. A gruesome death. His body would have been moving through the air at something like 60 or 70 mph. At the moment of impact, he slowed to zero. His internal organs didn't. They kept going and some of them tore loose. Lacerated liver and heart. The impact broke several ribs and some of them punctured his lungs. Extensive internal bleeding. An agonising death. Fitting for what had become a slow and agonising life.

That cunt Tweedie knew what he was doing, of course. He didn't admire my father. Not at all. But he knew that reminding me of his futile death, a death to which he was driven by mental torment, would play on my mind for a long time. Would eat away at me, as it had been doing, when I let myself think of it, for years. Would creep up on me as it crept up on me when I lay unprotected in sleep.

Chopin went away and something equally poignant came

on – Saint Saens, I think. I was sinking. Drinking myself morose and eating shadows. I woke up at blue o'clock in the morning, shivering and miserable, so I took myself upstairs and put myself very tenderly to bed, where I slept the sleep of the pissed and the despondent until well into the next afternoon.

I mooched around when I finally got up, ate little, smoked plenty, listened to the blues. Damn right I got the blues. Blues ain't nothing but a good man feeling bad. Blues with a feeling – that's what I have today. Okay; riffed on the blues thing long enough.

I needed to solve that Shakespearean conundrum, too. The Love's Labour's thing and the Lucrece quote too. What were they again? *O unseen shame! invisible disgrace!* Yeah. That was blackmail. Had to be. *Thy grace being gain'd cures all disgrace in me.* Oh, for God's sake! So bloody obvious! Why hadn't I seen it before? Grace! Grace being gained cured all disgrace in ... who? In Cairns, the man who was baying the moon for her. That was who. The quotes were Cairns's – Cairns's idea of suave smartarsery to smool a schoolteacher as he blackmailed her. We'd got that completely cock-arsed.

I needed to get a hold of Laura. But she was with her father. My resentment and grudge against Tweedie still smouldered like a dross fire. I wanted to get the ill-bred son of a bastard but good. If I only knew where he was, I'd burn some tarmac up there... Up there! Of course, up there! Where else would he be, but Aberdeen? Site of his first encounter with the Son of God, location of his lucrative dope-mongering. Where else would he go, at least initially? Nowhere fucking else was the answer. Obar Dheathain was the place for me. The Silver City with the Golden Sands. Get going, boy. And stand not upon the order of thy going. By Tummel and Loch Rannoch and Lochaber I would go. Headed for the Northern Lights.

I diverted my landline calls on to the Satanic implement of my cellphone. Then I packed my holdall again, picked up the laptop and left. Afternoon sun. A quiet enough drive. Einaudi on the player to help me mellow down easy. In a couple of hours, I approached Aberdeen on the A90. Not too many heavenly dancers in evidence but, when I crested a rise around Cove Bay, the sun was setting and the lights of the city lay sparkling in the twilit valley like sodium jewels in blue powder.

I found digs in a B&B in Bon Accord Street, off Union Street, the main drag. The landlady, Mrs. Wemyss, was provided by central casting, an axe-faced old crone instantly suspicious of me and my request for a single room for the night, possibly for the next two or three. She accepted my custom, although all the time she accompanied me upstairs and showed me the room, she enumerated the many things I was not allowed to do. I assured her I intended to do not much of anything in her premises, but that I had business in the city which would keep me occupied and out of there most of the time.

"This is a quiet house. There's no playing loud music in your room. Please don't bang the door or rev your car engine outside the house at night. No foodstuffs should be consumed in the room. And, of course, there's no smoking. Please do not bring alcohol into the house. And, if you do go out, please do not return under the influence of alcohol. I won't have that."

"No, I won't be doing any of the above, Mrs. Wemyss. I'm very tired and I will retire early. I'll try not to snore."

She looked at me, wondered briefly if she should just tell me to take my clientele elsewhere, but then continued with her litany. "You're not allowed visitors in your room, Mr. Black. I must stress that."

"That won't arise. And neither will anything else."

"Let me know if you want a bath and I'll put the immersion heater on again."

"I don't need a bath tonight, Mrs. Wemyss," I said.

"Breakfast is served between 7.30 and 9 o'clock."

"Thank you. I look forward to it."

Bon Accord my backside. I eventually jemmied the old hag out of the room and closed the door. A featureless cell. One single bed. A dresser and a chest of drawers. A window with a view of the buckets out the back. I opened the window and was deafened by the Aberdeen Herring Gulls Glee Club. I closed it again. Set up the laptop and Googled in "Aberdeen churches and missions". Over 790,000 sites were listed, so I restricted it to those in the UK, which brought the number down to a more manageable 20,000. I spent half an hour on it and got one or two useful items.

Then I went out and ate a rather good Chinese meal on Union Street, just a stone's throw from the digs. I could have spent a pleasant half an hour doing precisely that. But a glass of cold beer, some Won Tun Soup and a huge portion of Garlic Prawns restored my good nature somewhat. It was probably agin the rules to enter Mrs. Wemyss's establishment with garlic on your breath, but I decided to risk it.

I got back to my booth without incident. I wrote down the names and addresses of the one or two contacts I'd Googled earlier and decided to visit the Grampian carabinieri next morning.

51

Breakfast *chez* the Wemyss beldam was a quiet affair. Apart from one other man reading a paper at a table in the corner, I had the breakfast room to myself. Mrs. Wemyss was no more cordial than she had been on the previous eve. La beldam sans merci, right enough. You could feel the sedge wither from the lake as she put the rack of fawn and cooling toast triangles on the table. I broke my fast on porridge and then a smokie that was good enough at the time but kept coming back on me for the rest of the day, so that I felt I had it for breakfast, lunch and dinner. I couldn't help comparing it to the breakfast I'd had in Sheena's. The contrast could not have been starker. It didn't pan out to old woman Wemyss's advantage, I have to say.

Union Street glittered in the morning sunlight. I like cities. I can't remember the last time I had a holiday but, whenever it was, it was in a city. I'm not one for coating myself in Ambre Solaire and lying on a dune all day. I like to stravaig around the streets of Paris or Amsterdam and see the buildings, see the people. Union Street is an impressive thoroughfare, especially on a bright and sunny morning, full of shops and fine stone buildings, all glinting grey granite in the northern sunlight. I moseyed along it contentedly. Well, it was a while since I'd had a good mosey, and they can't touch you for it. When side streets presented themselves, I was gracious enough to spend some time making their acquaintance. I had a gad up Rose Street, and a daunder up Chapel Street, to say nothing of stravaigs up Summer and Silver Streets. A pleasant morning, with the occasional cigarette. And wilderness were paradise enow.

If you haven't experienced the granite city, then I call it a damned shame. And the glinting grey granite doesn't come any more imposing than in the Rosemount area. Halfway down Union Street, you hang a left along Union Terrace by the gardens and, there in front of you is the elegant curve of Rosemount Viaduct with the Central Library and His Majesty's Theatre. Terribly grand. A fine walk.

I'd a cup of coffee, bought a paper and then walked back

along the other side of Union Street, dipping down the side streets as they came along, meandering in the sunshine and scrutinising things as I went. The Megane was in Crown Street. Just like that. Just there, parked by the kerb as the street curves slightly away from Union Street after Windmill Brae and before it plummets down the hill towards Millburn Street and the Ferryhill area. No-one in it.

There was a space two behind it and I toyed briefly with the notion of returning to Bon Accord Street and bringing my own car to sit in there. But, by the time I'd done that, they might well have been gone. Even if the parking space was still there when I returned. So I took up position in the recess of a restaurant doorway, folded the Hootsmon at the crossword and reviewed the clues. 1 Across. "Fruitless hunt for barnacles and beans"; (4,5,5,). I inked in the solution, 'WILD GOOSE CHASE', and applied my mind to 9 Across: "Prey in an excavation"; (6). Prey in an excavation? Excavation – a dig, a pit, a quarry…

I looked up at the sky to think and, on the way up, my eyes registered a young woman passing. I let my focus fall again and rest on her. Split me, but she was certainly restful on the eye; everything her mother was. It was Laura, of course, looking like a model. Smart coat, rollneck sweater, blue jeans, high heels. Several large designer clothing bags in each hand. There was no sign of her father. Maybe made it easier, I'm not sure. I pushed myself off the wall with my shoulder and stepped out of the doorway. She was maybe two paces down the street, with her back to me. I stood and watched as she arrived at the car, fumbling in her handbag for the keys.

"Hello, Laura," I said.

She looked up, took a second or two to register who I was, then shook her head with a hairpin smile. "I knew it was a bad idea for him to phone you," she said. Then she unlocked the passenger door and put her bags on the seat. "People like you never give up, do you?"

"I'm paid not to," I said.

"So what is it now?"

"Payback time, I'm afraid, Laura."

"Payback for what?"

"Lots of things. Where's your father? Brother Gabriel?"

"I've no idea," she said, and then broke into a run past me.

It was a start and a flash, like some wild animal would give, and it took me utterly by surprise. The expensive heels went flying, one after the other, as she took it on the wing round Windmill Brae.

"Laura! Laura! This is crazy," I called, jogging after her. "You can't get away now! You're gonnae get caught! It's your father we need to find! You're not safe with him!..."

She was gone round the corner and into Union Street. I wasn't for chasing her. I know the steps for dances like these. To the public, I would be the one who looked like the aggressor. Picture it yourself: some pretty young teenager being pursued, even caught, maybe wrestled to the ground, by a thirty-something guy who wasn't the police or a doctor in a white coat. I'd look like a frothing sexual maniac. Some have-a-go hero would bean me with a bag of messages and then pummel me to a pulp on the pavement. What was I going to say? I'm a private eye? Aye, right son. Just you put this back-to-front-jacket on, then bite down on the dog-chew. Already, heads were turning as Laura took off down Union Street and I stopped at the corner, watching her go. She was certainly stepping along. Useless to tail her. There were one or two shopping centres down there – Trinity, is it? St. Nicholas Centre? Something like that. Retail Therapy's not my thing. Once she got in there, she'd be lost.

I made my way back to the Megane. It wasn't locked, but she had the keys with her. The bags were full of the kind of purchases I would expect a teenager to make – tops, dresses, shoes. A small carrier with two books in it – both shortlisted for the Orange prize. That, at least, I approved of. I checked the receipts. Paid in cash, all of it. A total of something like eight hundred and fifty pounds. Daddy was indulging his little girl, and then some. Making up for lost time. Dining on Finnan haddie, her heart belonged to Daddy. And neither wonder – eight and a half C's is a lot of beans in anyone's ready reckoner. I fanned the rest of the vehicle. A handful of receipts in the dash, from eateries, mainly. A tapas bar, A Brewers Fayre, a Chinese. No handbag. No phone. Okay.

The big Pig Parlour in Aberdeen is on Queen Street. I made my way there toot sweet and reported what had happened to the desk sergeant. She was interested enough in my little recitation to ask me to hang on and repeat it to their DS McIntyre.

McIntyre was a thin-faced guy with a number 1 haircut, and a beard and mouser trimmed down to the same stubbly brevity. He listened to me in almost complete silence. There was a female detective there, too, and she asked most of the questions. I told them about the murder of Brian Cairns. I told them about Brother Gabriel and Dominic Tweedie being the same man. I told them about his influence on the cult of the New Dawn, and told them what I knew of how the Angels had died. I told them that Laura was his daughter. I gave them a description of Laura as I'd seen her half an hour previously. And I described Tweedie, as he was the last time I'd seen him, and mentioned that he had been nowhere in the wings during the recent action. Brer Gabriel, he lie low.

Finally, McIntyre nodded and asked where I was staying. I gave him the address of old Wemyss's B&B for Quiet and Contemplative Gentlefolk. Then he asked me to stick around Bon Accord Street and undertook to give me the wire when developments occurred. He had no doubt his officers would pick up the young lady, and no doubt that she would lead them to where her father was bivouacked. His colleagues in Lothian and Borders F would be notified when she was lifted. As would the Tayside brethren. After that, I could dangle, as far as he was concerned.

The afternoon passed like a week in the jail. I lay on my bed – with my shoes off, just in case Mrs. Wemyss had a pillory out the back for men who dirtied their candlewicks – and completed the crosswords of the Scotsman, the Herald, the Press and Journal and the Guardian. Then I lay on my back, with my hands clasped behind my head, and alternately dozed and tried to remember as much of Hamlet as I could. I'd got as far as 'So lust, though to a radiant angel linked, Will sate itself in a celestial bed, And prey on garbage' when my mobile started to shake, rattle and roll.

"Mr. Black? This is DS McIntyre. Hi. We have apprehended Laura McGuire. She's in custody in Queen Street station as we speak. As yet, we have been unable to get any information from her as to the whereabouts of this Dominic Tweedie. We have, however, been in contact with Lothian and Borders Police, and with Tayside Police and I understand that representatives from those forces will be with us in Aberdeen tomorrow."

"Can I ask, DS McIntyre, will it be DI Saunders of Lothian and Borders who comes up?"

"I couldn't say, Mr. Black. I know that it was DI Saunders that our DI Stewart spoke to."

"Right."

I gleaned a little more. Uniforms, one male, one female, had collared the kid about an hour after she'd given me the breeze up on Crown Street. They'd gone round the shoe shops. Routine Plod work. And they'd hoovered the Megane off Crown Street, too. He rang off after that. So... the game was afoot, after all. If I was reading this right – and it was by no means a large print issue here – they'd let Bert or whoever from Lothian interview Laura. That meant I had to get a hold of Bertie boy and keep myself in the loop. I was on the pop of squeezing his number out when my mobile rang again.

I opened it up and said "Hello."

"Mr. Black?"

"Yes."

"This is Alistair McKechnie of Tayside Police."

"Ah, how are you, Sergeant?"

"I am well. Thank you for asking. It may interest you to know that our colleagues in Grampian have discovered Laura McGuire."

"I know, Sergeant."

"You know?"

"Absolutely. Sergeant, it so falls out that I am actually in Aberdeen at the moment. DS McIntyre has just phoned me with the news."

"He has?"

"Aye. I came up here on a hunch. I was sure Tweedie and the girl would be here. I came up for a couple of days' scouting around."

"My, my. A stroke of genius on your part, Mr. Black."

"Well, I'll be a little more modest. A stroke of inspiration, perhaps."

"Well, we have been invited, because of the connection with the New Dawn community. DCI Baird wants myself to travel to Aberdeen with one of our CID officers. He was wondering if you would help us out again, Mr. Black. A matter of identification. He supposed you to be in West Lothian but, since you are already in Aberdeen, perhaps that makes things a little easier."

"Of course."

"So, joining us tomorrow is a possibility?"

"Of course."

"We will be in Queen Street station at two o'clock."

"Ah. Right. See you then, then."

"Tomorrow, then, Mr. Black. Many thanks."

I clicked the phone off. This was the Story of the Three Wells. Well, well, well. There's none so blind as he who will not see. Or, as John Mayall once sang, Burn Out Your Blind Eyes. It had taken me a long time, but I was on the right track eventually. I opened the line again and phoned Bert Saunders's private number.

"Saunders of the River Almond," I greeted him when he answered

"Hello, Seamus. How you diddling?"

"Going to Aberdeen tomorrow?"

"I am. How did you know?

"Just had McKechnie of the Beautiful Silvery Polis on the horn."

"Want a lift?"

"No need, flatfoot. I'm here already."

I went through the explanations again, enjoying the sense of having been right and having beaten Bert to the punch on this one. We arranged to meet at the Queen Street ham curers and then I hung up. I treated myself to a night at the pictures. I watched a completely mindless action movie in the Belmont, had two pints in the Rosemount Bar on Union Street and even managed to get into Castle Wemyss afterwards without awaking Cerberus. And then I had a full and refreshing night of gathering zigzags.

52

Bert was with DS Emma Wood. Over lunch in the police refectory, I filled him on recent developments. Told him about my interview with Charlene McRobb and that I had formulated the near certainty that the one who had greased Brian Cairns was none other than the runaway daughter, Laura McGuire. That would account for why her mother had sent me off on the wild goose chase to Eden in the first place. Laura had gone to join the New Dawn to get away from the scene of the crime. So that it might look more natural and even less to do with her daughter being a murderer, Grace McGuire came to me with the distressed and bewildered mother act. Bringing my attention to the fact that her daughter had done something untypical of her would deflect suspicion. It was a sharp notion, I had to admit.

"Why would she kill Brian Cairns, though?" asked Bert, forking a boiled murphy and coating it in gravy.

"The way he was crawling after her mother. It was getting unpleasantly hot. I suspect he had threatened blackmail. I think the lines from Shakespeare were in his wallet because he was going to use it against Grace McGuire. I don't think it was put there after he was killed. I'm sure I read that completely wrong, right from the jump. There was a bit of snobbishness there. Why shouldn't a builder look up a line of Shakespeare? He probably thought it was a neat notion to put the bite on an English teacher with a line of the Swan."

"He might at that," said Bert.

"Did you pull those two in?"

"The boys are on it. If what you say is true, then we can nail them for perverting the course of justice. Both of them."

"Yep. Both. They were both in on it, I'm sure."

The interrogation room was small. You don't get many spacious interrogation rooms, or two interrogation rooms knocked through to make one big one. In it there was a table, bolted to the floor, and four chairs. Laura McGuire sat in one. She was wearing the dark roll-neck sweater and jeans. Her hair was brushed back from her face and put up in combs at the side. She wore no make-up. She looked like the art student that she might soon have been, had other things not intervened. Facing her, sat Bert, Emma Wood and the Tayside detective, a female DS Walker. There was a tape recorder on the desk and a video camera in the corner of the room. It was via this video link that I watched the proceedings in an adjoining room. The picture was not perfect; it was black and white and slightly angled. The picture rolled every so often. But it allowed me and some of the Grampian cops to follow the interrogation. Bert started the tape and began to speak.

"This is DI Robert Saunders and DS Emma Wood, Lothian and Borders Police, interviewing Laura McGuire in Queen Street police station, Aberdeen. It is 10.30 a.m. Also present is DS Elizabeth Walker of Tayside police. No legal representative present, at the suspect's request. Will you please state your full name, your age and your place of residence…"

I listened and watched as Laura gave the information as calmly as when I spoke to her in Eden. She was a cucumber, and no mistake. I'm no psychiatrist, but I've met psychopaths before, and I was pretty convinced I was watching one now. Little or no emotion. Flat, almost expressionless tone of voice. Nothing seemed to arouse her or annoy her. In fact, she looked inexpressibly bored by the proceedings.

"Laura," said Bert, "how well did you know the builder Brian Cairns?"

"I don't know any builders."

"Oh, I think you might have known this one. He and your mother shared a common interest."

"Did they? I wouldn't know."

"How well do you get on with your mother, Laura?" said Emma.

"I don't," replied Laura. "Not particularly."

"Why is that?"

"She has no interest in me. She has no interest in anyone, actually. Apart from herself."

"There must be some family affection there, surely," persisted Emma. "Mother and daughter?"

"She hasn't actually neglected me, or abused me. I'll give

her that."

"She has encouraged you to go on to university," said Bert. "Brought you up. Educated you."

"She has, yeah," retorted Laura drily. "Makes her look good. Must keep up appearances."

"Other than that, you claim there is no real warmth between you?" said Emma.

"Not much."

"Interestingly, your father, Joe McGuire, has stated that he thinks you two are really close."

"Does he? Dad always tries to see the upside. Always did. With everything."

"How is your mother on the subject of your love life?" asked Emma.

"I don't have one."

"But, in the past... How has your mother behaved towards boyfriends?"

"I haven't had all that many."

"Nonetheless. How has she been with them?" Laura shrugged. "Has she been protective of you? Over-protective, even? Or has she been quite relaxed about the situation?"

"Neither, really."

"Specifically. When you started going out with Billy McPartland, how did she feel about that?"

"She didn't like it. She tried to stop it."

"Why was that?"

"Because she thought Billy was rough and common. A threat."

"To you?"

"Bit of that," Laura shrugged. "Mainly to her image as a teacher."

"Did she dislike his membership of the Orange Order?"

"Partly. But he was loud and thick, over and above that. So he was 'beneath' her."

A pause of a few seconds was interrupted by Bert. "Not a shred of that is the truth, Laura, is it?"

Laura looked at him with withering contempt.

"Isn't it?"

"Isn't it the truth that Billy McPartland is your mother's

lover rather than yours, and...?"

"Hah!"

"And that they regularly take part in the sexual practice known as 'dogging', where they met a man by the name of Brian Cairns?"

"No idea..."

"And this man Cairns started to blackmail your mother?"

"No idea what you're talking about."

"And you killed him to put an end to it?"

"Me? That's ridiculous."

"You didn't kill him?"

"I never killed anyone. And if you're going to start accusing me of murder, I'm going to insist on a lawyer being present after all."

"We'll arrange one for you right away."

Bert nodded towards the camera. Emma took over, changed tack after an intense few seconds' staring.

"Laura. Why did you leave home and join the New Dawn cult?"

"I needed something in my life. I knew my life wasn't going where it should and I decided to do something about it."

"You found God?"

"Yes."

"Why didn't you just find him in the church in Armadale?" asked Bert.

With a characteristic sneer, Laura answered, "Because the church in Armadale, along with the community in Armadale, and the life in Armadale, was something I was trying to get away from."

But why specifically the New Dawn? Was it because the man you believe to be your natural father was its leader?"

"Yes."

"Tell us about him," Emma urged her.

"Where is he now?" Bert said quickly.

"I've no idea."

"You've no idea? Didn't you leave the Eden estate together at the time of the fire there? Or just before it?"

"Just before it, yes."

"And have you been together since then?"

"Yes."

"But you don't know where he is now?"

"No. He has meetings." She took a breath, sniffed and went on . "We stayed in a hotel. The Atholl..."

DS McIntyre, next to me, tipped his chair back and spoke quietly to a WPC. "Check it."

She left.

"... a big, old-fashioned sort of place. Big rooms. Old staircases and that. Victorian maybe. I liked it. It was quiet and the food was excellent. We checked out and spent last night in somebody's house."

"Whose house?"

"Don't know. Couple called Philip and Martha. They were friends of my father's from before."

"Surnames?"

She shrugged.

"Where was this house?"

"I don't know. I don't know Aberdeen at all. Ten minutes' drive from the hotel."

"And where is your father now?"

"Like I said, he told me he had a couple of meetings. We would meet up for lunch. Move on."

"Where for lunch?"

"That Chinese in Crown Street."

"That's twenty four hours ago. He must be frantic to know where you are by now."

"I doubt it."

"Why would you doubt it?"

"He doesn't get frantic."

We watched them probe her on the relationship with Tweedie, and what they had done since the fall of Eden. They were getting nowhere. I stood up and stretched my back. McIntyre looked at me.

"Cool one," he said.

"Aye. I'm off to snatch a gasp. Okay?"

"Sure."

Outside, I sparked up a burn and sucked the first draw down to my toes. Let's further think of this. Where was the old bastard? Doing what? Was he thinking of his daughter at all? Where would he be?

When I fanned the Megane, had there been any clues as to where he might have gone? What had there been? Not much. The togs. The tomes. The till rolls. The till rolls! The goddamn receipts... What was the name of that bloody eatery? Brewers Fayre! Those places were usually next door to hotels and things, weren't they? Bloody things, what were they called? Premier Inns, was it? Travelodges! Travelodges, yeah.

I spun a quick about-turn and spoke to the guy at the desk.

"Is there a Travelodge in the city?"

"Aye, two or three. There's one in Bridge Street here. One out on the Inverurie road... Bucksburn Manor..."

"Any of them got a Brewers Fayre nearby?"

He pursed his brow. "Bucksburn, I think. Got a Beefeater or a Brewers or one of these..."

"Cheers!"

Gone like a cool breeze.

53

The blade on reception was another one straight from Central Casting: mid thirties, peroxide blonde hair sprayed into a spun sugar basket, more cake than Gregg's, a red blazer with whiffy armpits that she disguised with cheap cologne. She looked up as I entered and plastered on the hypocrite grin that she'd learned at some Staff Development day. I was toting my laptop like a regular desk jockey.

"Good morning, sir."

"Morning. My name is Gerry Lawson. I'm here to pick up a colleague of mine, a Mr. Dominic Tweedie? I believe he may be travelling with a junior colleague."

She flicked her eye over the book.

"Yes sir. Does Mr. Tweedie know you will be picking him up?"

"He ought to," I laughed. "He set up the meeting with the MD himself. Ah – is this him?"

The door to the corridor opened and a man in a suit came out. It wasn't him.

"Never mind. What room is he in?"

The girl leant towards the phone.

"I'll tell him you're here, Mr. Lawson."

"No, don't bother. There are one or two things I've to run over with him." I patted the laptop.

"Of course, sir." She flung on the simper. "Mr. Tweedie is in Room 24. Second floor."

"Muchibus thankibus," I cheesed back at her and went.

Up on the second floor, there was a little woman with a trolley of bedding and cleaning materials. She was busy at Room 23. I approached 24 in a cartoon creep, lifting and placing my feet on the toes, undulating my shoulders. She stopped rattling her brush and pail and watched my impression of Goofy.

"Have you done my brother's room yet?" I hissed a whisper at her, nodding at 24.

She shook her head silently. I placed my ear to the door and listened for a moment. Nothing.

"You got a key?" I whispered.

"Can't do it," she said. "More than my job's worth."

"Aw. It's his birthday," I said and patted the laptop case again.

She shrugged slightly. I put the case on the deck and plucked a tenner from my wallet. I held it up, tipped my head meaningfully.

"It's the next one you're doing, isn't it?"

She looked round, shrugged again, then stepped forward, unlocked 24, relieved me of the banknote and was back rattling her tins of Vim before you could say 'venal'.

I slipped through the door. The curtains were drawn. The light was dim. The air was stuffy. Silence. Tweedie was lying on the bed, fully dressed apart from his shoes. He was as dead as dogshit.

54

Back at the nick, plots had been thickening too. By the time I got back there, having summoned the North East's finest to the deathbed of the Patriarch, all shit had broken loose. Bert met me and armed me back out the front door.

"Smoke time."

We lit up and smoked as we walked. Then leant our arses against a wall and talked. From one angle the police HQ is a brutalist block of a building, a concrete and glass shoebox with masts and coms dishes for roof garnish. We stood and looked at this inspiring vista as we talked.

"What's up, Doc?" I asked Bert.

"Her fucking mother's turned up."

"Grace?"

"Yeah. Fucking Jim Bryce pulled her yesterday back home, gave her the grill. Haven't heard how it went yet. Now she's fucking up here!"

"Lover boy with her?"

"Nah, don't think so. She phoned the daughter yesterday. Now she's up, demanding to see her."

"So what's happening now?"

"She's seeing her. They cut the interview short and took the lassie back to the cells. And now it's the family re-union. Lawyer on the way."

"One place round; change," I said.

"Aye, fucking right."

"Might be Endgame here, Bertie boy."

"Mair likely, it's just complicated things."

"Old Endgame," I said. "Lost of old, play and lose and have done with losing."

Bert scowled at me. "I wish to fuck you'd forget that Shakespeare shit sometimes," he groused.

"Shakespeare!" I said. "Did that sound like Shakespeare to you, ya tin-eared fuck? It was Beckett."

"Who cares? They're going to want you to formally ID Tweedie."

"Me?"

"You're the only one apart from the girl who's seen him

recently."

"Yeah, I guess."

"Same MO as Cairns?"

"Yeah, looks that way. The old mashed cranium."

"Lassie's a stick-on now."

"Should be."

A stiff on a slab is a stiff on a slab is a stiff on a slab. As Gertrude Stein would have said, if she hadn't been so hung up on roses. It may bear a superficial resemblance to a human being that once walked around and did regular everyday things like eating, working, reading the paper, having a shit and a haircut. But that's it. It's a stiff. Dead as mutton. Cold as any stone, as Shakey says.

Dominic Tweedie, Brother Gabriel, was just another stiff when they pulled back the cover. His hair was shorter and he'd shaved off the soup-strainer but it was him. He had that cheesy complexion that many stiffs have but the features were unmistakable. He didn't look too patriarchal or archangelic now, though. Just another cadaver, ready for planting. Like I said to Bert, the back of his head had been customised to let in some of the great outdoors. I nodded and the cover was replaced.

"That is Dominic Tweedie, sometime known as Brother Gabriel, the Patriarch of the religious cult, the New Dawn," I said.

"A West Lothian man?" asked DS McIntyre.

"Originally," I agreed. "Linlithgow, I think."

"Forensic history, that you know of?"

"I'm not sure," I confessed. "But there must be some."

I told them of the *Flash* computers fiasco, the disco fiasco and mentioned the distinct possibility of assorted other fiascos. And adverted, of course, to the immolation of the angels of the New Dawn.

"It looks like he escaped a culpable homicide rap," I said in conclusion.

55

I sat in the lounge area of Queen Street nick with Bert and Emma. They served a rather reasonable cup of java there. I'd had about four and a fistful of fags to accompany each one, while we waited to see what the Gramps would do with the Case of the Pulverised Patriarch. It looked very much like the bold Laura had struck again. Same M.O. Same result. A perforated heid.

"Why do you think she's done this geezer up here?" said Bert. "Her father?"

"Any one of a number of reasons. Maybe he tried it on with her. He's enough of a creep. And sex-obsessed. She might have creamed him for that. More likely, though, it could be because he deserted the mother after she was pregnant."

"You reckon?"

"Folk have killed for less," Emma pointed out.

"Oh aye, that's for sure. But ..."

"This lassie is only close to her mother. She doesn't care for anybody else. If she felt blackmail was insulting towards her, she might well feel that desertion was even more so."

DI Stewart of Grampian police sat down beside us. "Her mother has confessed to murdering the builder in West Lothian," he said.

Bert looked at me.

"Veri interesting," I said.

"Bound to get a result now," said Bert. "Think it was her, Seamus?"

"Na, not a chance," I said. "This is a play to haul the kid out of the gurgler. There's no way Grace McGuire did it."

"Why not?"

"Because the one who killed Cairns killed Tweedie. Bet the mortgage on that. And only one person up here killed the Archangel Gabriel. It wasn't the lovely Grace."

"Well, she should be interviewed about it, of course," said Stewart.

"Aye," said Bert.

"Do everybody a favour," I suggested. "Tell Laura that her mother has coughed. I think we'll see a different routine from her if you do."

Stewart sparked up too and asked Bert what he thought about the similarities between the murders.

"Well," said Bert, "it certainly seems to be the same M.O. Jack here is the one who has the case all worked out. He was hired by the girl's mother to find out why she had absconded and landed up with the New Dawn in Eden."

"A stall," I said.

"A ruse, of course, as we now think," agreed Bert. "It looks like a nap that Laura McGuire is responsible for your murder, tae. She was hidin' out among the New Dawn. Her mother hirin' Jack to investigate her flight was an attempt to throw us off the scent."

"But why the New Dawn, specifically?" wondered Stewart.

"There's a suggestion," I said, taking over, "that Brother Gabriel, or Dominic Tweedie, was her natural father. Maybe the flight from justice was combined with an attempt to forge a relationship with a long lost parent."

"Did this Gabriel fellow *know* he was her father?"

"Almost certainly not. He may have known he *had* a child somewhere, but I'm sure he had no idea who it was. However, I got a phone call from him not long before he died."

"Yeah? What was the call about?"

"To let me know he was extremely displeased at how I'd screwed things up for him. And to issue a vague threat. That we would meet again. No doubt, he would have a pleasant surprise lined up for me. Anyway, the point is that, during this call, he said to me that Laura 'claimed' to be his natural daughter. That's how he put it. Whether or not he believed her, I don't know."

"He didn't say where he was, or whether the girl was with him?"

"No. I asked him both questions. He said she wasn't physically with him at the time. I gathered she was in the neighbourhood."

"Okay. We'll grill her again in an hour or so. Want to hang around for it?"

"You can bet your bollocks to a barn dance."

56

I was right. This time round, Laura was quite different. I watched in the adjoining room. Emma asked her again what sort of relationship she had with her mother, given the fact that Grace had driven all the way up to Aberdeen and had spent the last hour embracing Laura and soothing away all them cares and woe.

"Laura," Emma said. "Would you describe your relationship with your mother, Grace McGuire, as close?"

"Very close."

"So not at all the ... distant one you described to us earlier."

"No."

"And, when you first talked to the private investigator, Mr. Black, in Eden, you gave him the distinct impression that yours was not a particularly affectionate relationship."

"Yes."

"Similarly, when your mother hired him, she was at pains to point out that your relationship was not particularly close."

"Yes."

"Why was that?"

"It was the plan we had agreed. Well, actually, it was the plan that she had agreed with Billy."

"Billy being...?"

"Billy McPartland, her lover."

"And a former boyfriend of your own?"

She shook her head. "No. That was a lie. I was never in a relationship with Billy McPartland. Or anybody else for that matter."

"So why were you and your mother, and Billy too, so keen to have Mr. Black believe that you and he had been an item?" asked Bert.

"Because that would give me a motive, among other things, for running away."

"So you have never been Billy McPartland's girlfriend?"

"No."

"How long has Billy been your mother's lover?"

"About a year, I suppose."

"And how do you feel about that?"

She shrugged and said nothing. I watched the screen, mesmerised. I wouldn't have wanted to have been in that little head, not for all the china in Wedgwood.

"You shrug your shoulders," said Emma Wood. "Does that mean you don't care? Or that you don't think very much of the arrangement?"

"It's her life. I wouldn't have anything to do with him. He's a moron. A ned. But that's the sort of thing she gets herself into."

"What do you mean by that?"

"Just that. She likes to be attractive to men. Even men like that."

"Does that anger you?"

"No. I'm not angry about it. It disappoints me. But I'm not angry at my mother. She's a wonderful woman. There's nobody like her."

"Laura," said Bert, "do you know what 'dogging' means?"

"Well, it can mean several things."

"Are you aware of the sexual connotations of the word?"

"Yes."

"Would that be part of what you called 'the sort of thing' your mother gets into?"

She looked down at her upturned fingernails, but only for the briefest of moments, before answering clearly. "Yes."

"Did Billy McPartland introduce the idea to your mother?"

She shook her head. "It's how she met him."

"And what do you think of it?"

"I despise it. It's playing right into men's fantasies. And doing that kind of thing gets her involved with all sorts of lowlifes."

"Lowlifes like Billy McPartland?"

"For one."

"And Brian Cairns?" Emma said quietly.

"Yes."

"What do you know about Brian Cairns?"

"Not much. A little. I know that he was a builder. And that

he went dogging. I know that he started to stalk my mother. Developed an obsession about her. That's the kind of men you meet dogging."

Then, all at once, on Bert's prompt, she coughed her guts up. Said she had twice overheard her mother and the Buhll discussing how Brian Cairns was obsessing about Grace. They sat in the conservatory on warm nights and talked about stuff like that, assuming Laura was upstairs at her studies. The first time, she overheard Billy saying he was going to kill 'the cunt'. She thought it showed just how he was eaten away with jealousy. Grace was trying to calm him down, saying that it didn't matter, it wasn't all that important. Grace said there were always people who screwed things up, no matter how hard you tried to prevent it. She told Billy that there was no danger of her ever agreeing to go out with this man, or do anything else with him. She was trying to reassure the meathead that he was the only guy for her. Eventually, Billy calmed down and just started to take the piss out of the guy.

"And was that all that was said?"

"That time, yes."

Emma took over again, reminded Laura that she'd spoken about two occasions. Laura said that, the second time, it was obvious to her that Grace was genuinely concerned about things. She had been getting phone calls. And letters, Laura thought. But she couldn't be sure. She never saw them, only over heard her mother refer to them in her conversations with Billy. She thought that Cairns was threatening to show Grace up in some way if she didn't agree to go out with him. The Buhll was going ballistic, roaring and screaming about what he would do to 'that bastard builder', if he got a hold of him.

When Emma asked what happened then, Laura said she went into the conservatory and asked them what was going on. At first Grace said it was nothing, that it was a storm in a teacup, nothing to concern Laura. Billy said 'Nuhun a dae wi' *yew'* or something equally articulate. Then Laura sat down opposite her mother and said Grace *had* to tell her; she was he daughter. If some man was sexually fixated on her and was threatening to expose her, they had to do something about it. Grace had some standing in the town. They couldn't afford to let anybody take that away from them.

At first, they had looked at her as if she had just appeared out a hole in the ground. Then Grace told her the whole deal: that she and Billy were doggers and that Cairns had started to get kinky about Grace. That Billy, being just a few generations down from the trees, had threatened violence. That Cairns had then tried a different plan, phoning Grace and threatening to expose her. He knew a journalist and shit like that.

Bert asked if they, all three, had made any plans to deal with the situation. Laura said they hadn't. But she had thought about it all night, couldn't sleep for trying to think of a way to get back at the man who was giving her mother such a hard time.

Bert looked at her. "And did you come up with any ideas?"

"It was easy, really."

"Tell us."

"I got his works number in the book. When I phoned, I got his receptionist. I asked if I could please speak to Mr. Brian Cairns. She asked me my name and what it was in connection with. I told her my name was McGuire and he would know what it was in connection with. She put me through to him."

"And?"

"I told I wanted to talk to him and he said he would phone me back in ten minutes. He took my mobile number. I knew he was going to call from his own mobile. Get out of the office and get some privacy. He was excited about the idea. I could hear it in his voice."

"And he phoned you back?"

"He did. In five minutes. He must have got out of the office and driven round the corner or something."

"What did you say to him?"

"I told him that my mother was very interested in him. But she couldn't afford to take any chances, with Billy being the way he is. He said he could understand that. And I said, but there must be a way they could get together without Billy knowing, and maybe he and I should meet up and see if we could find a way out of it. Then I said that my mother had told me he was a very attractive man himself, and that he liked younger women. I implied that I would be very interested in meeting him for my own satisfaction, if for no other reason. Ha ha."

She laughed a short, humourless and bitter laugh. A dry laugh. A vindictive one.

"And did this plan work?" Bert asked.

"Like a charm. Men are so gullible when it comes to sex. All you have to do is pander to their ego and give them a suggestion of getting their hands on flesh. Easy."

"So tell us where you met him."

"He suggested the old grounds at Bangour Village. I drove there and he was there already. He suggested the walk. I don't know why. Maybe it was an added refinement he had in mind. So we walked down this wee path."

"When was this?"

"The Sunday evening."

"So – the … 12th?"

"Whatever."

"Were you talking about the situation with your mother?"

She shook her head. "He never mentioned it once. He was full of himself, trying to come on to me. Saying I was extremely attractive, even more beautiful than my mother, if that were possible. Asking me if I preferred older men. He said he knew that some young women, especially more intelligent young women, liked older men. All that crap."

"And you hit him?"

"Yes. He turned away – a bird made a noise in the trees, I think. And I thumped him on the back of the head."

"With what?"

"An axe. There are some tools in the shed at the back of the conservatory. I got the axe from there. Concealed it under my top, stuck in the top of my jeans at the back. When he looked away, I hit him."

"How many times?"

"I don't remember. A lot. He screamed the first time and fell over. I just knelt on his back and thumped and thumped him. It was like splitting sticks."

"What did you do with the axe?"

"I took it away with me. Dumped it in a skip. Round the back of some industrial units in Bathgate. Covered it over with the rubbish that was already in there."

"Where in Bathgate?" asked Bert.

"Behind the Regal."

"You must have been covered in blood."

"I was. I walked back to the car. I had a change of clothes in the boot. I stripped off and put on the fresh clothes. Put the messy ones in a plastic bag in the boot. Drove off. There was nobody about to see me."

"But you must have had blood on your face and hands."

"Nobody can see that when you're driving a car. It was getting dark by the time I was driving back."

"Was anyone at home when you got back?"

"My mother. She screamed when she saw my face. It must have been covered in blood. I told her what I'd done."

"And how did she react to that?"

"She got hysterical. Crying, shivering, shouting at me that I was a bloody fool. She shouted at me to get a shower. When I came out of the shower, I was all cleaned up. She calmed down a bit then."

Silence.

"A little water clears us of this deed," I said half to myself.

"I hate Shakespeare," said a female tec. "We had to do *Macbeth* for Higher. I hated it."

"And now it's being acted out before your very eyes," I said, concentrating on the TV.

Bert said, "And when did you hatch out the plan to come up north?"

"That night. My mother phoned Billy at his work. He was nightshift. He came out the next morning and we talked it through."

"Tell me what you decided."

"I should get away from the area completely. Eden seemed the obvious place, what with my father and everything. Mum said she would try to wrong-foot the police by going to that man Black and hiring him to find out if I was okay, as if I'd run away and done something right out of character. We weren't sure that anybody would associate me and Cairns but it might have come out about Mum and the dogging. Then Mum and Billy agreed that they should try and make Billy look suspicious. That would take attention away from me again. And Billy had cast-iron alibis for the whole week. Nightshift at work. Visiting his own mother and various pals during the day, going to the pub, going to the flute band rehearsals – all that."

"You happy with all those plans? Did you agree to them all?"

"I thought Black was a bad idea. These idiots never give up. My mother's been calling me on my mobile, telling me about his rooting around."

"Blame your mother for involving him," said Emma.

"So you killed Brian Cairns with an axe in the grounds of Bangour Village Hospital, on the night of the twelfth of August?" said Bert.

"Yeah."

"Interview terminated..."

DS McIntyre scraped his chair back. "Just like that, eh?"

"Sang a different song that time," said the Macbeth hating tec.

"A mother's love's a blessing," I said.

Bert and I sauntered up the afternoon streets, smoking, taking the air and talking things over. Then we'd a coffee and a sticky bun in a café.

"Miss McGuire's a composed little bitch, isn't she?" said Bert.

"Yeah. Unflappable, I would say. Nothing touches her. Her schoolmate says she's like that at school, too. Very detached. Doesn't let any of them get close to her. Except this Charlene one. And only sometimes with her."

"Psycho."

"I think so. The only one she feels anything for is the mother. What we got here, Bertie boy, is a younger and female version of Norman Bates."

Bert immediately gave his award-winning Anthony Perkins imitation: "Mother! Oh God, mother! Blood! Blood!"

I laughed. A young couple sitting opposite looked at him and then raised their eyebrows at each other.

"Well, after all," I said. "A boy's best friend is his

mother."

"Twelve cabins; twelve vacancies," countered Bert.

"We all go a little mad sometimes."

"I don't set a fancy table but my kitchen's awful homey."

"Okay," I said, "enough with the quotations, already."

57

This time, it was McIntyre and Elizabeth Walker of Tayside interrogating Laura. They started by asking her about the events of the night of the 19th, the night that Eden had been torched. Laura said she wasn't there, that she and Tweedie had left the afternoon before. She had been sewing in the little cabin with Sister Margaret when Brother Ira came in and told her to go to her cabin until further notice. He didn't say why. This was mid afternoon. Three or four time. Asked if she heard anything like gunfire, she said categorically not. Nothing like that.

When she got to her cabin, her biological father was there. The Patriarch. He told her to pack up her belongings and go with him. Didn't say where. He simply said that he had important business which would mean he would be away from Eden for the foreseeable future. Since she was his daughter, he wanted her to accompany him. He hadn't known about her for 18 years. Now he didn't want to be out of her company any more than he had to be.

"How did he know you were his daughter?"

"I told him. That private investigator Black had been up in Eden, footering around like we thought he would, after my mother hired him. I thought it best to make myself known to the Patriarch."

They left Eden in her maroon Megane. She'd asked him why not take the sports job but he told her it would be better to take hers. It would be less conspicuous. And they drove to Aberdeen. The first night, they stayed in the Athol – what she called "a big hotel in the centre of town." They had separate rooms. She did not do much. Got bored. Her father told her he had to go out on business, though he never specified what kind of business. He gave her money to go and buy clothes and books. They moved out of the Athol the next day. Tweedie told her it was a 'tactical necessity' to move out of the centre of Aberdeen. They moved to what she called 'a wee travel place'. In the middle of nowhere. Nothing to do, nowhere to go, nobody to see.

"Did your father go out during the day here, too?" asked

DS Walker.

"No. He stayed in. We both did."

"Right. Did you fall out about something?" continued Walker.

She took a sip from a glass of water on the table, like a celebrity being interviewed for a magazine programme, before answering. "Yes. I asked him about my mother. About how he felt about her. He said he couldn't remember her all that well. I asked him if he knew she was pregnant with me at the time."

"And what did he say?"

"He said he heard that, but a lot later. He only was with her on three or four occasions, he said.

"Is that true?"

"It's what my mother says," said Laura.

"Go on."

"He said he didn't know she was pregnant. Then I asked him if he thought he'd deserted her. And he said no. They were two mature, intelligent people and they both knew what they were doing. He was surprised my mother wasn't on the pill or took some precautions. Not a word about taking any himself."

"Is that why you felt angry with him?" asked DC Walker.

"Partly. It was getting worse. He started to talk about my mother. 'Wee Grace' he called her. He said she was really into sex when she was young. She couldn't get enough of it, he said. He said she had the body of an angel and the soul of a devil."

She stopped, looking ahead. Over their heads at the wall. Re-living it. But she didn't flare up or betray any other sign of emotion. She simply paused for a while.

"Cool bitch," whispered Bert, as we watched. I nodded. Said nothing.

Then Laura had a second sip of water and resumed. "He said that my mother was fonder of him than he was of her. More than that. She had a fixation about him. She wouldn't leave him in peace. And eventually that was what drove him away. He needed to be free to be with other people if he wanted. He was sorry to hear that she was pregnant, later. But he just couldn't be doing with the possessiveness and the angry scenes. He said she got to be a pain in the backside. It got so that he was glad to be shot of her."

She stopped again. For a longer time. Eventually, Walker spoke.

"What did you say to him about all that?"

"Mmm?" She snapped out of a reverie. "Oh, nothing, really. He just sat there with that inane grin on his face – the Patriarchal one? And all the while he was saying these terrible things about my mother. He asked me if he'd hurt my feelings. I said no. I was just interested in everything about them. When they were young. How they got together and how they got on when they *were* together. That sort of thing. He said, 'Yeah. I understand. It's a natural feeling. A natural feeling.' And not once did he ask about her. Not once did he ask how she was doing, or whether she was married, or how the two of us got on together. Not once. No interest in that. No interest in her. Or in me."

"And what happened?"

"At the end? Oh. He said he was going to have an hour's nap in his room. I sat and thought about what he'd said about my mother. And I thought about what he'd said to that man Black. He'd told Black I wasn't there but I was. I was in the room and I listened to it all. But I was *never* really there for him, in a way. He had no feelings for the New Dawn or anybody else, either. I thought about it a long time. Then I went down to the car and brought up that metal thing for changing tyres or something, what's it called?"

"A wheel brace?" suggested McIntyre.

"Yeah. That, probably. It's a big metal pipe shaped thing."

"Yep. A wheel brace."

"I brought it upstairs and I sat in my room for a quarter of an hour."

"What did you do for that quarter of an hour?" asked Walker.

"I watched the TV with the sound down. Let him fall asleep."

"And then…?"

"I went next door to his room. He was sound asleep on the bed. He was facing away from the door. He didn't wake up or turn round. And I hit him with the wheel brace. The first one nearly broke my hand and he kind of moaned and tried to move. But I hit him – twice more? Twice more, I think … And he kind of shuddered and lay there. And then I just hit him and hit him and hit him till his head was all caved in."

They let a silence follow. It was so profound I swear I could hear the tape turn in the machine. DS McIntyre shifted in his seat and spoke quietly. "Did you know he was dead?"

"Of course."

"What did you do after that?"

"After that? I took his wallet off the bedside table, and I left him where he was and I locked his room door. Put the 'Do Not Disturb' sign on the door handle. Then went back to my room. There was nobody in the corridor. I stripped and showered all the blood and yuck off. I put my stained clothes in a plastic bag. I dressed and dried my hair. I put the brace thing in another plastic bag and put that in the first bag. Then I went out, with the plastic bags."

"Did anybody see you go out?" asked McIntyre.

"Yes. The girl on the desk smiled."

"What did you do?"

"I drove to the harbour and I dropped the stuff in the water."

"Did nobody see you do that?"

"No. I strolled about the docks till I got to a place where nobody else was about. I kind of slipped in behind a boat so that I was out of sight. I found a big stone and put that in, and then I dropped it in the water. Then I strolled away again."

"Have you no regrets about killing your father?"

"He wasn't my father. In every sense of the word, apart from the biological one, Joe McGuire is my father. Dominic Tweedie was another vain, self-centred man. He insulted my mother. He belittled her. I couldn't let him do that."

McIntyre let the tape run for a few seconds and then said, "Interview terminated at 3.05."

Bert stood up and stretched. None of us in the little room had said anything while the interrogation was going on.

"Cool as fuck," observed Bert.

"Chilling," agreed Emma Wood.

"She was like that when I spoke to her in Eden," I said. "You'd think butter wouldn't melt…"

"Yeah," agreed Bert. "They're often like that. Looks like you were right on the money, Seamus."

"Looks that way," I agreed.

"And she just spilled it all there to protect the mother," said Emma.

"Mainly," I agreed. "But also because, now that Grace fouled things up by making her own play, she doesn't rate it as important enough to keep quiet about. She thinks she's better than other people. She has nothing but contempt for people like Cairns and Tweedie. And for people like us," I said. "Same reason she refused legal representation. Contempt."

"A contemptuous wee bastard," said Bert, and slipped his jacket on.

58

The fine weather continued. I sat on a bench in the Steelyard, next to Sky Blue. Jim Dandy stood by the side of the bench, smoking his cigarillos and watching the buses come and go in King Street.

"Papers are sayin' that the lassie done it," he growled.

"She's been charged with the murders, aye," I replied.

Jim Dandy shook his head wonderingly. "Fucksake, you cannae be sure ae nuthin' these days. Eh? What kinna fuckin' world is it where an eighteen year old lassie kin batter fuck oot a two guys heids – wan a thum her faither, mind ye? Ah mean tae say, the world's gaun too fast, that's what's wrang."

Sky Blue turned his head in the direction of Jim Dandy and fixed his gaze on a distant cloud, so that he could draw a bead on the coupon of the gibbering dwarf.

"Will ye take a listen tae yersel'? What a heap a shite you talk half the time. How kin the world be gaun too fast? Anybody measured the speed ae the earth when it turns, tell me?"

"Well, since you ask," I said, "aye. The earth spins on its own axis at a thousand miles an hour. I read somewhere that the speed it goes round the sun at is 67,000 miles an hour."

Sky Blue revolved his pow and looked upon another aspect of the heavens.

"See, what it is tae hae brains, Dandy. You nor I never kent that. Nae cunt chucked your brains intae the pig-bin, son. Aw they years at the university done you some good, eh? What it is tae be an educated man."

"An educated man?" sneered Jim Dandy. "Educated fuckin' Archie."

"Edinburry Uni wis it ye went tae?" asked Sky Blue.

"Edinburgh, aye. I lived in a flat in the New Town for four years."

"Well, fuck me blue," said Jim Dandy. "Think aboot that, then. We're rubbin' shooders wae the quality. Ah'm surprised he condescends tae live in Bathgate. Him huvvin' been a tounie. Gaun tae the theatre wae a wumman in lang white gloves and her tits spillin' oot 'er evenin' goon, nae doot."

"Hardly that, Dandy, I think. More like something out of Dickens. You know? Wee gloves with the fingers snipped off, and suckin' gruel off a spoon."

Sky Blue chuckled quietly.

"Twinty tae a room, lik' the Pakis," guffawed Jim Dandy. Casual racist remarks were part of his lack of charm.

"Yes, you're not far wrong," I agreed. "We had to fill the house. A student grant doesn't go very far."

"Far enough," spat Dandy. "Enough tae keep thum in LSD an' French letters, onywey. As faur as I can see, that's aw students dae – hoor aboot an' smoke yon LSD. Lie in their scratchers aw day an' fuck aboot aw night."

"Sounds good to me," I laughed.

"See? Nae cunt willin' tae work, these days," moaned Jim Dandy. "Whit the fuck happened tae leavin' the school an' gittin' a joab?"

"Like *you*, ye mean?" I said.

"You can fuck off ya cheeky young get," snapped Dandy. "Ye kin see I'm no fit tae work."

"Maybe not to join the Scots Guards," I said, "but you could have worked in an office. If somebody gave you a dooky-up to the stool."

"Ya impident young cunt!" Jim Dandy hollered, lividly spitting. "Get yersel tae fuck!"

"Noo, noo, calm doon, Dandy," said Sky Blue, "Jack's jist jokin'. You started it, takin' the piss, an' Jack's jist giein' ye some back. Don't dish it oot, if ye cannae take it."

"Ach, cheeky bastart," subsided Jim Dandy.

The people of Bathgate went about their daily business. Cars droned along by the traffic lights. People bought the messages and went into the café for a cuppa.

"Whit aboot the mother and the toy boy?" asked Sky Blue.

"Accessory after the fact," I said. "They've been charged with conspiracy to pervert the course of justice."

"Aye? Whit sentence wid they git for that?"

"Well," I said. "It is possible to get life. But most likely they'll get three or four years, I think."

"'Pervert' is right," opined Jim Dandy. "How onybody kin stand at a car windae an' caw theirsel's aff watchin' other folk humpin' an' *no* be a pervert is beyond me."

I let him ponder the matter in silence for a second or two before I spoke.

"Well, Dandy," I said. "It's like Shakespeare says. There are more things in heaven and earth than are dreamt of in your philosophy." And I meandered off.

59

I lobbed the packaging of my sandwich into the office bin and drew the crossword towards me. But I couldn't be hacked trying to finish it. Apathy surge. I stared at the wall like Belshazzar. Many, many tickle the parson. Nothing in my career so far had been quite as dramatic as anything that had happened in the previous fortnight. I felt like a bairn when the circus leaves town.

My work took on the routine of small potatoes again. Humdrum. Mundane. Quotidian. Worked all the summer, worked all the fall; had to take Christmas in my overalls. But, as some old Warwickshire scribbler has it, 'If all the year were playing holidays,/ To sport would be as tedious as to work.' So, at least for a while, there was no more rubbing shoulders with devotees of the lifestyle, or anyone who claimed to be the last prophet, the only man with a rope-ladder to the Elysian Fields. My life got marginally less interesting and a lot less dangerous.

I followed folk to see if they were cheating on their partners. I examined the hard drives of PCs. I tried to trace some long-lost ne'er-do-well of a youngest son to tell him that his old man had croaked and that he – the son – had, as a consequence, fallen heir to a sizeable bag of berries. I listened to dead bluesmen. And I still did two crosswords a day, just to keep the old grey matter grey and mattering. Whatever happened, I needed my mind to be, and remain, Wilkinson sword edged.

I read the papers carefully over the days. I caught every TV news bulletin I could. Tayside Police discovered a total of 36 bodies: men, women and children. All but four of them had died in the Meeting Hall of cyanide poisoning. One of the bodies in the burnt-out remains of Scriddan House turned out to be that of Brother Ira. I wondered if he died like a gunslinger.

Like it always does, the focus of the news shifted gradually until there came a time when the demise of the New Dawn was not referred to. In due course, the papers would be full of the trial of Laura McGuire for the murders of Brian

Cairns and Dominic Tweedie. That would be a cause celebre around West Lothian for a while. The county is still a place where sensational murder trials that revolve around sexual desire, jealousy and revenge are not all that common. It would shift the doings of the council (Britain's best in 2006, as they never tire of pointing out) off the Courier's front page. If only temporarily.

But I chewed at it myself, for a much longer time. I couldn't get it out of my head. It kept popping back up like an applet you can't shift. Dominic Tweedie, a figure from my father's past, a man I had met once before, to have been so significant in all of it. A madman. A man who had burnt out several circuits in his brain with his consumption of base, bomb and acid. And then to have taken to religion like a duck takes to oranges. But it confirmed my view. I was with the misquoted Marx on that one. Religion *is* the opium of the people. Delusions, grandiose talk and readiness to credit any old rubbish are symptoms common to both.

I had lost religion finally and fully when my father jumped off the Forth Bridge. Not long after that, my mother started to bark. I'd been doing the REM number for a while before it. That's me in the spot…light. But God just went away forever after that.

I couldn't mark the day it happened, but it happened. There was no darkening of the sky, no pyramids of fire in the west, no ear-shattering report as the Lord died in thunder and smoke. Mighty statues did not deafen the world with the reverberations as they toppled in Valhalla. There was no Bang, comparable to the Big one, as God suddenly ceased to exist and the entire history of theology imploded into a dot as small as a full stop with the mass of a planet. I was just sure he was not there any more. Probably never had been.

But Tweedie had other motivations. He was not a party to any Pauline conversion on the road to Domestos. He had set up another business venture, pure and simple. In the course of this venture – much more successful than his previous efforts – he indulged his hobbies of narcotics and sex. This is not so unusual. I am always entertained at how often these conduits of the Lord are caught with their cassocks round their ankles and a spliff in their fingers. I must admit to enjoying my Schadenfreude with sauerkraut when these American TV evangelists are dug out of the fleshpots like badgers and brought into the open air. And it happens with a pleasant degree of regularity. They may be bound for Glory but they don't object to a whack or two of Mammon before they go. Tweedie got his coffee, though. Espresso doppio, in fact. And hell mind him.

Grace McGuire. Now, there was a case to ponder. She was a strikingly attractive woman with a great deal of culture and education, not to mention a good name in the county. Strange that she should jeopardise all of that for a sexual kick. Oh, I know, sexual behaviour can be strange and compulsive. I've checked out what some folk download off the Internet. Apart from what is universally regarded as vile and subhuman, the number of fetishes catered for on websites is truly staggering. You can wander through the world of leather, if that lights your candle. Women walking on each other in heels and nothing else, wallabies wrestling in mud – whatever's your kink, you'll find it. But most of these interests are pursued in private, behind closed doors and behind pulled drapes. Grace got her quivers from the old five-a-sides in the public park. And, however snobbish it might sound to say it, her meeting with Billy the Buhll eventually wrought her undoing. From their sexual dalliances, all the tragedy of that week or so flowed. Billy just got lucky. A yob whose beefcake impressed a classy lady beyond measure.

And young Laura. A sad case. So young and so untender. All of her woes stemmed from her mother's hot-arsed behaviour too. But I was sure that Laura would have made her mark on the world in some other chilling fashion before long.

All profoundly depressing, the more I thought about it.

I locked up, leaving the crossie undone, and drove home. Locked the door, pulled the curtains. I put an old Stones LP of my father's on the player and stretched out on the settee beside Black Jack, who lifted his head in irritation at the disturbance, then sniffed and settled again. I lay with my ashtray on my chest and kippered my lungs with a pack of Benson & Hedges. While I listened to some old 60's words of wisdom.

*You know, sometimes you get what you want.
Then you go and lose what you had...*

Printed in Great Britain
by Amazon